Husband Fur Hire

Husband Fur Hire
ISBN-13: 978-1518783159
ISBN-10: 1518783155
Copyright © 2015, T. S. Joyce
First electronic publication: October 2015

T. S. Joyce
www.tsjoycewrites.wordpress.com

NOTE FROM THE AUTHOR:
This book is a work of fiction. The names, characters, places, and incidents are products of the writer's imagination or have been used fictitiously and are not to be construed as real. Any resemblance to persons, living or dead, actual events, locale or organizations is entirely coincidental. The author does not have any control over and does not assume any responsibility for third-party websites or their content.

Published in the United States of America
First digital publication: October 2015
First print publication: October 2015

Husband Fur Hire

(Bears Fur Hire, Book 1)

T. S. Joyce

ONE

"You get out of my house!" Elyse screamed.

She chugged breath and blinked fast to hold the moisture that rimmed her eyes at bay. She would not cry for this man, not one tear.

"Our house, Elyse. It's *our* house!" Cole yelled. He looked insane. Hazel eyes blazing, face red, veins popping out of his forehead, he was pacing their bedroom like a caged animal.

Cole McCall was the biggest liar she'd ever met.

He'd lied about being a good man, and about being faithful. He'd broken every promise he'd ever made her, and now this? Elyse wiped her throbbing lip with the back of her hand, and it came back with a smear of crimson.

He'd lost his damned mind if he thought she was one of those women who would take a hand to the face and stick around.

In a rush, she ran out of the bedroom and bolted for the gun rack near the front door. She yanked off an old shotgun, snapped it open, shoved two shells into the barrel, then popped it back into place with a satisfying crack of metal.

"What are you doing?" Cole yelled as he came out of the bedroom, hands in his hair, eyes wilder than she'd ever seen them. He was going crazy. Crazy. She'd watched him slowly

4

lose his mind over the last few months, and she'd been patient, but this was where the horse got off this buggy.

"I said get the fuck out of my house!" Her lip throbbed in time with her racing heart, and her arms shook with shock, but when she gripped the gun and aimed at his chest, her hands steadied. "I hope you know me well enough to understand I don't bluff."

"Baby," he crooned, holding out his palms. Cole's eyes cooled, and he smiled apologetically, the snake. "You don't want me to go."

"I really, really do."

"You won't make it through winter without me hunting for us."

"You gave half our food away to your good for nothin' brothers, Cole. I sincerely think I'll be better off without you pissin' away my money and depleting my winter stock. You don't even work with me! You don't. You've left me alone to do everything, and you come back only when you want something or when you need someone to hurt. You're broken. I can't fix you, and I don't want to try to anymore." She cocked the gun. "Gather your shit."

"I didn't mean to hit you—"

"Oh, don't you dare." She shook her head hard and glared. "Don't you dare insult me with that garbage. You will never be forgiven for lifting a hand to me, Cole. Never."

"I love you, Elyse." He took a step toward her, hands out in surrender. "It was an accident."

She huffed a humorless laugh and raised the barrel of the rifle to the vicinity of his forehead. "Take another step, and I'll blow a hole in you so big I'll see the fucking kitchen through you. Get your things and never come back. If I see you on my property again, I'll shoot you for trespassing."

Cole's shocked gaze lowered to the barrel of the shotgun pointed at him. Elyse gasped when he gripped the end and pulled it to his head for a moment, but he released it and strode into the other room. God, he'd almost forced her hand. Cole really was losing his mind.

The rustle of his duffle bag against the bed was loud in the silence of the small living room, and it seemed to take him hours to pack, though it couldn't have been more than ten minutes. Ten minutes to exit her life. That should've told her everything right there. He had never really been in this.

He would have to take his snow machine to get to Galena, but she didn't care. She would get her other one working again. She could move on and forget Cole McCall had ever existed. She hoped.

His hair was mussed when he came out of the bedroom with his belongings strapped over one shoulder. Even if his eyes were pooled with regret, he didn't have any tears for her. Crazy didn't cry.

Crazy Cole, like everyone in town had called him, and he'd gone and proved them right. Her disappointment was infinite.

"I'm sorry," he murmured with one last, long look. It was the sincerest she'd seen him in months.

Then he walked out of her house and into the dark winter, and Elyse knew with certainty that this would be the last she ever saw of him.

****

The worst thing about being a grizzly shifter wasn't the Change. It wasn't the pain that came along with it or having to hide his true nature from the humans he interacted with. It wasn't even the violence he was called upon to perform as a shifter enforcer.

The worst thing about being a grizzly shifter was the hunger.

Ian Silver huffed three frozen breaths in the depths of his den, preparing himself for the pain of the Change back into his human body. The one right after hibernation was agony, but it would be easy after this. Or if not easy, at least less painful.

Closing his eyes, he tucked his animal away. It was a slow process, and he had to concentrate on each area of his body. The small, dark room echoed with the sounds of snapping bones and grunts of pain and the snarling of an angry animal that didn't want to be pushed inside yet. But then, his bear never wanted to be stifled.

It wasn't until he lay on the cold wood floor of his den as a human, naked and shivering, that he noticed the manila envelope someone had shoved under the thick wood of his door. He'd built this cabin inside a cave more than a decade ago on the land his ancestors had made their dens, and no one knew his whereabouts except for his two brothers, who wouldn't pay him a visit even if he was dying, and Clayton Reed, head of Alaska Shifter Enforcement. Fuck.

Ian was hungry—starving, in fact—and the last thing he wanted to deal with after six months of hibernation was an enforcer job.

With a growl and a glare for the damning envelope, he dressed as quickly as his sore muscles allowed. Thick sweater, jeans, warm socks, and hiking boots on, and he was up, stretching his aching joints. He caught a glimpse of himself in the mirror. Gaunt face, emaciated body, clothes hanging off him, hollow eyes, and one gnarly beard. Even the blue of his eyes was dull. He always hated the way he looked after hibernation—as weak as a dried twig, and just as ready to snap.

Ripping his gaze away from the reflective glass, he reached for his jacket draped over the dresser and beat off a healthy layer of dust. It was dark in his one-room den, but his night vision was impeccable, so he didn't have any problems finding his way around. This place was for sleeping only and lacked the amenities he needed to refuel his depleted body. Tonight, he would stay in a hotel in town and eat until he was glutted. Whoever's file that envelope contained was going to eat him for breakfast if he didn't build up his strength.

Ian pocketed his wallet along with all the money in the safe that shadowed the corner, then picked up the envelope. The weight was too substantial for a warning order. Clayton had definitely sent him something big.

He'd planned on eating before he opened the envelope, but it had been a couple of years since he'd done a thick-packet kill order, and one of the shifters around here must've fucked up royally if Ian was being called to hunt them.

He took one last glance around his den before shoving open the door, allowing the dim cave light to filter in. Even as muted as it was, the brightness hurt his eyes after sleeping so long. The envelope crinkled in his hands as he pulled the stack of papers and pictures from it. A strange jolt blasted through his body as his gaze landed on the first image. It was a color picture of a woman. Honey-colored hair tied back, long neck, pursed lips, and troubled, hollow eyes that looked eerily similar to his right now, except she was human and hadn't been asleep for the past six months. She had a hoe in her hands and was working a garden, and the look on her face said the photographer had caught her at a moment when she'd only just glanced up from her work, then likely returned her attention right back to it. Her eyes were a strange gold-green color, and she didn't wear a stitch of make-up.

Ian shook his head and gritted his teeth so hard his jaw ached. Clayton knew better than this. He knew better than to give him a kill order on a woman. Ian spat on the ground and pushed the picture aside. Cole McCall stared back at him with wild eyes that said his inner wolf had taken the last of his sanity. That was more like it. Ian scanned the paperwork to make sure it was McCall he was supposed to hunt and not the pretty woman in the photograph.

An unreasonably large wave of relief washed through his chest as he read the name. The lady was an innocent. Elyse Abram. Pretty name for a pretty woman, and not his intended target. She was just Cole's bad decision to try and hold a mate while his inner wolf slipped into madness. The McCall boys were all the same, descended from a long line of crazy werewolves. And man-eaters, every last one of them. Dumb fuck had involved a woman in his final year of sanity. Cole was even stupider than Ian had thought.

When Ian looked at the picture of the woman again, a strange warmth tingled in his fingertips where they connected to the glossy paper. Any man with eyes could see a woman like her was fine-bred and beautiful. Much too good to couple up with a McCall. Troubled by his sympathetic thoughts, Ian shoved the entire file back into the folder and slammed the door of his den closed, then strode out of the stone-encased tunnel and crawled through the small opening in the rocks and out into the sunlight.

Inhaling deeply, he closed his eyes and tilted his face up toward the sun. Even with half a foot of snow still covering Afognak Island, he'd never felt anything better. The woman was safe from him, and soon she'd be safe from Cole McCall and whatever idiot thing he'd done to get a price on his head. He was about to eat for the first time in six months, and he'd survived another winter. Life wasn't all peaches and berries, but this was the best a grizzly shifter could ask for.

Getting off Afognak meant uncovering the boat he'd hidden at the start of winter and dragging it to the beach. Not many came to this island, especially in this season. Hunters and hikers mostly, but no one lived here except him. There were a few cabins dotting the island that weren't made for permanent residence, but provided temporary protection for visitors from the wild brown bears that called this place home. Only the bravest hunters, or the most desperate, went after black-tail deer at the risk of running into a grizzly. Afognak was also said to be haunted, a rumor probably started by his ancestors and one he fueled if anyone asked because he liked his peace and quiet. The untamed land felt like home to a half-feral shifter like himself.

The boat engine was frozen and needed work and new fuel, so getting the dinghy in the water and hearing the whine of the little motor took a couple of hours. And all the while, his stomach growled.

The waters of the Marmot Bay were passable, but there were still ice chunks everywhere, so he had to be careful not to damage his hull as he maneuvered toward Kodiak Island. By trade, he was an Alaskan bush pilot, like one of his brothers and father before him, but he kept his plane in Pilot's Point to keep the werewolves off his trail when he went to sleep for the winter.

Damn, he was hungry. The second he set foot on land, he pulled his boat out of the frigid waters and tracked down his traditional post-hibernation restaurant to tuck into. It was an old inn that didn't get much traffic outside of tourist season, and the wait staff never commented on how much he could eat in one sitting.

It was here, in the back corner of the darkest room, that he pulled the envelope from his inside jacket pocket. The thick, heavy packet had been burning a hole against his chest. Or so it felt because the entire way here, he'd craved to take it out and stare at the woman's picture again. This hibernation had apparently made him lose his damned mind.

The server was friendly, a local he'd seen before, and she only hesitated a moment when he ordered one of everything on the menu.

Galena, Alaska the paperwork read—the last place Cole McCall had been seen. That would be one helluva flight for a warm-up, but anything was doable for his old red and white Cessna 182. He'd get her up and running and probably get there by tomorrow, depending on how many places he needed to stop for fuel and food.

He frowned at the photo of the woman again. It was hard to tell in the grainy picture, but it looked like her lip was split. Ian swallowed a snarl that started deep in his chest, and tried to convince himself that the growl was about being hungry and not his protective instincts kicking up. He had no claim on this woman, and it came as zero shock if McCall had mishandled her. Asshole. Ian shoved Elyse Abram's picture to the back of the stack and tried to concentrate through the rage that was boiling his blood.

"Are you okay, sir?" the waitress asked in a concerned tone.

She'd put plates of food all over the table, and he hadn't even noticed her working beside him. Shit. *Focus.*

"Yeah," he rasped out. It had been a long time since he'd used his voice, so he cleared it and tried again. "Yeah, I'm fine." *Smile. More genuinely.* "Thanks."

He read as he ate. McCall had been on a tear for the last month. Two trapper attacks, one fatal, but that wasn't the worst of it. That wasn't what got Cole hunted by someone like Ian. It was the picture of the little six-year-old girl. Dark hair and dark inquisitive eyes, probably Alaska Native. She'd been attacked right outside of Kaltag by a single, unprovoked wolf with McCall's dark gray saddle back markings.

"Mother fucker," Ian rumbled, more growl than words.

He read faster. The girl had been care-flighted to Anchorage. The doctors were hopeful for her to survive, but as of last week, she was still in the ICU, listed in critical condition. When the hell had Clayton dropped this packet off? Ian searched for a date, but all of the printed numbers in the top left corner of each page were a week old. Cole was probably in the wind by now and would be harder to track.

Ian huffed an angry sigh and relaxed into the seat cushion as he stared out the window, his thoughts racing. A little girl. The food in his stomach turned to a block of cement. A little innocent girl, and Cole went after her. Why? Because that was what McCalls did. They should've done the world a favor and let their line die off generations ago, but no, they just kept procreating with unknowing humans. All the pups were males because female offspring didn't live past childbirth, and all male McCalls grew up just as crazy as their ancestors. There was poison in their bloodline, and now the present-day pack was apparently old enough to start letting the madness in.

A week. What if Cole had gone after Elyse while Clayton was waiting for Ian to wake up? He swallowed hard. Elyse Abram. Best to keep her name formal in his mind since his heart started pounding every time he thought of her. It was dangerous to imagine himself attached to anyone. He had a better moral compass than to pass his bear shifter shit onto an innocent.

He needed to get it together. Eat, find a hotel, and scrub himself clean until he felt like a human again, charge his long-dead cell phone, check and prep his plane, and head to Galena to track down that psycho sonofabitch that would split a woman's lip and harm a little girl just as easily as armed trappers.

Cole McCall had hell coming for him, and the damning fire that was about to engulf him had a name.

Ian Silver's hunt started now.

TWO

Elyse wiped sweat from her brow and pulled another bunch of rotten potatoes from the wooden box in the root cellar. She was so desperately low on food that each one felt like a slash to her stomach. Each represented another meal she wouldn't eat because stupid Cole had stolen half her danged vegetables and most of their meat as well, just to pilfer off to his no-account brothers. She wasn't totally off the grid, but there was no money for red meat. Red meat was hunted during the warm season and rationed, and if someone in the community needed help, people helped, knowing they would do the same for them if they could. But the way the McCalls did things was stealing. They never repaid anyone, and when she and Cole had started dating, the mooching had begun early. And the last couple months, when Cole was out drinking and kicking up some awful rumors with a couple of townie girls, his two brothers, Miller and Lincoln, had become aggressive with their freeloading.

She'd fought it, but Cole never defended her from their treatment and yelled at her for resisting his brothers. "They're family," he said, as if that gave them an excuse to abuse her hard work. Well, they were no relation to her. She'd worked her ass off to gather enough food to last the winter for her and Cole, and he'd just thrown it away, as if his no-good brothers were more important than her. So many red flags she'd ignored because she'd loved him. Or thought she did, but thinking back, perhaps she was just so desperate not to be alone through the long winters that she mistook companionship for love. Being with someone and still feeling completely alone was the worst feeling in the world.

She would never, ever make that mistake again. Love, or whatever amounted to love, was off the table from here on. Love had starved her and hurt her heart, and he'd been able to walk away so easily. From day one, she'd told him what she was and wasn't willing to put up with, but he'd broken every rule, one by one, as if he was testing her to see how long until she cracked. Fucker. Elyse sniffled and wiped her eyes. She'd let a man ruin her. Uncle Jim would be rolling over in his grave if he saw how weak she'd been with Cole. He would've never given her this place in his will if he'd known how pathetic she would turn out. Well, no more!

She knew what she could and couldn't do. She couldn't run this homestead by herself. Not with the cattle and the other livestock to take care of, and not when she couldn't leave the animals long enough to hunt game meat for the winter. She needed a helpmate, and this time she was going to do it better. She was going to be stronger. Uncle Jim had put an ad in the newspaper for a helpmate when he'd needed one, and he'd been rewarded with Marta, who'd worked this place beside him for twenty years before she passed. He'd found the exact partner he needed to run this place, and that's just what Elyse aimed to do, too. No more romantic bullshittery or fairy-tale notions. She would find a good, capable husband who would just happen to be fantastic at leading the subsistence lifestyle this place required. She was going for the man with the strong back and leaving love off the table completely. A wise woman learned from her mistakes, and Cole McCall had been the biggest, most disappointing mistake of all.

Her cell phone rang, and she tossed it a glare before she moved to a box with precious few carrots left in it. Half of those were rotted, too, and it became abundantly clear that her rationing hadn't been doing her any favors. The vegetables were old and going bad. No amount of cool, moisture-free air and sawdust packing could keep them edible forever.

Another ring, and she wiped the sawdust from her palms to her jeans and picked up the phone that was about to jump off the wooden stool she'd set it on. She didn't recognize the number.

"Hello?"

"Uh…" There was a pause that was too long to be polite.

Elyse narrowed her eyes. "Cole, if this is you, fuck off."

She went to end the call, but the man said, "No, no, wait," in a deep, gravelly voice that was definitely not Cole's. "I'm sorry. I didn't think you would pick up."

"Well, you called me. What do you want?"

"Cole McCall. Have you seen him?"

Elyse sank down to the stool and bit her thumbnail. "Who wants to know?"

The man gave off a nervous laugh. Deep and rich, like his voice. "Look, I'm sorry for interrupting—"

"Does he owe you money?"

"No."

"Did he bang your sister?"

The man cleared his throat and sighed. "No."

"Mister, I haven't seen Cole in months. I booted his ass out of here mid-winter. I haven't seen him at my homestead or in town. His brothers still hang around the bar in Nulato, though, if you want to ask them."

"Okay. Thanks for taking the time to talk to me. Miss, are you crying?"

"Of course not." She wiped her tears with the back of her hand and swallowed hard. "I never cry." Stupid sniffles were giving her away.

"Over Cole?"

"Ha," she huffed.

"I'm a complete stranger who you'll never meet."

Elyse forced herself to stop biting her nail—a bad habit she couldn't seem to break—and leaned back against the stone wall of the root cellar. "Not over Cole. Over the situation he left me in."

"What situation?"

"It's nothing. I'm fine, just angry with myself. Everything will work out. It always does." She'd been repeating those lies for the last three snowy months.

"Hmm," the man said noncommittally, as if he didn't believe her lies either. He had a nice sort of voice. Calm and deep, but with a gravelly rasp, as though he didn't use it often. She couldn't get a grasp on his age, though. He could be twenty or sixty. She smiled and imagined he was twenty-six like she was. Food for thought since there weren't many people her age in Galena.

"Elyse Abram?"

She froze. He knew her whole name, and the way he said it, so formally, sounded so strange against her ear. "Yes?"

"If you need anything, you call this number, and I'll get it to you. Food or anything. No strings attached."

"What?" She sat up straighter against the cold stool. "But…you don't even know me."

"That's okay."

She waited the span of three breaths, her mind racing round and round. No man had offered her help out of the blue…well…since before she met Cole, and even then, it was kind neighbors who had a stake in helping her out. She had repaid their kindness and more as soon as she had been able. But complete strangers didn't offer help. They just didn't.

The line was quiet, the man still waiting, and for lack of a better answer, she murmured, "Okay," knowing she would never call this number again. Her pride was as big and wide as a canyon, and asking for help from someone she couldn't repay reeked too much of charity. And she was no charity case. "It was nice talking to you."

The man's voice softened as he said, "You, too, Elyse Abram."

The line went dead, and Elyse stared at the screen until long after it had gone dark. She couldn't believe that five minutes ago she was thinking there wasn't a decent man left on earth, and then one had called her unexpectedly.

Perhaps that was a sign.

Not everyone was as broken as Cole McCall, so maybe she could stop being so mad at the world and get on with living already.

And the first step to doing that was putting the ad in the newspaper, just like Uncle Jim had done all those years ago.

She would be damned if she was going to come out of another Alaskan winter this hungry.

****

Whatever situation Cole had put Elyse Abram in made Ian want to kill him twice. Some put-down orders haunted him. The ghosts of his marks seemed to cling to him. His animal wasn't a killer for sport. He was defensive when cornered and could hold his own with any shifter who went on the attack, but being an enforcer wasn't a choice. It was a career chosen for him by his lineage. Grizzly shifters were rare, and they were the biggest of all the were-animals. He and his brothers existing at all kept most of the shifters in Alaska in line. But sometimes when his hand was forced and someone went mad, hurt humans, or threatened to expose their kind, he had to hunt them when his animal didn't see the point.

With Cole, it was different.

Inside, his bear was snarling to get the damned deed done already. And for the first time in as long as he could remember, Ian was concerned his bear was actually going to enjoy putting someone down. It was that little sniffle Elyse

17

had made. That tiny noise had his bear churning in his gut, roaring to get out and bleed something.

What Elyse hadn't known when she gave him the whereabouts of Cole's brothers was that Ian was calling her from the bar in Nulato. Currently, he was sitting a mere thirty miles down the Yukon River from her homestead. So close.

Ian fingered the napkin under his beer and lifted his narrowed eyes to a pair of scraggly werewolves talking low between themselves in the darkest corner. Even from here, his nose burned with the stink of alcohol wafting off them. They must be in some kind of important conversation if they'd missed him sauntering in. He'd showered and trimmed his beard, and sure, he looked human enough right now, but there was no mistaking the scent of bear that clung to him, and werewolves had impeccable senses of smell.

Miller's nostrils flared, and he jerked his pissed-off glare to Ian. There he was—alpha of the McCall pack and general asshole. Lean as a whip, dishevcled, greasy hair, and a shade of blue eyes that screamed "somethin' ain't right." Wild Miller, dipping his toe into the insanity pool, too.

He stomped over, his untied boots clomping with every step. "I know what you're doin' here."

"Sit down."

Miller slammed his fist against the table and leaned into Ian, eyes lightening by the second. "You tell that cunt-licker, Clayton, to take the order back."

Ian kicked the chair across from him out from under the table and looked pointedly. "Sit down, or I'll be hunting you next."

Miller glanced back at his brother, Lincoln, who was still glued to his chair in the corner, ear turned, listening easily. Gritting his teeth, Miller sat down across from Ian and clasped his hands on the table. "He didn't do nothin' wrong."

Ian laughed once and shook his head. "That's the way you want to play this? You know what he's done. Three strikes, McCall. If you didn't want this, you should've kept your dog on a tighter leash."

"He bit one trapper, but it ain't like we can Turn anyone. Just a harmless little nip."

"Bit one multiple times and dragged him through the woods, killed the next, and I know about the little girl, Miller, so stop the bullshit and tell me where he is."

"I ain't tellin' you shit." Miller leaned back in his chair with a smile and spat onto the wooden floor. "And you ain't never gonna find him, Silver, you big. Dumb. Fuck. He's off grid and out of your swatting range. You can give Clayton a personal message from me and my pack." Miller lifted his middle finger and canted his head, his mad grin stretching even wider.

Off-grid and out of swatting range, and Miller was narrowing down his search area quite nicely. Cole would be in an old rundown cabin he thought everyone forgot about then. One without an airstrip around for Ian to land his plane.

Ian gave him a dead smile and downed his beer, then stood. "You have a nice day now, Miller. I'll see you around." Probably sooner than later and at the order of Clayton.

Miller stood so fast he blurred, breaking the rules and showing some of his strength to the unassuming humans staring at them from the bar top.

"Careful, doggy," Ian said low.

"If you go after my brother, know this, Silver. I will summon every McCall in Alaska to my side. Me and my pack will hunt you down. You won't be able to find a safe enough place to hide from us. And we'll take our time about it, too. Maybe we'll kill your brothers first. Eye for an eye and all that."

"Tell them hi," Ian said blandly. "I haven't talked to the pricks in three years. Stay safe, McCall."

The threat in that was intentional, and Miller had the good sense to keep his trap shut as Ian walked out of the bar.

The urge to visit Elyse Abram's homestead was overwhelming. It was more than idle curiosity that had him hesitating before walking back to the airstrip outside of town. He was so close and hadn't visited Galena in two years. He'd been all over Alaska, both on tracking jobs like this one and as a bush pilot, delivering anything and everything that needed to be delivered. But now that he was thirty miles away from her town, the instinct to linger was almost too hard to ignore.

She was the recent mate of a werewolf, though, and a sensible bear didn't touch another predator shifter's claim. But even so, when Ian had talked to Elyse Abram on the phone, it had sounded like whatever Cole had done to her had hurt her badly, and the want to comfort her somehow made it hard to put one foot in front of the other right now. His gaze was drawn time and time again to the main road that led out of town to where she lived up in the wilderness.

No. Ian shook his head to rid himself of the temptation. The best thing he could do for her was put down Cole, and make sure the crazy wolf didn't lose what was left of his mind and go after her. She'd dodged a bullet by escaping a relationship with a shifter, and Ian would be damned if he was the bigger, more damaging, bullet she stepped in front of. She deserved a nice, normal, human mate, or husband, or whatever they were called.

His boots crunched through the late winter snow as he strode purposefully toward the landing strip where he'd parked his plane.

Meeting her, and allowing his bear see and smell her, was a terrible idea. What did he have to offer anyone? He slept half the year, and the other half was filled with enforcing and running plane deliveries in a mad rush to earn enough money for the food he needed to eat for the next hibernation.

No, she was much better off without knowing he even existed.

Everyone was.

THREE

The little girl had been attacked twenty miles outside of Kaltag, and the trapper attacks were within a thirty mile range of that as well, so Ian would start there. If Cole had moved on, he would have a better chance of finding where to if he canvassed the village. McCalls were notorious freeloaders, and unless Cole was going straight wolf, he would be in town begging for food, money, gas for his snow machine, whatever.

There were a dozen old homesteader cabins that had been abandoned out there, too, so he would check those out while he was in the area and hope to get lucky.

Outside of town, he prepped his plane and took off. It was a short flight to Kaltag, and he began circling out from there. From the plane, he could make out two old dilapidated one-roomers through the trees with a lot of animal tracks around them. Cole would've traveled here by snow machine, or maybe he'd gone wolf to get way out here.

Another sure sign that Cole had been squatting here and not just passing through was there were no manicured landing strips. Cole would want to make it difficult for Ian to get to his hidey hole, and from way up here, scanning the snowy tundra below, dotted heavily with evergreen trees, Ian was going to have a hard time landing safely.

If he was Cole, he would've picked a similar place to hide out. *Think like the prey.* That's what dad had taught him, Tobias, and Jenner when they'd first shifted at age sixteen. And Dad had been the best tracker there ever was. Any advice Ian had gleaned from him during his youth was now worth more than gold.

He took the last bite of yet another apple and tossed the core onto the pile in the passenger's seat of his little four-seater plane.

Ian narrowed his eyes at a strip of smoothish landing space, covered in what looked like thinner snow. From the long tracks, someone had used it since the last snowfall to land, so that was going to have to be good enough. He had the skis on the landing gear, but still, one wrong move and his lightweight plane could be smashed to pieces with him in it. Now, he had decent shifter healing, but he sure loved his ride, and he hadn't crashed yet. A couple of close calls, but nothing too damaging.

He circled around, assessing the makeshift landing strip, and sure enough, there were definitely sled marks in the snow, revealing it was thin enough to land if he took the angle just right. He lined up and dipped the nose slightly, lowering himself slowly to the glittering snow. It would be dark soon, and he needed to make some tracks before nightfall. If Cole was still here, his brothers would've likely called to warn him. But if he'd been spending time as a wolf all day, Ian still had a shot at catching him by surprise.

His heart drummed against his sternum as he lifted up enough to straighten out, and his landing gear skied across the snowy straightaway. It was rough and jostled the plane, and at the end, he turned a bit wonky, but it was a better landing than he could've hoped for way out here.

It was cold as balls, so he blanketed the plane to make less work for him when he returned. It took time prepping the Cessna, but it would be worth it later, especially if he came back out here after dark.

He tossed the apple cores in the woods for the hungry winter birds to pick up, then pulled on his fox fur hat, sunglasses, and mittens. He could stand the cold a lot better than humans, but Alaska was brutal at night, and any windchill made it even more miserable. Despite the frigid temperatures, this was just how he liked to hunt. Snow made it easy to track anything. Animal scat was stark against the white, and tracks were easy to see and identify. He could read entire stories in the snow if he took the time to interpret the signs.

Ian pulled a giant pack of beef jerky from his backpack and tore into it as he made his way from the plane toward the woods in the direction of the most promising cabin he'd seen from the air.

How was his stomach growling while he was feeding it? Little beggar was always obnoxious until he put on that first twenty pounds.

It was nearly dark when he scented animal fur. He was close to the cabin now, and the tracks in the snow were definitely wolf. He couldn't have gotten this lucky. It wasn't possible. Cole wasn't this stupid to be right out where he could see from a plane.

But when he stepped through to the clearing of the cabin's yard, low and behold, Cole McCall himself was standing in the doorway, as if he'd been waiting for him.

The hairs on the back of Ian's neck lifted, and he slowed to a stop just inside of the tree line.

"It ain't a trap," Cole drawled out. His head twitched, and his eyes blazed for a moment before they dimmed again.

"Cole, you gotta problem, man," Ian said as he lowered his backpack to the snow beside his boots.

"Clayton?"

Ian nodded once.

It was hard to tell behind Cole's thick beard, but it looked like his lip ticked once. He inhaled deeply and pushed off the door frame. "Is it death?"

Ian nodded again, then looked around pointedly. The cabin was old, maybe eighty years, and the roof had gone to rot and caved in at some point. "You didn't pick the best hiding spot. You made it too easy."

"Yeah, well I wasn't hiding from you. I was hiding from her."

"I don't understand."

Cole twitched his head again and let off a long, low snarl, then swallowed it down. The hairs lifted on Ian's arms despite the warm winter jacket. Crazy always heckled his instincts. Crazy was unpredictable and could get a man killed if he wasn't careful.

"My wolf wants Elyse."

Now Ian was the one letting off a growl, and he didn't feel inclined to stifle his as Cole had done.

Cole swallowed audibly. "He settled for the little girl, but she just bought me time. I thought you'd never fucking get here, Silver."

"You are prepared then?"

Cole uncrossed his arms and nodded. "I know what I am now. I can feel it. Dumbass that I was, I thought I could be saved and outsmart the McCall curse. I thought Elyse could save me. And then I beat on her."

"Fuck," Ian muttered in a snarling voice as he tried to keep his head. Everything was red now. Red Cole, red woods, red snow. "You know a wolf bride wasn't ever going to save you, McCall."

He lifted one shoulder in a half-shrug. "If it were you, and you thought you could be saved, wouldn't you try?"

Ian inhaled the mountain air, but it stank of wolf and fur. Cole looked human enough, but he wasn't in control. His animal even smelled unsettled. "I'll give you an honorable death if you want it."

"Even after I hurt the girl?"

"Didn't say you deserved it, asshole, but I have sympathy for a man losing a war to his animal. You and Lincoln are the least shitty of the McCalls."

Cole huffed a laugh, though his expression stayed exactly the same. Defeated. "I'll take that as a compliment coming from you. Can I ask you one last favor?"

"Don't push your luck." Ian cocked his head and narrowed his eyes, curiosity piqued. "What is it? Not saying I'll do it, but I'll consider it."

Cole pulled a folded piece of paper from his jeans' pocket and held it out. "It's a letter to Elyse. An apology. I'm not safe to give it to her myself."

"I don't think that's a good idea." In fact, putting Elyse in front of his protective grizzly was the worst idea ever. He'd come to that conclusion over the plane ride here.

"Please, man," Cole pleaded, uncertainty slashing through his lightening eyes. "Dying will be easier if I know she'll get this."

Ian scrubbed his hands down his face and nodded. "Sure." He approached and took the letter from Cole's outstretched hand. Maybe he could put it through the post, or pay someone in Galena to deliver it to her. "You ready?"

Cole nodded and pulled his thick sweater over his head as Ian began to shuck his clothes. "Hurry," he said in a strained voice as his neck snapped back.

"Shit," Ian muttered as he rushed to undress. His bear would destroy his clothes ripping out of him, and he needed them to get back to the plane frostbite free.

Cole's Change was instant, more proof of how in control his animal was. It should've taken minutes as each bone, tendon, and joint broke and reshaped, but Cole's wolf exploded out of him and charged before Ian was ready. God, this was going to hurt.

He pushed his Change, but it was hard to focus with Cole's teeth ripping into him. The snow in front of his face splattered with red. His red. Pain blurred his vision. The snapping of his bones was deafening, and Cole's wolf was going at him in earnest now, tooth and claw. The law of Alaska was simple. Kill or be killed. His wolf knew why Ian was here, and apex predator shifters didn't die easy, even if the human side of Cole saw the necessity.

Ian closed his eyes and pushed his Change harder than he ever had. A smattering of pops echoed across the clearing just before millions of stinging needles blasted through his skin and covered his body in a thick, winter coat. He roared his fury at the little, cheating shithead and shook his massive body, dislodging Cole's teeth from the muscular hump over his shoulder blades. Even skinny and right out of hibernation, he was still ten times the size of the wolf.

Cole charged, but Ian was ready for him now and pissed as all get-out that he was so badly injured going into this. He batted him down and lunged. Engaging, they both snarled and snapped and bit and clawed, ripping into each other in a battle to the death.

It didn't last long after that. Ian was quick—a skilled killer. Just the snap of his neck, and Cole was done. As Ian paced a tight circle around the body to make sure the wolf's chest didn't rise again, a deluge of emotion washed through him. Anger that Cole had talked so freely about hurting Elyse and the little girl. Pity that Cole had tried to save himself with love but had been unsalvageable. Regret that he was the one who had to end a life. Relief that it was done.

Ian forced himself back into his human skin. He wished he could explore these woods as a bear, but there was work to do. He had to bury the dead, or he couldn't live with the lives he had to take. He had to break through still frozen ground to dig a grave, and he had to make it back to his plane before the wild wolves came out hunting for the night.

But before all of that, he had to make a couple of calls from the satellite phone he'd brought.

The first went to voicemail, as it always did, because his asshole brother, Tobias, didn't ever bother to pick up his calls. He left a message—a short, sweet, to-the-point warning. Hopefully Tobias would check it at some point.

On the second call, his brother Jenner answered. "What?"

"Hey to you, too." A soft, impatient rumble filled the line so Ian told him, "I just killed a McCall on order."

"So?"

"So Miller made a threat against you and Tobias. Just thought I should warn you."

Jenner made a single clicking sound across the line. "I'm offended you think Miller and his pack of pups is anything to warn us about."

Looking down at the freely bleeding gashes that covered his ribcage, then the giant red smears in the snow near his feet, Ian huffed a quick breath of steam and nodded. "Stupid me. How is everything else"—the line went dead—"going?"

Fantastic. As always, a pleasurable experience talking with his brother.

Ian chucked the phone into his bag and hooked his hands on his hips as he looked down at the dead wolf. At least Cole's brothers had cared enough to make a threat against him.

The McCalls were bat-shit crazy, but they were loyal.

At least Cole died knowing that someone in the world had his back.

Ian winced and dragged his gaze away from the limp gray and cream-colored wolf. He redressed slowly, careful of his gaping side. It would heal soon enough, but it hurt like hell right now, and sure as anything, the heavy iron scent of his blood would bring in the predators.

A little more effort, and this would be behind him. He could call Clayton, tell him it was done, and hope that was the last enforcer job he got this season.

The hunt was over, and now he could get back to his life.

Eat, sleep, fly, deliver, prepare for next winter, and above it all…forget about Elyse Abram.

FOUR

Elyse cocked her eyebrow at the seventy-five-year-old mountain man doing his best to convince her he would make the perfect homesteader husband. Even if she could ignore his foul odor, she couldn't ignore the three pain pills he'd popped in the last fifteen minutes or the deep limp he blamed on a bum back.

She wasn't going to do this again, choose someone who wouldn't pull their weight. The entire point of her putting an ad out for a helpmate was so that she didn't have to run this place alone. She wasn't looking to be pampered, but she wasn't tacking on more work than this man was worth, either.

A strong back. That was the first requirement she'd listed in the ad, so why had she interviewed three lame men now? Because apparently the only ones who took a husband-for-hire advertisement seriously in modern times were drunkards, moochers, and men old enough to fart dust who were tired of living alone. One of them had even called her his "retirement plan." Hell nope.

"Thanks for coming by, Mr. Daltry. I'll be sure to keep you in mind when I make my final decision."

He was murmuring incomprehensibly as he listed all of his finer qualities, too fast for her to understand, but she was pretty sure she heard him say, "I only drink on weekdays" as she led him gently to the door.

And when she finally closed it on him and his truck engine roared to life, she rested her forehead on the rough wood of her door and sighed. Seven months since Cole had left, four months since his brother, Miller, had informed her that he'd died in the backcountry from a bear attack, and now it felt like she would never feel normal again. Tears stung her eyes as she pulled the newspaper off the table by the door. She had the damned thing memorized, but re-read it anyway. She had a couple of months left of warm weather, but she was so far behind on stocking up for winter, she felt as if she couldn't breathe. Perhaps if she re-worded the advertisement again.

Husband for Hire
Good Alaskan man wanted. Must have strong back. Hunter preferable and bonus points for good marksmanship. Must not be prone to cabin fever and must be self-entertaining. Works well under stress for long hours. Good hygiene. Romantics need not apply.

Any longer and she'd have to pay for a bigger ad, and she was low on money as it was.

A knock sounded on the door, and she tried not to groan out loud. The damned barrier wasn't sealed well, and old man Daltry would hear her. Perhaps he'd left his pain pills on the chair he'd sat in, or perhaps he was back because he'd just remembered some fascinating tidbit that would be sure to change her mind.

Steeling herself, she tucked her loose hair behind her ears, gripped the handle for a moment to plaster a polite smile on her face, and opened the door. She jolted at the sight of the behemoth before her, and from the startled expression on his face, she'd surprised him just as badly. He was definitely not Mr. Daltry.

"Holy shit," she murmured as she looked hungrily at the powerful legs encased in his jeans to a tapered waist and strong, wide shoulders pushing against the fabric of his blue sweater. He had the top button undone, and layers of muscle underneath led to a thick throat where his Adam's apple bobbed as he swallowed hard. It was his face that held her frozen, though. Sure, a reddish beard covered his jaw, but at least he'd trimmed it recently, and looking past the scruff, any red-blooded woman could tell this man was a vision. Smooth, sun-tanned skin, and a straight, narrow, proud nose. A crop of sandy brown, messy hair covered his head, but it was his eyes that had her knees going wobbly. Piercing blue and hard to look away from. And now he was smiling. Kind of. He looked a little uncomfortable, but that was okay.

Elyse stepped outside onto the sagging porch and looked him up and down as she shuffled around him in a wide circle. She even kicked the back of his locked knees with her boot, but he didn't wobble at all. Sturdy as a pine tree, this one. "You're not even hideous to look at."

"I beg your pardon?" the man asked, twisting around and following her with his gaze.

"You aren't repulsive."

He frowned. "Thank you?"

"It's just, everyone else who answered my ad…you know…was missing most of their teeth." And smelled, but not this one. She leaned forward and sniffed. Soap and animal. Nice. He could probably ride a horse, *and* chop wood like a demon, *and* had definitely read the part of her advertisement about good hygiene. Oh, and he was a big, muscle-bound brawny man. She gripped his bicep and gave an approving whistle when her hand wouldn't reach around it by half. So firm. So big.

The man wore a troubled frown, so she quit poking him.

"Are you all right?"

"And caring. Nice touch. Do you hunt?"

His eyes narrowed, but he nodded once.

"Good aim?"

"With a rifle?"

She nodded and crossed her arms, waiting and trying her best not to look at those powerhouse legs again. She'd already established his back was strong enough.

"I'm a fair shot."

"Good. And are you a self-entertaining sort of man?"

"You mean am I independent?"

She'd never seen a more confused look on a man's face. Maybe he'd forgotten what the ad said, so she reached inside the doorway and picked up the paper, then handed it to him and pointed at the article.

She waited while he refreshed his memory.

His lips moved as he read, and then suddenly he reared back and his eyes went round. Oooh, such a pretty color, even if he was looking at her strangely right now. "Husband for hire?"

"That's why you're here, right?"

"Why would you need to pay for a husband?"

"Not pay, per say. We would split the duties around my homestead as helpmates to begin with, and after a week or two, we can marry." She nodded definitively.

"We can marry," he repeated in an odd tone.

"Yes. And I won't be trading money, more like a barter for you coming here to be the man of this house. I have cattle, and you'll have a say in the running of this place and a safe cabin to live. I'm a loyal sort and will have your back. And…you'll have me."

His animated eyebrows jacked up. "You? You mean…"

Cheeks heating over the thought of sex with a titan like him, she cleared her throat and delved into more favorable conversation. "Were you born in Alaska?"

"Why?"

"Because I don't want one of those mainlander men who think it'll be fun to homestead for a few seasons, then leave me high and dry once they grow bored with it. This isn't some Alaskan reality show, mister. I need someone to stick around for me."

The man frowned down at a folded piece of white paper he held clutched in his hand. Slowly, he tucked it into his back pocket and said, "Let me see your freezer."

"My freezer?" she asked, utterly baffled.

"Yes, woman. Let me see how much meat you have stocked up. I want to know your situation. This is some sort of interview, right?"

"Yes."

"Well, doesn't it seem fair that I interview you, too? Picking a mate—" The man shook his head and tried again. "Picking a *spouse* sure seems like a big enough deal that both parties should be agreeable, don't you think?"

Huh. She licked her lip and thought on that. He was the first to ask her any questions back, besides the normal, "How many acres do you own?" and "Will I inherit the land if you die?"

Feeling vulnerable, and a little more than embarrassed, she twitched her head. "The freezer is this way." She led him around the outside of her cabin to the back porch where she removed the padlock from her deep freeze and stood back.

The man cast her a quick glance before he opened the lid all the way. He locked his arms against the edges and stared down into the nearly empty depths, then wiped his beard against his shoulder, as if it was a habit he did when he wasn't happy. "Is this your only freezer?"

"Afraid so. I had a man, but he gave everything to his brothers, and I've been just trying to get by for a while now. That's why I put an ad in the paper, you see. I don't want to just survive anymore. I need help so I don't lose this place. It's been in my family for a long time."

He cleared his throat and wouldn't meet her eyes. Instead, he stared into the abyss of her freezer as he said, "Your man. What happened to him?"

Cole's slap burned across her memory like a brush fire. "He wasn't very nice to me, so I asked him to leave. He died four months back from a bear attack."

"Four months, and you don't think this is too soon to look for a husband, or helpmate, or whatever it is you're doing?"

"What are you doing here?" she asked angrily, tired of the judging.

The man scratched his head in an irritated sort of way, then set those biting blue eyes on her. He rubbed his hand thoughtfully over his beard, then lifted the newspaper as an answer.

"Then why are you asking me if it's too soon?"

"Because I want to make sure you're stable enough to do this before I consider your offer."

"My offer?" The nerve. She hadn't made anyone any offer.

"Yeah," he said, standing to his full, imposing height. "How many have responded to this?"

Smartass. She lifted her chin primly. "A dozen."

"And of that dozen, how many were under the age of sixty and fully capable?"

Zero. Elyse glared and clamped her mouth shut.

"That's what I thought. Good Alaskan man, strong back, you won't have to worry about me going crazy over a dark winter, I can work from sunup until sundown and beyond, and I am one fuck of a good hunter. You won't go hungry, and I *will* put weight on you. From the looks of it, you didn't fare well this past winter, and you haven't made up your reserves. This," he said, letting the lid of her freezer fall loudly, "isn't acceptable, and it won't be this low again if I have any say in the matter. I have good hygiene, and as far as the *romantics need not apply* slice of this lunatic pie, I don't have a romantic bone in my body, so you're good on not losing your heart to me. That's the point of this, right?

Shack up for help around this place, but safely after your last man turned out to be a piece of shit?"

Elyse made a shocked noise in her throat, but the man spun on his heel and strode for the house. He set his narrowed gaze on the woodpile and counted the cords she had cut, which were a pathetic few. Then he made his way to the horse shelter and leaned on the fence, not inviting one sentence of conversation from her while he studied her horses and the chicken coop that now housed exactly zero chickens on account of Cole giving her poultry meat away for booze.

"I have goats in the barn."

"How many head of cattle?"

"Only fifteen now," she murmured, feeling dizzy for reasons she couldn't explain.

"Where are they?"

"Twenty miles up the river on better grazing grounds. My brother checks on them to make sure predators haven't got them, and I'll pay him with a one to butcher when he helps me drive them back here for winter. I go out there a couple times a week if I'm able."

"Hay?"

"I got it planted. It'll need cutting soon."

"You got snow machines?"

"One. It needs work to run."

"And the garden?"

"Out back. It's overrun with weeds and not producing much right now. I've been having trouble keeping up."

The man strode away from her on those long legs, his boots squishing over the muddy drive. Elyse rushed to follow. On the porch, he kicked his shoes off and pushed open the door to her cabin. She winced at what his attention hesitated on. Dishes in the sink, dead flowers in the vase on the table, un-swept floors, dust on everything.

He hooked his hands on his hips and shook his head.

"I must look pathetic to you," she whispered.

"No." He turned and gave her a sympathetic glance with those striking eyes of his. "I'm pissed at your last man for draining you like this, but I can see you've tried. It's been months since he left, though. You should've rebounded." He gave a long, irritated sigh. "I'll consider your offer and give you an answer before weeks' end."

"Okay," she murmured, shocked. Had she made him an offer? She was supposed to be in charge of negotiations, but he'd come in here and dumped her off balance.

He strode out of her house and shoved his feet into his boots. Without bothering to tie the laces, he strode off for an old cream and brown Ford truck with fat tires and mud all down the sides.

"Wait!" she said, lifting her voice as he drove away. "What's your name?"

"Ian." With one last flash of blue eyes before he drove away, he called out the window, "Ian Silver."

FIVE

Ian pulled over to the side of the road about a mile from Elyse's homestead. "Dammit!" he yelled, slamming his open palm against the steering wheel.

Wrecked by how different she looked, he couldn't drive like this. His skin prickled with the first tingles of the Change, and if he didn't get it under control, he would destroy his truck and Change way too close to Elyse. And he could feel what his inner bear was planning. The monster was pissed that he was driving away from her right now. He would be back at her cabin in a minute flat if he gave the animal his skin right now.

Skin and bones. Fuck. She looked so different from the folded picture he'd been carrying around in his back pocket for the last four months since he'd put Cole down. She was thin in the picture, sure, but now? Her damned collar bones were sticking through her thin, gray shirt as though she had no meat on her at all. And her hands were shaking, but she didn't smell nervous. And it wasn't the drink or any other kind of self-medication that was making her this way, either. He would've smelled that, too. No, she was hungry and working herself to death to keep that place running.

There had been two salmon in her freezer. Two. The first snow would come in two months if she was lucky, and all she had stocked up for it was two goddamned fish. He hated

Cole all over again for not being stronger. Giving her chickens away to his no-account brothers. That wasn't the crazy part of him. That was the learned, freeloading part of him. He'd thought Elyse could save him, but Cole hadn't ever stood a chance of her doing him any good. Not when he used her up like that.

For the hundredth time, he wanted to read the letter Cole had given him to deliver to Elyse. Ian had kept it neatly and tightly folded over the last four months. It was private and none of his business, but dang it all, he was curious about what Cole could've possibly written to make an apology this big.

She was hiring a husband!

Ian didn't like it, but he got it. Homesteads around here usually went to sons, but Elyse had been handed one and was stubborn enough to work herself into a grave to keep it up. *Romantics need not apply.* Ian wanted to spit. She was screwing herself out of any chance at a happy life by the way she was going about this, and all for the sake of keeping her homestead.

Ian leaned his elbow on the open window of his truck and gritted his teeth. He would make a damned poor husband, but even he could see the merit in him helping her. He could work harder and longer than a human man, he slept all friggin' winter so she wouldn't have to worry about him getting cabin fever, and he could help her in the warm season to stock up. He could provide for her. Make sure she lived comfortably during the snowy months.

But…

His secrets could get her hurt, or worse. He'd just come back from checking his den on Afognak, and the McCalls had burned his cabin in the cave. They'd been thorough about it, and now it was nothing more than ashes. How they'd tracked him down, he didn't know. He'd used that den for a decade without problems. Miller was hunting him slow, and burning his den was a warning. They hadn't forgotten about their brother, and if Ian stayed here, a mere thirty miles upriver from where the McCalls lived, Elyse could get caught in the crossfire.

But then again, the last place Miller would expect to find him was with Cole's ex-mate.

Ian could prepare her homestead for winter, hunt the meat she needed, then go bear and find a natural den on Kodiak Island with the wild bruins. It wouldn't be a fancy cabin in a cave, but his animal wouldn't care overmuch as long as he got to sleep peacefully. Or as peaceful as possible knowing Miller would be searching every den in Alaska to kill him in his sleep.

His stomach soured at the thought of dying like that. Miller didn't know anything about giving an honorable death. Miller would do it when Ian couldn't fight back.

He leaned over his window and glared at the muddy road that stood between him and Elyse's homestead. He could be happy here, and that was a truly dangerous thought. He was having a hard enough time leaving after talking to her for five minutes. What was going to happen when he fell for her completely? Her life would always be in danger because of him.

A scarred-up grizzly shifter enforcer could make no woman happy.

But from the way she acted back there, she wasn't looking for happy. She was looking for security.

He would make a shite husband, sure, but he could get her fed.

Ian growled and jammed his foot on the gas. Putting distance between them was vital. He was compromising with himself, justifying staying and putting her in danger. This is why he had stalled on delivering that note. This is why he'd waited four months and then decided, in a moment of weakness, to give it to her himself. He had harbored an unhealthy amount of obsession over the woman in the picture since he'd awoken from hibernation.

His damned bear was clearly broken, and now he was convincing Ian to shack up with a needy human.

No. She would find someone decent to fill her advertisement and live a longer, happier life for it.

Ian was no better a choice for a mate than Cole McCall.

****

Ian Silver had lied.

He'd said he would give an answer by weeks' end, but it had been nine days since he'd graced her doorstep and given her freezer that judgmental look. He'd backed out, and the brute hadn't even had the decency to tell her in person.

And now the applicants for her advertisement had waned to no prospects, and she'd wasted all that time interviewing for nothing.

Now, she was further behind than the last three years, and by a lot. Uncle Jim would be so disappointed in her if he saw his place now. This land had been in the Abram family since 1914, and it had never been more at risk than when it fell into her lap. And most nights, she still stayed up wondering why her uncle had thought it best to give her the land instead of her brother, Josiah.

Josiah was strong, had a good head on his shoulders, and wouldn't have ever let this place fall to ruin. He would've never been duped by someone like Cole.

Elyse grunted as she scooped another heaping pile of chicken poop-matted hay from the coop floor. It was late August, and the layers of scat from the winter were thawed out. There wasn't any hope for more chickens until she could figure out how to make more money and purchase the animals plus feed, but the coop was smelling up the clearing, and she'd set aside the morning to clean it up in hopes that someday, perhaps next warm season, she would be in a better place to house hens again.

A soft noise outside made her draw up and frown, but when she listened harder, there was nothing out of the ordinary. Birds and rustling grass and the ever present sound of bugs. Shaking her head and fancying herself crazy, she bent back down and scooped another pitchfork full of smelly muck into the bucket.

There was that noise again.

Elyse set the fork against the wall and made her way out of the coop door, knee-high rubber galoshes squishing against the filth with every careful step. Her gaze was drawn down the dirt road toward the noise that was getting louder now.

The muddy nose of a brown and cream pickup was bouncing slowly toward her. Ian Silver was back.

With a gasp, Elyse wiped her hands on her jeans and patted her messy hair she'd piled high on her head. Her pants were smeared, her black rain boots were covered in an inch of fragrant muck, and she was about to see the man she'd been thinking of constantly all week. He would definitely tell her no when he saw her like this.

As he eased his truck in front of the cabin, he was pulling a trailer with a snow machine behind it, and sudden hope bloomed in her chest. The bed of his truck was piled high with belongings, and even the back seat of his truck looked full.

She patted her hair again and smelled her shirt, but scrunched up her nose at that bad decision. The scent of old chicken poop had a tendency to cling to everything. Maybe he wouldn't notice.

Ian Silver got out of his truck and strode around the front on his long, powerful legs. He was more intimidating than she'd remembered. Was he even bigger? She thought so. More filled out and muscular somehow.

She fidgeted until he looked up from the ground and stopped her cold with those bright blue eyes of his. "I have a few negotiations."

"Uh. Okay?"

He hooked his hands on his hips and glared. "One, I'm not marrying you."

"Non-negotiable. I want a husband."

"Why? I can work just as hard whether I'm your husband or not."

"Because I want you to have incentive to stick around, Mr. Silver. I'm not looking to hire labor for a season." She gave him an empty smile. "I want to grow old with you."

Ian inhaled deeply and rolled his eyes. "Oh, God. Fine, but you have to go through an entire year with me before we talk marriage."

"What? No! You're just buying yourself time to escape. I want a husband."

"You don't want a husband, woman. You want loyal help."

"I know what I want."

"Well, you're being unreasonable."

"I'm twenty-six years old, have horrible taste in men, and no prospects. Galena isn't exactly teaming with available men my age, Mr. Silver. I put an ad in the newspaper for a husband, not charity work. I want someone I can depend on to work beside me, and what reason would you have to stay if we don't say vows in front of a preacher?"

"My answer is no. We can talk about it after you see how it is living with me through the winter season."

"Well," she said, crossing her arms stubbornly over her chest and swallowing the lump of disappointment down her throat, "then I'm afraid we don't reach an agreement."

"Dammit, Elyse Abram, why are you turning away good help?"

"Because I want more than that." Shit, it was out there now, and her eyes were burning with tears. "I want someone to be there for me. I'm not asking for love, Ian. I just don't want it to be so easy for a man to leave. It took ten minutes for Cole to pack up his belongings and leave my life, and just like that," she said, snapping her fingers, "he was gone."

"Yeah, and what if I end up to be as bad as him? Huh? You don't know me!"

"I know you well enough. I know you looked in my freezer first thing. Cole only opened that lid when he was taking something from me. You counted how much wood I had chopped and asked about my garden and took stock of my animals and for fuck's sake, you even asked about the hay I'd planted. Cole didn't care. He was on a bender in town while my brother and I planted those fields by ourselves. Will you raise a hand to me, Mr. Silver?"

"Never."

"Then you're all right by me. I want vows. I want a man legally tied to me. I want a man to see me and have pride that he is making something work with me, and I never want to wake up again wondering if my helpmate is going to leave."

"Gah!" Ian barked out, his eyes blazing in irritation as he paced in front of her.

He ran his hands through his mussed hair and then flung them forward. Fuming, he turned and got back in his truck, and before she could muster up the words to stop him, he was pulling away and out of her life for the second time.

And it was back to square one. Again.

SIX

Elyse dumped another bucket of water over the floorboards in the chicken coop and stood back to inspect all her hard work. It had taken well into the afternoon for her to get it cleaned on account of the stupid tears that were blurring her vision half the danged time.

Stupid Ian Silver had teased her. She'd been so close to having a good man and the promise that life around the homestead would be less overwhelming, but he'd been here a total of five minutes before he left. Typical.

With a growl, she stomped out of the newly cleaned and entirely empty coop, then stabbed the earth with the pitchfork with every step she took toward an old water trough. Running water up here was sketchy. Uncle Jim had set it up to feed from a natural spring at the back of the property, but the water pressure left a lot to be desired, and it was cold as icicle piss. She grabbed the old rusted handle of the water pump and worked to get the water flowing. When it trickled an acceptable amount, she hurried to wash her hands and arms with the bar of soap that sat on the ledge. And when she was done with that, she turned her attention to the shelter for her two horses, Milo and Demon, the last one aptly named because he was a biting, bucking asshole to anyone in his saddle.

Shoes squishing in the mud, she swatted at a bug that was hovering right in front of her face, then skidded to a stop as she spotted Ian's pickup coming down the road again. He wasn't being careful about her driveway this time. Instead, he was skidding this way and that, pulling the trailer behind and going faster than she would ever advise with the short clearing she had for a yard.

He locked up the brakes, and the tires stopped spinning. The truck, however, took a good extra twenty feet to skid to a stop. Ian got out and slammed the door behind him, then marched over to her. He stood a good foot taller than her, so she had to arch her neck all the way back to take in his angry face. From the fire in his eyes, she thought he would ream her out, but instead, he held up a simple gold band between his pointer finger and thumb.

"This is a bad idea," he muttered. Clearing his throat, he sank down to one knee in the mud and dragged his furious gaze up to her. "I can't in good conscious marry you without you seeing what kind of man I am for one full winter. I can't explain to you why, but I don't feel right tethering you to me legally until you know all of what you're in for. But I can give you this." He held up the ring, and the sunlight glinted off it like newly washed miner's gold. "I've never asked a woman to marry me, never even considered it, and this is the first and last ring I'll ever buy. This ties me to you and to this place as well as any marriage license would. I'll be your man, Elyse Abram. I'll make sure you don't go hungry and that you are safe. As long as I'm alive." The last part he said in a quieter voice as the heat cooled from his eyes. "Wear my ring, and it'll make me a part of this place. This is the only vow I can give you right now. It's my final offer."

Her mouth was hanging open, so she closed it with a small snap. Her breath trembled as she looked down at her dirty clothes and muddy, floppy galoshes in shock. "You're proposing?"

Ian pursed his lips and nodded once.

"But I smell like chicken poop."

He nodded again. "That you do. What's your answer?"

Stunned, she gulped and shook a strand of loose hair out from in front of her eyes. "I accept your negotiations."

Ian frowned slightly, then stood to his full, towering height and shoved the ring roughly onto her finger. He spun to walk back to his truck, but hesitated with his back to her. He turned and stared at her, his stormy eyes troubled. His throat moved as he swallowed, and slowly he rested his hand on her waist. She froze under his touch as warmth pooled in her middle. He leaned in and kissed her on the cheek, his rough beard tickling against her skin. His lips lingered there, and she closed her eyes to savor the unexpected moment.

Easing away, he dropped his hand from her hip and nodded toward his truck. In a deep, growly voice, he murmured, "I brought you an engagement present."

"You did? What is it?"

"Chickens."

And as she stood there stunned, with the weight of the gold band heavy on her finger, watching her new fiancé unload cardboard boxes with holes poked in the tops from the back of his truck, a weight lifted from her shoulders. The advertisement had worked, and better than she'd ever imagined.

Ian Silver was hers, and not only that, but the man had already pegged the clear and direct way to her heart.

Pretty promises and poultry.

Forcing her legs to move, she squished up to him and took a box from his hands. It was heavier than she'd expected, and when she heard the mature squawking and fluttering from inside, she understood. He hadn't bought her chicks to raise. He'd bought her adult hens that would already be egg producers. He'd probably paid a pretty penny for these, and now her respect for him as a capable man bloomed.

"Have you worked a homestead before?" she asked, suddenly feeling overwhelmed by how much she didn't know about her fiancé. *Fiancé*. Geez, she'd really done it.

"No, but I know what needs to be done to keep you alive through the winter."

"Oh." She toted the heavy box toward the coop, ignoring how noodle-like her legs felt as she bounced this way and that as if she'd taken a half dozen shots of tequila. She'd been proposed to. Like, handsome-man-on-his-knees-in-the-mud-asking-for-her-hand proposed to.

She swayed at the door, but a firm hand gripped her upper arm. In a worried tone, Ian asked, "Are you feeling poorly?"

"I think I'm in shock," she admitted as she allowed him to guide her into the giant coop. "I thought you'd left for good."

"Well, you were stubborn and asking for it."

She would've been offended if it weren't for the teasing edge in his tone. She set the squawking, scratching box down with an unintentional thud.

"I'll get the rest of them," Ian murmured. "You go fill their water dispenser."

"Okay." Her voice sounded dreamy and strange to her own ears, as if it belonged to someone else.

She wasn't used to being bossed around, and it should've rankled her, but by his worried tone, she got the distinct feeling Ian was asking her to do the easy job. She wasn't making a good impression on him. She was much tougher than she looked and had made it through much bigger than a little engagement shock.

The coop was tall enough for her to stand to her full height. It was lined with nesting boxes along one wall with roosting polls, and there was a small door at the bottom of the opposite wall that allowed the chickens into the outdoor pen when it was open. It seemed she had cleaned this place just in time.

Elyse hauled water from the pump with a pair of buckets that sloshed against her legs with each step and filled the two water dispensers while Ian hauled another three boxes of chickens into the coop. Then he filled the grain storage box with bags of chicken feed while Elyse opened the cardboard lids and set the poultry free. They were all different colors. Browns, reds, and black with white speckles and oh, they would make a lovely array of colored eggs for them to eat. They were mostly grown but still young chickens, and she laughed as the last box revealed four adolescent turkeys that were just getting their adult feathers in.

When she turned, Ian was staring at her lips with the most peculiar look on his face. Another wave of heat burned her cheeks, so she busied herself with breaking down the boxes to save for later use. Nothing went to waste around here.

With the chickens, turkeys, and one mean-ass rooster fed and settled, Elyse turned to offer Ian help with unloading his belongings, but the man had vanished like a ghost. And when she peeked outside the coop, he was backing his snow machine off the trailer and onto a ramp as though he'd done it a million times. Then he turned it for the barn and disappeared through the open sliding doors.

Okay then. Elyse meandered to his truck, pulled open the back door, and guffawed at what he'd brought. There were a couple of trash bags of what must be clothes, sure, but most of his belongings seemed to be old, second-hand tools. Limb cutters, a chainsaw, an ax, and a giant silver metal box of what was probably wrenches and the like, along with a tackle box and a pair of fishing poles.

When Cole had moved in last year, he'd brought a duffle bag with him. That was it.

Pleasure unfurled in her stomach as she enjoyed the difference of this time with Ian. He was bringing his get-shit-done belongings, as well as clothes. She could already imagine his ax near the chopping block and his tools in the barn. He was about to imprint himself into this place as surely as his ring was imprinting itself onto her finger.

With an emotional smile, she pulled the hard case of his chainsaw out of the back and hefted it toward the barn. Wait, what if he got mad at her for touching his stuff? Did men get possessive of their tools? Uncle Jim hadn't, and she'd never seen Cole lift a hand to help so he wasn't any indicator on normal male behavior. Josiah hadn't ever minded her touching his stuff, but he was her brother and the patient sort. Maybe she should rush back and put this where she found it.

Ian strode from the barn and nodded to her. The corner of his lip lifted, and he said, "Thank you," as he took the burden from her hands.

As he sauntered off, Elyse froze there with her empty palms out, then turned and went back for another load. And when the tools were all in the barn and she'd settled the ax blade into the chopping block, she rushed inside to do a speed clean while Ian was still busy in the barn. At least she'd found the energy to wash the dishes this morning, but she hadn't set foot in the guest bedroom in months. She dusted the dresser, swept the rustic wooden floors, and then replaced the bedding with fresh linens. After angling and re-angling the rocking chair in the corner just so, she turned and let off a yelp as Ian stood right behind her with a quirk to his lips.

Her heart threatened to leap from behind her breastbone. How was a man so big and powerful so silent when he wanted to be? He stepped around her, so close she could smell his piney, masculine scent and feel warmth radiating off his skin.

Ian set his trash bag luggage on the bed. "This'll do. I'll unpack later, but I think you should eat."

She thought about her now empty freezer, and shame, not shyness, heated her cheeks.

Ian narrowed his eyes and cocked his head suspiciously at her hesitation, then turned and strode out of the house, his heavy boots echoing against the floors. The creaking of the freezer sounded a moment later, and a muttered curse directly followed. And now Ian was back in the mouth of the room, his lips pursed in a thin, angry line. "Woman, what did you plan on eating today if I hadn't a shown up?"

She ran her tongue over her teeth, stalling and debating whether to lie or not.

"The truth," he demanded, as if he could read her mind.

"I picked some carrots."

"Carrots?" The volume of his voice made her hunch her shoulders to her ears. "Why haven't you been hunting and fishing?"

Anger snapped through her like a rubber band popped against her skin. "If you must know, I have been hunting and fishing, but I'm pretty shitty at it, so I haven't got anything. Yet. And when I'm not out in the woods failing epically at hunting, I'm racing daylight running this place. None of this has been easy on me, you judgmental beast."

"Judgmental beast, am I?" His animated eyebrows quirked up. "Fine. Since you have me so pegged, you're too damned skinny."

Elyse let off an offended sound. "Well, you're too muscular and probably require eighteen thousand calories a day. I do not. I'm not skinny. I'm efficient."

"Horseshit. I can see your bones poking out through your shirt, and your stomach's been growling since I got here."

She narrowed her eyes and crossed her arms over her chest like a shield. His words hurt. There. There it was. Him calling her skinny burned her pride. Oh, she knew she'd lost weight. She was the one who saw herself withering away in the mirror, but Cole had taken all of her damned seed potatoes, bartered them for God knows what, and left her so low on everything she was struggling to get ahead. And she hadn't lied. She was shit at hunting. That was one lesson Uncle Jim failed to teach her before he passed, and Josiah had never offered to show her how to track animals. She had more pride than to beg people to teach her something a good Alaskan woman ought to know by instinct.

Furious at Ian for being harsh, and even angrier with herself for caring, she brushed past him, knocking against his irritatingly firm arm, and strode for the living room. The rifles were hung on wall pets in the front corner beside the door, and she picked the one that recoiled the least, then stomped out of the house.

She made it deep into the woods before Ian's voice called out from behind her. "Where are you going?"

She bit back a curse that he followed her. "Hunting. Obviously."

"No, not obviously. What the fuck are you planning on taking with that pea shooter? It's good for muskrat and ptarmigan. Rabbits maybe. And you're rushing off pissed with no supplies and no pistol."

"Why would I need a pistol, Ian? I have a rifle."

"If you can call it that. And as to why you would need a pistol...slow down. Elyse Abram!"

"Stop calling me that!" she fumed, rounding on him. He backed up from her, step for step. Wise man.

"It's your name."

She shoved her ring finger in the air like she was flipping him off. "We're engaged. You can drop my last name."

A low rumble emanated from his chest.

"Did you just growl at me?"

"No."

"Yes you did!"

"Give me the gun, and let's go back to the house before you find a pack of wolves."

"Piss off. I'm going to bring home dinner, honey."

"I brought food with me. We don't need to do this tonight and, anyway, it'll be dark before you find any game. Just…" Ian grabbed the barrel of the gun over her shoulder and yanked. Only she wasn't ready. He startled her, and she jerked the trigger.

A deafening boom echoed through the woods.

Ian's bright eyes looked downright terrifying as he yanked the gun from her grasp. "Are you fucking kidding me? You had it loaded with the safety off? You could've killed yourself or somebody else."

"I wasn't pointing it anywhere near you or me. It was up in the air."

"Gun safety basics, Elyse *Abram*. Safety on until you're ready to pull that trigger, and furthermore, your finger shouldn't even be on that trigger unless you have your intended target in the crosshairs. Now get your ass back to the cabin before I carry you my damned self. I'm mad enough to do it right now."

Elyse gave him a slit-eyed glare. "You aren't the boss of me."

"I offered you the protection of my body when I gave you that ring. You aren't going out into the wilderness when it's this late in the day on a fool's errand. Your kind can't even see in the dark."

"My kind? *My kind*? I suppose you mean women." She poked him in the chest, but jammed her finger painfully, which only pissed her off more. Irrationally, she growled out, "I'll have you know I was doing just fine before you came along."

"Bullshit. You're skin and bones."

"Stop it!" Her lip trembled, and she bit it hard. "Don't you know anything about being nice? If you have something mean to say, swallow it down, man. I get it. I'm too skinny for your liking, but this is the only body I have, and insulting it isn't helping. You think I want to look like this? Do you even know what it's taken to get this bad? I was pretty once, you arrogant sonofabitch." Stupid tear as it tracked down her cheek and stupid tremor in her voice. Furious that he'd gotten her so riled up, she made her way around him and stepped over the knee-high grass, headed back home.

She used to be strong before Cole mishandled her. She never cried or worried over the opinions of men, and now she'd been reduced to tears by a stranger.

"Fuck," Ian muttered from behind her, but if he was following, she couldn't tell.

At the water pump, she dragged over the biggest bucket and began pumping the handle to get the water flowing. She filled the bucket nearly to the top and hauled the insanely heavy burden toward the horses' shelter.

"Here, let me," Ian said in a resolved voice as he slid his hand over hers to take the bucket.

"I can do it on my own. I have been for the past three years. Don't worry. You don't have to have a dick to do this kind of work, Ian. Women can do it, too."

He released her hand and walked beside her. "I was wrong for the things I said."

"Great. Forgiven. Fight one down, only sixty more years of me pissing you off to go." Water sloshed all over the leg of her jeans and, great gads, it was cold, but she was used to it. She always fatigued at the end.

Demon and Milo waited at the fence for her as she hoisted the water bucket to her hip and dumped it through the fence into their trough. "And just so you know," she said, clutching the bucket handle to steady her shaking hands. "I have goats. I was working my way up to...you know...killing one."

Ian ghosted a glance toward the barn where the goats lived, then nodded his head. "I shouldn't make snap judgements on things. I just don't like how thin you've become."

"How thin I've become? You've only seen me one other time, and I assure you, I'm not much worse off."

Ian opened his mouth as if to say something, then snapped it closed again. He ran his hands through his hair and admitted, "I don't know how to talk to girls."

"You never had one before?"

He shook his head, and if she didn't know any better, she could've sworn his cheeks were turning red.

"Well, you've just shocked me to my bones."

Ian leaned on the fence and watched the horses drinking deeply. "How so?"

"Because I thought a man who looks like you would've been with a dozen girls, at least."

Scrunching his face up, he glanced over at the sunrise and murmured, "I didn't say I haven't slept with women. I just mean that I haven't had one of my own." He turned those bright eyes on her. "To keep happy. You understand?"

"Are you backwoods?" Being raised in the wilderness without access to girls was the only thing that explained why a big, strapping, sexy-as-hell man like Ian Silver hadn't held down a relationship with a woman.

He huffed a soft laugh. "You could say that. And just so you know, you aren't too skinny for my liking. I think you're pretty enough. I just don't like thinking you're hungry. I've been hungry before. It sucks."

"Yeah it does," she said on a sigh as she rested her chin on the fence and watched the sinking sun beside him. "And thanks for saying that. You didn't have to."

"What, that you're pretty?"

She nodded slowly, her chin rubbing her protruding wrist bone.

Ian shook his head, whatever that meant, then said, "Come on. I'll put a few more buckets of water in the trough. You go wash up, and I'll get dinner on." He picked up the bucket, then turned and walked away. "You smell like chicken shit," he said over his shoulder.

Elyse snorted, but bit her lip to hide her amusement. She really did smell rough after cleaning out the coop. Ian was one lucky man to have landed such a fine woman as herself. "Sorry I almost shot you!" she called.

She couldn't tell for sure from here, but his cheeks looked like they swelled with a smile as he walked away. "Forgiven. Only sixty more years to go."

SEVEN

Ian had hurt her.

A few hours here and, already, he'd made her tear up. Even though she'd let him off the hook, his guts still felt all ripped up that he was the cause of any more hurt. This is why men like him had no business taking on a woman. They were soft, and he was all claws and teeth and grizzly moods.

He dumped a second giant can of beef stew into the pot and stirred.

The woman had taken to nesting worse than he did right before hibernation. While he'd unpacked the pallets of food he'd brought with him from the bed of his pickup, she'd swept the floors and thrown out the dead flowers from the vase that decorated the kitchen table. He was pretty sure she'd even cleaned the outhouse. There was running water here, but just barely since, according to Elyse, it was fed by a natural spring that wasn't a huge producer. There was enough for a quick, trickling shower, but not enough for toilet flushes, so the outhouse was going to be part of life now.

"Is your heat oil?" he asked. Lame. God, he didn't know how to talk to women.

Elyse bent down with the dust pan and scooped a mound of dirt into it. "I couldn't afford the three thousand a year to do oil, so I'm all wood burning. I mean *we're*. We're all wood burning." She stood, cheeks flushed in the soft glow of the lanterns hung around the room.

"I'll need to start cutting as soon as possible then. You only have enough chopped to last you the first couple of weeks of snow. And I think we're going to have to butcher at least one of your cows."

"What? Why?" she asked as she dumped the dustpan's contents out the back door. "I need those to sell. That's where my money comes from. I'm not totally off the grid or subsistence. I buy some of the things I need, and I only have fifteen head of cattle left, if no predators have run off with any of them."

"I thought you said your brother was watching them."

"Part of the time. More like checks on them, but Josiah's no range rider. He has a life of his own and a little piece of land he's managing close to the summer grazing range."

"Hmm," Ian said low in his chest. That wasn't good. Predators were thick around here, thanks to all the wilderness around them. Galena was nothing like Anchorage. It was population five-hundred, and other than sitting on the bank of the Yukon River, it was surrounded by the Alaskan wilds. It was a wonder Elyse had any cattle left.

As if she could hear his thoughts, she said quietly, "When my uncle was alive and running this place, he had eighty cattle. It's hard thinking about losing any more of his herd."

"It's not about the meat, Elyse." Ian banged the extra stew off the spoon on the side of the pan and moved the boiling meal off the burner. "I looked at your hay, and if we cut it at peak time, when it will give the most nutrition to your animals—"

"Our animals."

Ian sighed and leaned against the natural wood counter. "It won't be enough to get a herd that big through the winter. Honestly, we need to butcher one or two and maybe even sell off a couple more. If you want to build the herd next warm season, then we need to figure out how to purchase more later, but we can't feed what we have now. Not with that little hay."

"I worked my ass off to plant that. Josiah helped, but most of that was me."

Ian hated the disappointment on her face. He got it. Right now she was thinking about how hard she'd worked. She'd probably bled and sweated all over that field, and here he came, telling her the work wasn't enough. "Next year will be different," he said softly. "If you still want me around after this winter, we'll get more hay planted, and I'll buy you more cattle, okay? Between you and me and Josiah, we'll get you where you want to be."

Elyse's hair was down and still damp from her shower, and as she picked at a little piece of masking tape on the counter, she'd let her tresses fall forward, hiding her face. He couldn't stand not being able to see her eyes right now, so he reached forward and tucked a strand behind her ear, then lifted her chin with a hooked finger. "Okay?"

"You're a good man," she said so softly he wouldn't have heard it without his heightened senses.

God, he wished that were true. If she knew her ex boyfriend's blood was on his hands, though, Elyse wouldn't be looking at him so gratefully right now. She was the good one. He was just here hoping some of her decency rubbed off on him.

Ian focused on pouring stew into the two wooden bowls Elyse pulled from the upper cabinets.

"Are you feeding an army?" she asked twitching her chin toward the vat of canned stew he'd heated up.

"Oh. I should tell you now. You'll have to accept and get used to the fact that I eat a lot."

"We're going to eat all this in one sitting?"

"Look, I can't explain why, but my body needs a lot of food to sustain itself. I'll get sick as all get-out if I don't eat constantly."

Her delicate, sandy-colored eyebrows arched up in surprise. "Constantly?"

Ian handed her a bowl and settled his hip against the counter to tuck into his meal. But Elyse had other ideas about the way meal-time should go and made her way through the small kitchen to the table. She even pulled a chair out for him before she sat in the one right next to it.

"I usually eat standing up."

"Why?"

Ian took a bite to stall as he mulled over why he was so damned comfortable avoiding tables outside of restaurants. After swallowing, he shuffled to the chair and sat down beside her. "I guess because I've always been alone. Tables are for families."

"Well, now you have me."

Now you have me. Her words lifted the hairs on his arms, and he sat there stunned, watching her eat. He had someone. Really had her. Elyse was wearing his ring as proof.

Ian Silver wasn't a lone grizzly anymore.

Elyse was wrong, though. He wasn't the one who had her. She'd had him since the day he'd woken up on Afognak Island with her picture tucked into that envelope. He'd wanted her. Feared her for what that attraction could mean for him. Deep inside, there was this warm tendril that unfurled like a fern frond a little more each time she spoke to him, or each time he learned something new about her. It wasn't love yet, but if she kept declaring things like that, she was going to own him, heart and soul. A dangerous game for both of them.

"Where are you from?" Elyse asked between bites.

The temptation to tell her the truth was overwhelming. He was from a dark den in a dark cabin in a dark cave made for long sleeps. In his mind, he'd always called it the Monster House. That had been home base until Miller had burned it. She didn't need to see the darkness of his life, though, so instead, he answered, "Everywhere. Here and there."

She stopped eating and stared at him. With a slow blink, she said, "You know we'll have to actually get to know each other at some point."

"Alaska."

Elyse pursed her lips. "Where in Alaska?"

Stifling a growl at her getting too close to his secrets, he leaned back in his chair and listed off the places he'd stayed this warm season. "Fairbanks, Coldfoot, Nome, Kodiak Island, specifically Port Lions and Larsen Bay, Afognak, Trapper Creek—"

"Okay. I get it. You don't want to talk about where you're from."

"I'm from everywhere, like I said."

"Or you're from nowhere." Elyse cocked her head with a challenging look glinting in those gorgeous green-gold eyes of hers, then went back to eating and completely ignored him.

Nowhere. A good place to hail from for a ghost.

"What about you? Where are you from?"

"Anchorage."

"City girl," he said, teasing in desperation to see a smile on her face again.

She scraped the bottom of her bowl, so Ian stood and refilled it for her. When he sat back down and settled the steaming beef stew in front of her, she said, "I used to spend time out here with my Uncle Jim in the summers when I didn't have school. He and his woman, Marta, didn't ever have children of their own, and my mom was overwhelmed raising me and Josiah by herself. She got the summers off of being a parent when she sent us here. And it was fine by us, because we got to help my uncle around the homestead." Elyse ghosted him a glance, then returned to her food. "I fell in love with this place when I was seven."

"Is that why you're so hard on yourself for struggling here?"

"Yeah. When I stayed with my uncle, I thought there was nothing he couldn't do, you know? He could fix anything and come up with a solution to every problem. I watched him dig a water filtration system to get water in this cabin, just because Marta wanted it. I saw him treat her like a queen as much as he was able, and he never got impatient with explaining how and why he did things around the homestead. My dad wasn't in the picture, so Uncle Jim filled this void in me I couldn't figure out how to fill up when I lived in Anchorage. Josiah always loved this place, but me? I *loved* this place." She pursed her lips and shook her head, shrugging her shoulders. "It always felt like home, and my real home in the city felt temporary. I think my mom saw that, too, because even when Josiah started wanting to stay in the city and spend the warm months shooting the shit with his friends, she kept sending me here."

"Why didn't your uncle teach you to hunt?"

"He got me through the hunter safety course, but by the time most of the big game seasons came about, I was back in Anchorage going to school. And when I turned eighteen, Mom wanted me out of the house the second I graduated high school, so then I got a job in the city and my visits out here were few and far between. Life, you know? I got caught up trying to cover my bills. I missed the last of Marta's life, and I missed the last of Uncle Jim's. And I missed this place. I was unhappy and uncomfortable in my own skin. I didn't know a damned thing about myself and couldn't figure out what was missing, and then Uncle Jim left me this place in his will when he passed three years ago. And suddenly, everything made sense. It was like coming home after being away for a really long time. And I was proud of myself for the first time in a long time because the first year I did okay. Josiah helped a lot and settled twenty miles away. The grazing was better over his way, so we figured out how to run the cattle together. Sometimes I think he moved here to make sure I was okay, though. He liked Anchorage more than I did. He has friends there."

"And you didn't have friends after all that time there?"

"I did, but it wasn't like with my brother. I have trouble connecting with people. No, that's not true," she said with a deep frown. "I have trouble picking the right people."

Ian nodded slowly. He could see that. She was trusting and gave too many chances, and sometimes in this world, innocence like that drew in dark people who liked to take advantage. She'd put herself in a submissive position and drawn in the dominants who would feed off what she could provide, be it emotional or material. It was the easiest thing in the world to see why a woman like Elyse would want to make a life way out here where she didn't have to make those decisions on who to trust.

"Is that why you let Cole come around?"

Elyse gave him a faraway look and an empty smile, then pushed her half-eaten bowl away as if she'd lost her appetite. "Cole came around because he found a good mark to use. And being too big a pussy to break it off with me, he made himself unacceptable so I would pull the trigger on our relationship. I'm going to go to bed." She stood and walked abruptly into her bedroom, leaving Ian's head spinning on what had just happened.

What had he said? He'd just asked about Cole because he was honestly curious on why a smart, hard-working, level-headed woman like Elyse would allow a free-loading asshole to drain her like that.

Elyse closed her bedroom door behind her, and from the other side, he heard the trickle of water from her bathroom sink. Troubled, he ate slowly, going over and over their conversation. He didn't want to be done talking yet. He was only just getting to know her. But maybe that was the problem. Perhaps she wanted to get to know him, too, but he'd shared nothing about himself and had asked her to share her deepest regrets with him. This shit right here was why he was going to make a terrible mate…er…husband. He had no social skills and was baffled by every single thing she did and said. Grizzly bear shifters were solo creatures. Too dominant to hold relationships with each other, as highlighted by his non-existent bond with his brothers, and the instinct to settle down only struck on rare occasions. And that usually turned out awful by the first hibernation because what woman on earth was going to deal with their man sleeping for six months of the year instead of carrying on a relationship with her? None. Even his own damned mother had been done with his dad long before she delivered his triplets. Overwhelmed and uninterested in mothering multiples, she'd given Ian and his brothers to Dad for full custody by their second year.

Maybe he should've told Elyse that part. Maybe she wouldn't feel like she was giving too much for nothing in return then.

Ian washed their dishes and turned off the lanterns, and with one final troubled glance at her closed bedroom door, he made his way across the living room to his own bedroom.

The bed was lumpy and the pillows flat, but that wasn't what kept him awake tonight. It was a small sniffle, just like the one Elyse had given off when he'd talked to her on the phone all those months ago. It gutted him.

Had he caused her tears? Had memories of Cole made her cry like this? The quiet kind where she was trying to hide her heartbreak. Ian made his way silently through the living room and pushed open her door. Illuminated by blue streaks of moonlight that filtered through the window, she lay with her back to him, knees curled up to her chest, her shoulders shaking. He couldn't stay, but he couldn't go any farther. Elyse hadn't asked for his comfort, and he was an intruder on her private moment, but still, he couldn't force his feet back to his own bedroom.

Trapped, Ian rested his back on the door frame and slid quietly down the wood.

And long after Elyse's shoulders stopped shaking, he finally, finally fell asleep.

EIGHT

Elyse stretched and squinted at the early morning sunlight that was assaulting the room. She rolled over with the intention of snuggling her pillow for a few more minutes before she forced herself up to start the day, but a giant figure on the floor near her open doorway had a screech clawing its way up her throat. Swallowing it back down, she remembered all the events from yesterday and fidgeted with the gold ring around her finger.

Why on earth was Ian curled up in a giant ball sleeping on the floor?

As quietly as she could manage, she slipped out of bed and made her way into the bathroom, careful not to disturb him. Her reflection in the mirror was atrocious, but after she put her hair in a messy bun, brushed her teeth, and washed her face, she didn't look as rough. That enormous bowl and a half of stew she'd eaten last night had done her some good, even if her eyes were a little puffy from…crying. Crap. Maybe that's why Ian was on the floor. Maybe she'd been too loud.

Tugging the hem of her sleep shirt lower, she padded across the cold wooden floorboards and shook his waist gently. "Ian," she whispered. "Ian."

"Hmm?" he asked sharply, sitting up so fast he nearly bowled her over. "Shit," he rasped, catching her arms before she put her tailbone through her throat on the floor. "You okay?"

"I'm fine." Elyse lowered down to sit by him and pulled her arms gently from his strong grasp. "Why are you sleeping on the floor?"

Ian blinked hard at her lap, then ran his hand through his hair as he looked blearily around her bedroom. "You were crying."

Scrunching up her nose, she said, "I was trying to be quiet about it."

"I have good hearing. Why?"

"Why was I crying?"

"Yeah, why?"

Elyse shook her head, not ready to admit all her demons. He already thought she was pathetic. Best not go proving he was right.

Ian rolled up much more gracefully than she'd expected and offered her his palm, upturned. "Purple panties," he rumbled low.

Sliding her hand against his, she allowed him to pull her up. "I'm sorry?"

"You're wearing purple panties." His gaze dropped to her hips, then back to her face. "When you sat down, I saw them. Just thought we should get that out in the air."

"Great, anything else?" she asked, mortified.

Ian cleared his throat and nodded once. "I like them. They're a good color on your skin. And I like the cut. And you smell good. And your hair...it's...nice. And your eyes."

"What about them?" She swayed slightly, feeling yet again that she was unbalanced around Ian.

"I like those, too."

She was fighting a smile now. Damn, sleepy Ian was a flattering little flatterer. "Anything else?"

"Yes."

"You want to tell me what it is?"

Ian shook his head and stepped around her and into the bathroom. "Your turn," he said in a sleepy, rumbling voice as he squeezed toothpaste onto his toothbrush.

"Okay. You're tall and strong, and I like watching your pec muscles move under that undone button of the sweater you wore yesterday, and your eyes are also very nice, and twice I noticed you had a boner, and I was intimidated because it looks huge all pressed up against your jeans, but I like it." There. Honesty for honesty, but now Ian was staring at her in the mirror as if she'd lost her mind. "What?" she asked with a frown.

"I wasn't asking you to compliment me, woman. I meant why were you crying?"

"Oh." God, this was embarrassing. "If you could just wipe that boner comment out of your mind, that would be great."

"Hell no. That was my favorite part." Now Ian was smiling behind his toothbrush as he scrubbed, and her cheeks were so hot that she pressed her palms against her face just to cool them down.

"I was crying over Cole," she blurted out, then slapped her hands over her mouth. "I shouldn't have said that. It's not right to you."

Ian's smile slipped away, and he dragged his bright blue gaze away from hers in the mirror. "You miss him?"

"No. I feel…" God, how did she put this where he would understand? "He told me once I was the only thing that could save him, and I kept him around too long trying to be that for him. He died alone, off in the woods somewhere in some awful way. Bear attack. They aren't quick, you know."

Ian's eyes tightened in the mirror, but whatever argument he'd been about to give, he kept it to himself.

"I feel guilty. I did love him. Once. There. I feel bad that I wasn't enough. How pathetic, right? The man wasn't even nice to me, and still, I can't stop replaying those words in my mind. He was so serious, like he really thought I could make him into a better person. It's guilt that has me weak, and you don't deserve the ghost of that man in this house. *Our* house."

Ian spat toothpaste and rinsed, took his time wiping his face with the hand towel, then turned and leaned back against the sink ledge. "You have nothing to feel guilty for."

"But he died alone—"

Anger flashed across his eyes. "He died like he was supposed to, Elyse. There was nothing you or anyone else could've done to change that man's ending."

"But—"

"No." Ian reached for her and crushed her against his chest, squeezing the air and her argument from her lungs. "Going over it in your head and feeling bad won't change anything. This isn't your fault. Listen to me." He hugged her tighter and lowered his lips near her ear. "His death isn't on you. That's just you scratching at a cut and keeping it raw. It won't heal if you don't leave it alone. You're *enough*, Elyse. Cole wasn't."

Something changed inside of her. It was instantaneous, breathtaking, and warm. He'd said she was enough. No one had ever said that to her before. Before this moment, she'd been the kid in school who needed improvement. The daughter who couldn't maintain the relationship she wanted with her mom. The girlfriend who couldn't hold a man's attention. The sister Josiah had to pack up his whole life for, just to make sure she was okay. The homesteader who'd steadily failed at carving out a life here. The niece who'd missed the last years of Uncle Jim's life chasing an empty life of her own.

But here, in Ian's arms, he was telling her differently with such conviction in his voice. You. Are. Enough. What that combination of simple words did to her middle was incredible. Where she'd shunned compliments before, convinced anything nice said about her couldn't be true, these words stuck to her ribs. They rattled around in her head and landed right in her heart, and in this instant, she believed him.

To Ian, she was enough.

Slowly, she slid her arms around his waist and rested her cheek against his chest, over his pounding heartbeat. It felt so good to be right here with his words warming her from the middle like a good shot of whiskey. His arms were so strong around her, hugging her close as if he didn't want to let go any more than she did. She'd been freefalling before now, and Ian Silver, a man she had no right to have this strong a connection with, had just reached out and plucked her from the sky.

Exhaling a shaky breath, she clutched the back of his shirt. No more tears for Cole. Ian was perfectly right. Even if she'd let him stay, the truth of the matter was that Cole had gone long before she kicked him out. He was staying with other women and drinking all night in Galena, avoiding domestic life. Avoiding her. How could she be expected to save a man like him? He hadn't even tried.

"Thank you," she whispered, her knees going soft as she melted against him farther.

Ian nuzzled her cheek until his beard tickled her skin. "For what?"

"For coming here. For sleeping on my floor because you were worried. For saying I'm enough. For all of it. Everything."

His heart raced under her cheek as he eased back by inches. His lips were so close to hers now. So close. If she just turned her head...

Ian's hand slipped to her cheek and around to her neck, cupping her gently as he stayed frozen there. This felt big. So big her hands went cold and damp, and her heart raced to match his. His bright blue gaze was at her mouth. Ian leaned forward and pressed his lips against hers, and Elyse's legs locked completely. If it wasn't for one of his arms around her, she would've fallen, but Ian was there to catch her. He was good. Right down to his marrow, he was a good man.

He moved his mouth against hers, and an embarrassingly helpless noise escaped her throat.

In the moment that followed, a strange noise came from Ian's chest. It was short and low, like a hum, but it made his chest vibrate in a strange and exciting way. Oh, sexy growly man. He angled his head more and brushed his tongue against her lips. Elyse opened for him because she could trust him. He was worth being vulnerable for. His tongue stroked against hers in a slow rhythm that had her gripping his shirt even tighter, hugging him even closer. Feeling brave, she pressed her tongue just inside his lips and the hum was back, only louder this time. His erection was thick and hard against her belly, and desire unfurled inside of her. His fingers were tightening around her neck now as he kissed her harder.

How long had they been here, entangled like this. Minutes? Hours? Time lost meaning as he showed her just how tender and how sexy he could be. The man was building a fire inside her, and he was taking his time with it, letting her savor the feeling of his affection. Slowly, he backed her against the wall. Intertwining his fingers with hers, he lifted both of her hands over her head and slowed his kiss again. He altered their pace over and over, slower, faster, softer, harder, making her anticipate when he would let his control slip.

Ian's mouth moved against hers smoothly, as if he'd kissed her a hundred times and knew what she liked already. Another soft noise came from her—this one relaxed and happy—and Ian gave her three soft pecks, nibbled on her bottom lip, then rested his forehead onto hers. His breathing was deep and slow as he closed his eyes and seemed happy to just be. He lowered their intertwined fingers to her sides, but didn't let go of her hands. She loved this. Loved everything about this moment. Ian wasn't pushing for more, or kissing and running. He was giving her affection like she'd never experienced before. Her stomach fluttered with how much she liked standing here, pressed between him and the wall as he squeezed her hands. With a smile, she tilted her chin up and kissed him softly, just a small smack to let him know she'd liked that. The corners of his lips lifted, but when he opened his eyes, they weren't the blue she remembered. They were darker.

"Your eyes," she whispered, canting her head and blinking hard. Perhaps it was a trick of the lights. His face was in shadow.

Ian squeezed his eyes tightly closed and shook his head. His hands slid from hers, and he brushed her hip with his fingertips as he leaned forward again. Lips so close they tickled her ear, he said, "I like you."

And then he left her there, legs splayed and locked, leaning heavily against the wall, wishing it wasn't over yet.

Ian Silver, her own personal stranger fiancé had just given her the most meaningful kiss she'd ever received.

She brushed her fingers over her swollen lips, staring at the open door he'd disappeared through as she whispered, "I like you, too."

NINE

Elyse had one snow machine that needed parts to work and a four-wheeler that Ian was hard-pressed to figure out why the engine wouldn't turn over. He muttered a curse and wiped his hands on the oily rag. Glaring at the damned thing, he went over everything that could possibly be keeping the engine dead. He needed to cut wood, but to get the dry stuff, he needed to cast his net wider. And to do that, he definitely needed the four-wheeler.

A soft, pretty sound perked up his ears. Rubbing the dirty cloth absently over his hands, Ian strode from the barn, but froze when he saw Elyse on her knees in the overgrown garden behind the house. Her jeans were covered in dirt, and her hands worked constantly to pluck weeds from the soft ground, but it was her lips that held him captive, heart drumming against his chest.

Elyse was singing.

He stepped back into the shadows beside the barn and watched her. Listened to her. Her voice was beautiful. Not the beautiful, yeah-she-can-hold-a-tune kind, but Elyse had a voice that rivaled any he'd ever heard on the radio stations. Soft and bluesy, perfect pitch, perfect vibrato, tone as clear as a bell. He couldn't sing for shit, but Elyse...Elyse's voice was enchanting. A siren's voice.

Huffing a surprised breath, Ian leaned against the side of the barn. She'd been freed up to work on the weeds that were choking out her garden while he took care of the animals this morning. Perhaps she sang all the time, but a tiny, selfish part of him hoped she was singing as a response to something he'd done. Because he'd made her happy. Because of that kiss they'd shared in the bathroom this morning. He couldn't stop thinking about it, and he hoped to God she was having the same trouble. And listening to her now with that clear-bell voice that drifted this way and that over the breeze as she worked, he was falling even harder for her.

He gripped his shirt, right over his heart that was aching right now for no damned reason at all. Looking at a woman shouldn't hurt, but when he tried to look away, the ache deepened. Elyse had done something to him he couldn't explain. From the moment he'd seen her picture, she had seemed important. It had taken months to get to this place, and now, no matter how much he tried to convince himself he was just here to help a woman in need, with every minute he spent with Elyse, she was feeling more and more like his woman.

And then that kiss…

He'd let his control slip, and she'd noticed. She'd pointed out his eyes. The curse of a shifter was the changing color there. It was proof he was just pretending to be human, and she'd drawn his bear from him with just the touch of her lips. With just the taste of her.

For the first time in his life, Ian was scared of someone. A five-and-a-half-foot tall woman with no meat on her bones, who was singing an old love song and plucking weeds from a garden, was more intimidating than any enforcer order Clayton had given him.

What a pathetic monster he made.

With a frown, he forced himself back around the corner and into the barn. Staring at Elyse all day wasn't going to make his extensive to-do list any shorter. Taking care of her was instinct now, and one he couldn't ignore. Ian didn't want her to just survive the winter while he was sleeping. He wanted her comfortable and well-fed. He wanted her happy. Happy. Yeah, she deserved that after everything. He wouldn't be here for her in a couple of months, and he needed to get this place up and running, manageable for her even, so she could get her confidence back. Oh, his Elyse was tough, but she'd buckled under the weight of the last couple of years, and she needed to find her strength again. And he was going to show her how strong she could be. She would have to be if she was going to help keep his secret someday.

Keep his secret? Ian shook his head at how much he'd lost his damned mind. She couldn't ever know he was a bear shifter. Just the thought of her looking at him like he was a freak soured his stomach. She'd looked at him like he was everything earlier when he'd kissed her. Those strange colored eyes of hers had pooled with adoration for him. *Him.* If she found out what he was and what he'd done to Cole, she would hate him.

Forcing his mind onto the task at hand, he spent the next two hours fixing the four-wheeler. And when it was finally running again, he filled it with gas and drove around Elyse's property to familiarize himself with the acreage and outbuildings. Her land was covered in rolling hills and ancient pines. Even when the winter dumped white over the landscape, there would still be plenty of green thanks to the trees that grew here. The beetle infestation had blown through these parts a few years back, but this place hadn't been hit too badly. And the dead trees left over from the pine beetles would make good firewood now. The ATV paths were overgrown or non-existent, which meant this four-wheeler had been out of commission for a while, but it was powerful enough to handle the sharp inclines of her land. At the highest peak, he could make out a large, jutting rock in the distance. He stood on the four-wheeler, bent at the waist and arms locked on the handles just to take in the place better. She had a beautiful piece of land, and as he stood here, dragging his gaze over the lush wilderness, he understood how she found magic in this place.

A wooden structure in the distance captured his attention, so he revved the little engine and drove toward it. It was a dilapidated cabin, probably long ago abandoned by some of Elyse's relatives. And when he drove a nearby trail, it led to a second two-room cabin, the roof of which had collapsed. Ian shook off the urge to eye them as possible den sites for winter. He couldn't hibernate this close to Elyse. Not with Miller hunting him. Still, it was nice to imagine sleeping so close to her.

When he drove the four-wheeler back down the dirt path near the house, Elyse stepped out of the chicken coop and waved, then shielded the sun from her eyes as she waited. Damn, it felt good to have her here when he came home. Chills blasted up the back of his neck at the thought of that word. Home. Was this place home already? It was strange to think so, but that ring she'd accepted from him said he was a part of this place now. And it was a part of him.

"You said you need to eat a lot," she called over the roar of the little engine.

"You hungry?" he asked.

"Yeah, and I was going to make you lunch, too. What do you want?"

Pleased to the bone she'd been thinking about his constant need for food, he grinned and patted his leg. "I want you up here, woman. Ride with me into the barn, and then I'll cook you something."

Her face transformed as her full lips lifted, and she graced him with those straight, white teeth of hers. She approached slowly. "I'm filthy, Ian Silver. Are you sure you want to cuddle me?"

Ian reached for her and tugged her hand until she was standing right beside the ATV. Then he picked her up by the waist and settled her over his lap, hooking her knees around him. Playfully, he nipped her neck as she giggled. God, he loved that sound.

Revving the engine, he said, "Your dirt don't bother me, Elyse. Hold on."

Her arms went around his neck as he maneuvered them into the barn. His lips were on her before he even turned the four-wheeler off. He'd been thinking about doing this all day since she'd let him get so close to her this morning. Only this time, she wasn't letting him lead. The minx bit his bottom lip, hard, and rocked against his erection. Reckless, he gripped the back of her hair and pulled her head back, exposing her neck. He trailed biting kisses down her skin. Fuck, he wanted her. Wanted to be inside of her, claiming her, but he had to take it slow with Elyse. Cole had hurt her, and she was still crying over him. Ian didn't want to bed her too soon. Elyse needed more time to be ready for all the emotional weight that would come with them sleeping together.

And sure as rain, if Ian slept with Elyse, it wouldn't be fucking. It would be loving, and the difference was almost as terrifying as the woman in his arms.

Elyse slipped her hands under the hem of his shirt and ran a smooth touch up his stomach. His abs clenched under her palms as he trailed his kisses to the base of her throat. He pulled her tighter against his erection, so the next time she rocked those sexy little hips of hers, she caught his length and, holy hell, she felt good against him.

When he kissed her lips again, Elyse gave off a pained noise, and instantly, Ian released her hair from his grip. "Did I hurt you?" Dammit, of course he had. He was being too rough. She was human and fragile, and he didn't know his own strength.

"No." She touched her chin gingerly. "Yes. I'm not used to kissing a man with a beard."

"Oh," he murmured. "Here, let me see." He pushed her hand gently away and lifted her face in the muted barn light. She was looking red and a little raw, and he felt like grit. He should've shaved. With a sigh, he kissed her neck softly, then lifted her off and settled her on her feet. "Come on, let's go eat."

"Are you mad?" she asked, sounding confused as she stood her ground.

Ian held out his hand and shook his head. "Not at all. I feel bad for hurting you. We'll give it a rest, okay?"

Elyse's face fell as she slipped her palm against Ian's. "I don't know if I want that."

Ian chuckled and pulled her along beside him. "You like kissing me then?"

Bumping his shoulder, she said, "You know I do. Don't be that guy."

"What guy?"

"The guy who knows he's hot but still fishes for compliments."

"So you think I'm hot?" he asked through a grin.

Elyse laughed and shoved his shoulder. Before she could retreat, he picked her up and threw her over his shoulder, then slapped her ass as she peeled into a fit of giggles.

"Brute. You put me down, or I'll—"

"You'll what?"

"I'll never kiss you again."

Ian loved that challenge, so he settled her upright and gripped her shoulders, staring intently into her eyes until her breath went all shallow and ragged. Then he leaned forward and angled his face, but at the last moment, froze mere millimeters away from her lips. He brushed her hair from her face and cupped her cheek. "Never?"

She let off a sexy, helpless noise, then blinked hard and shoved away from him. "Tease."

"I heard you singing," he said low as he followed her in the house.

There was a smile in her voice when she said, "I used to sing all the time."

"What stopped you?"

"Life."

"And now?"

She tossed him a coy look over her shoulder and headed straight for the kitchen. "Now I'm going to make lunch."

Hmm, who was the tease now?

Lunch was sandwiches—one for her and four for Ian. And when they were done, he told her to, "Go get dressed for town."

"Why?" she asked, her eyes sparking with curiosity and something more. Excitement. Town must be a rare treat for her.

"We need to get you a hunter and trapper's license."

"Oh." Her face fell in disappointment, and she took their plates to the sink.

"What was that look for?"

"I don't trap."

Ian narrowed his eyes and stood behind her as she scrubbed their dishes. Her honey-colored hair was soft against his fingertips as he moved it out of the way to expose the length of her pretty neck. Showing the neck was a sign of submission, and even if she didn't know what he was, he liked when she let him see it. She'd called him a brute once. Elyse had been right.

"You'll learn to trap so if you get in a bind this winter, you can go out there with confidence and bring something home. And if you need money or supplies from town, you'll be able to barter with the fur. Now what were you really going to say?"

Her neck flushed, white as porcelain to a soft pink. "Nothing."

"Tell me."

"I thought you were going to take me into town to…you know…spend time with me."

"We are spending time."

Elyse let off a human growl that was about as intimidating as a kitten hissing. "I thought you were asking me to go to town for a date."

Ian dropped his hand from her hair and took a step back, shocked. "A date?"

Elyse sighed and put the dishes away. "You asked, and from your tone, dating isn't for you. I really do get it." *Cole was the same.*

He could almost hear that last part, though she didn't say it out loud. He felt bear-slapped, so instead of saying something intelligent like, "Sure I'll take you on a date. We're engaged anyway, so what's the big deal?" he stood there like a lump on a log and watched her disappear into her room. The sound of rustling fabric sounded a minute later, as though she was getting dressed, so Ian headed into his own room and cleaned up. He could seduce a woman, and he could make one happy in bed, but outside of the bedroom, he felt like an off-balance bull driven through quicksand. Words had never been his gig, and he messed up a lot with Elyse. She seemed frustrated, but if she knew the animal she'd managed to tame in no time flat, she would probably be easier on him.

Cole had laid out a long path of disappointment for this woman. But unlike Cole, Ian would keep trying, because Elyse—*his* Elyse—deserved the effort.

TEN

Elyse slathered on a layer of lip gloss and shoved the make-up she'd used into the tackle box she stored it in. Ian might not be taking her out on an actual date, but she had dolled herself up anyway, because dangit, she didn't get to go to town very often, and especially not with a man. Cole's idea of date night had been coming home drunk, boozing it up even bigger in the living room, and trying to convince her to play strip poker for his pleasure, not hers.

Her chin was tender and chapped, so she put a small dollop of lotion on to hurry the healing process, then grabbed her purse and checked herself once more in the floor-length mirror. She wore her nicest dark jeans, her cleanest hiking boots, and her most flattering red shirt clung to her curves. At least it would cling if she didn't look like a friggin' skeleton. She was going to do better. She was going to be better. The way Ian was around this place said he knew a lot about living off the land, and he would make a great asset as a teacher around here. She was bound and determined to be a good student so that she could be strong again. So she could be the good Alaskan wife Ian deserved.

She stepped into the living room, but Ian had his back to her and said, "Close your eyes."

"Why?"

"Because, woman, I have a surprise for you. Just do it. No peeking."

Elyse stifled a smile and squeezed her eyes closed. "Okay, they're closed."

The sound of his boot prints echoed over the old floors, louder and louder as he came closer. A zing of anticipation sent a tremble up her spine as he came so close she could feel his warmth. He radiated heat like her own personal sun encased in a man's body.

"Listen, I'm not always going to say the right things," he said on a breath as he slid his hand over hers. "I'm not good with words, and I'm not good with anticipating a woman's needs. Not yet. I'll ask you to be patient with me and to know I'll never mean to hurt you, but sometimes I will, because I'm a bullheaded man with no experience making someone else happy."

"Oh, Ian." She squeezed her eyes more tightly closed and clutched onto his hand harder. "I'm sorry for making you feel like you're always saying the wrong thing. You're doing so well around here. Around me. I suspect we'll both poke at each other's nerves while we get to know our way around one another. And you don't have to apologize about not being good with words. I can tell you don't talk much. You're a quiet man, and I like that about you. When you say something, I know you mean it, and that you're only talking because it's important to you. I'll be more patient, okay? And Ian?"

"Yeah?"

"You do make me happy."

Ian inhaled sharply, then let his breath out slow, as if he was releasing all his tension with it. Then he lifted her hand slowly to his cheek.

Elyse gasped at how smooth his skin was under her touch. Lifting her other hand, she felt her way around his clean-shaven face, imagining what he looked like without it being shielded by scruff. Ian held his palms pressed against the backs of her hands, as if he didn't want her to stop touching him, and when she ran her thumbs under his eyes, she could tell they were closed from the way his lashes rested on his cheeks. With emotion filling her heart, she smiled and sighed in contentment. He'd shaved for her because he didn't want to hurt her when they kissed. Big, burly, leather-tough mountain man, and he'd done the nicest thing any man had ever done for her. He'd thought of her comfort above his own.

She tilted her head back and stood on tiptoes, eyes still closed as she pressed her lips gently against his. There was no more scratch, no more tenderness, no more ache blooming on her skin. There was just this connection that she could fall into and get lost in. His mouth moved slowly against hers, as if he was savoring her and reveling in this moment. She was falling. Falling for her fiancé so hard it was scary. She didn't want to hit the rocks below. She just wanted this dipping stomach feeling to last on and on.

Ian eased back and hugged her tight, lifting her feet off the ground. "I'm going to take you on a date, but not today. It don't feel right after you being upset earlier, and I've been to Galena before. There's nothing there that would be big enough for our first date. I'll take you out tomorrow, okay?"

Elyse hugged his shoulders tight. "Will it be your first real date?"

Ian huffed a laugh. "First real one, yes."

"Will you tell me what we're doing for it?"

"No, I want it to be a surprise."

"Can I see your face now?"

Ian hesitated. "Okay." He laid a soft peck on her cheek and let his lips linger there, stalling.

Leaning back, she beheld his clean-shaven face for the first time, and it drew a gasp of aw from her lips. The lines of his face were sharp and strong and too beautiful to be hidden behind facial hair. His bright blue eyes were worried as he searched her face, but he didn't need to be. He was the most handsome man she'd ever laid eyes on. His hair was cut short on the sides, and longer on top. Where it had looked shaggy before with his beard, he now looked devastatingly perfect. Like a model on the billboards in Anchorage.

"You don't have to say anything," he whispered as the corners of his lips turned up. "You say enough with your eyes."

"You're intimidating," she admitted, unable to take her gaze from his face. Ian Silver was too handsome for her plainness.

Ian brushed his thumb across her cheek and cupped the back of her neck, massaging gently. He let off a shaky breath and murmured, "Not as intimidating as you. Tell me, Elyse, did you put on make-up for me?"

Her words stayed clogged in her thickening throat, so she nodded.

"Why?"

She swallowed hard and dropped her gaze to the off-white T-shirt that clung to his powerful torso. "Because I want to be pretty for you. I want you to like me the way I like you."

Ian lifted her hand to his chest and pressed it there, right over his heart. It pounded as fast as hers was right now. "I do. Make-up or no, you have me."

"I thought you were bad with words."

Ian chuckled and led her to the door. He grabbed both of their jackets off the coat rack with one oversize hand, then closed the door behind them. And when they made their way over the yard to his truck, he surprised her utterly by pulling the door open like a gentleman. And as she buckled her seatbelt, he watched her with an unfathomable expression. One that made her draw up and smile shyly at him.

He said he could read her eyes, but he didn't see how animated his own face became when he was around her. Earlier he'd said he liked her, but his eyes said more than that. Whatever was happening between them was bigger than *like*.

And as he strode around the front of his truck, she could see it in his smile. He made her happy, but she made him happy, too.

The inside of his truck was clean and smelled like old leather. Ian turned the key, and the engine roared to life. His radio only got one station, the one out of Galena, but the DJ was on a role with songs she remembered from high school. Every time Ian looked over at her with a smile that was now easier to see without his beard, she felt like she was flying. Window rolled down, she let her fingers catch the late-summer breeze as Ian turned onto the main dirt road that led to town. It was a forty-five minute drive, and he was quiet on the way, but it wasn't an awkward silence. Ian was a man who didn't waste words. He didn't talk just to hear himself as Cole had done. And back in the cabin, he hadn't charged in there after their spat and demanded she admit she was wrong. He'd gone into his room, thought about why she was disappointed, done something sweet by shaving for her, then compromised about taking her out. He was thoughtful in ways that surprised her, coming from a man who looked like him.

The mysteries around her fiancé stacked up, layer by layer, and because he hadn't given her any real explanation as to what made him the way he was, her curiosity was growing cavernous. She'd met men with handsome, rugged looks like Ian when she'd been in Anchorage, but they'd all seemed the same. Arrogant, and they knew their place at the top of the food chain. And while there was no question Ian was a powerful man and knew his abilities to fix equipment and hunt, he didn't have that air about him that said she was beneath him. On the contrary, he seemed determined to lift her up. He could've made her promises that he would provide the meat for their house if she took care of the garden and the canning. Instead, he was taking her into town to get her hunting and trapping licenses because the man seemed bound and determined to make her self-sufficient. It scared her because a secret part of her wanted to become dependent on him until she could find her strength again. She didn't like how he'd talked about getting herself out of a bind in the winter. She wanted them to get out of any situations that arose together. But she understood he wasn't trying to keep her reliant. He was trying to make her more capable, as she needed to be to make a life out here long-term. The idea of trapping during the winter season scared her, but it also excited her. Ian was taking over the lessons where Uncle Jim had left off. For that, her respect grew deeper and wider for the man sitting next to her.

Feeling brave, she scooted over as close to him on the bench seat as her seatbelt would allow. He responded by draping his arm over her shoulders. She rested her head against his shoulder and smiled out the front window at the lush, green landscape. Summers in Alaska were beautiful, and she was sharing this one with Ian. Twenty-six, and she had the giddy fluttering in her stomach like a teenager with a crush.

"How old are you?" she asked. He looked younger now without his beard.

"Thirty." He arched his eyebrows and cast her a quick glance as he pulled past the Welcome to Galena sign. "An old man compared to you."

"Robbing the cradle," she murmured, waving to Janet Graves who was watching the truck from in front of the radio station.

"I like 'em young and tender," he teased as he pulled into a parking spot in front of the general store.

Elyse laughed and poked her bony arm. "I don't know how tender I am, old man."

"I'll get you tender enough," he said so softly, she had to strain to hear him. "Wait there, and I'll get your door."

Stunned, she murmured, "Okay," through a baffled smile. For a backwoods man, he sure had a surprising amount of manners.

Galena was a small town, but that didn't stop it from being a natural hub for the small villages around it. Settled right off the banks of the Yukon River, this was ground zero for boat deliveries for the outlying towns. Even with the small population, the town had a local police force, radio station, and hospital facility. It even had a feed store for all the homesteaders who called this territory home base.

Getting her licenses from the guy behind the counter at the general store only took twenty minutes, and while she waited, Ian stocked up on groceries. She was so ready to start filling the freezer. Meat was expensive, and she was feeling mighty guilty about the money he was spending on food. Ian didn't seem to mind, though, and was cordial to the cashier as he checked out. Even when he paid the sixty-two bucks for her hunting-trapping-sports fishing license, and an extra five bucks for waterfowl stamps, he didn't even bat an eye. He just told Mr. Neery he sure appreciated it and led her out of the store with his two armloads of groceries.

"Favorite store in town?" he asked as he loaded his wares into the back seat of his Ford.

"Easy. Feed store."

"Why?"

"Because sometimes they have baby chickens in there, and they're so little and cute and fluffy." Her voice had gone all squeaky as she mushed her fists together in front of her face, so she cleared her throat and finished, "And there is, you know, horse feed in there."

Ian let off a single, booming laugh and shut his door. "Well, we need some feed anyway, but I have a feeling you don't think dusty bags of oats are as cute as baby things."

Ian's nostrils flared, and he gave a thoughtful frown at the feed store down the street. But before she could ask what was wrong, he hooked his arm over her shoulders like a proud rooster with a new hen, and damn, he dumped all those butterflies back into her middle. He led her slowly down the street, looking in each store window as they passed. He told her he'd only been here a couple times, a long time ago, and that the town had built up a lot since then.

"What were you doing in Galena?" she asked.

"Deliveries." He didn't explain beyond that, and anyway, she was taken with a wire cage set up in front of the feed shop. Dawna Summers was sitting behind it reading a newspaper, but inside were three little balls of fur.

"Puppies," Elyse said on a breath as she picked up their pace double-time. "I just want to pet one. Just one, and then we can get what we need. I'll just be thirty seconds. A minute, tops."

Ian was chuckling that warm sound behind her. His voice was easy and relaxed when he said, "Woman, pet those dogs as long as you want. I like that you go mushy for animals."

"I am not mushy," she argued half-heartedly. Elyse turned her attention to the woman sitting behind the puppies. "Hi, Dawna."

"Elyse!" The older woman stood and gave her a spine-cracking hug. "I haven't seen you in town in forever. Heaven's girl, you are skinny as a stick. Are you ill?"

"No, I'm fine. It was just a hard winter."

"Well, land's child, winter has been over for a while." Dawna pushed her glasses farther up her nose and cast a quick glance over Elyse's shoulder, then leaned forward and lowered her voice. "Do you need help? I don't have much, but I can spare a couple of rabbits Robby snared."

And this—this right here—was why Elyse loved this place. She'd been too proud to ask for help, but that didn't mean people weren't willing. Dawna and her husband, Robby, struggled too, but she hadn't even thought twice about offering Elyse some of her hard trapped food. "No,

Dawna, you keep your rabbits. I got me a husband now. Or a fiancé, rather."

Dawna's gray, bushy eyebrows nearly lifted to her hairline. "The advertisement landed you this strapping fellow behind you?"

The strapping man in question stepped forward and offered his hand for a shake. "Name's Ian."

Dawna shook his hand slowly, her eyes bulging round from behind her thick glasses. "You're the new man of the Abram's homestead?"

"I am," he said in that rich tone of his. "I'll get her healthy again." There was steely promise in his voice that brought a grin to Elyse's face. Oh, she believed a man who gave oaths with conviction like Ian did.

"Can I pet one of your puppies?"

"Oh, sure, hon. Business is so slow today. Serves me right for trying to sell them on a Tuesday. My Sheba had five of them, but lost two."

"Oh, poor momma and poor babies," Elyse crooned as she picked up a little gray and white one, cradling it on its back like an infant. The sleepy pup whined and wiggled, but eventually gave into Elyse's affection and went limp in her arms.

"Malamute or husky?" Ian asked, picking up one by the scruff of the neck and lifting its lips to study its teeth.

"Husky. My husband and I breed sled dogs. Some of our pups have gone on to place in the top five in the Iditarod."

Ian grunted thoughtfully and replaced the pup, only to pick the last one up and check its teeth, too. This one, the runt from what Elyse could tell, growled at Ian.

A low laugh came from deep within Ian's chest, and if Elyse didn't know any better, he sounded impressed. "Snuggle this one, woman, and see if you like him."

"He won't be any good for pulling a sled," Dawna warned. "Too runty, and we had to hand-feed him when he wouldn't eat. Weak composition. He's a fighter, sure, but he won't ever have the endurance for a team dog."

Elyse put the gray, softly snoring pup down and took the little black and white ball of fluff from Ian. One of his eyes was blue, and one was a soft brown, and when she made kissy sounds, he barked a tiny ferocious sound. "Oh, he is a handsome little scrapper," she crooned as the pup licked all over her face and wiggled his little curled tail.

Dawna grinned. "If you take that runt off my hands today, I'll only charge you half for him."

Elyse shook her head sadly and said, "Oh, we can't buy—"

"How much?" Ian asked.

"A hundred-sixty bucks, and he's yours. I'll even throw in a bag of puppy food I brought with me."

"Ian, that's too much, and he's another mouth to feed."

"I'll make sure you both have enough to eat. I think we should have a dog, especially in the winter when the wolves get bad." The gritty way he said *wolves* blasted chills across her forearms.

"Wolves?" She frowned. She heard their howling plenty, sure, but they'd never approached the cabin.

A flash of emotion washed over Ian's face like a wave, there and gone before she could decipher what it meant.

"You have tracks all over your land, and a good dog will come in handy in the cold months when the predators get hungry and too brave. A couple warning barks could save you from a bad situation."

"You're wanting a watchdog then?" Dawna asked. "He'll be a good one for you, especially if you aren't wanting him to do sled training."

Ian was already pulling his wallet out, and hope and guilt churned in Elyse's chest. "I can't ask you to buy me a dog," she whispered, hugging the pup closer.

"Then we can call him my dog if you want." Ian handed Dawna a stack of twenty dollar bills and smiled at the leather-skinned woman. "I thank you kindly for giving us a discount on him. We'll give him a good home."

Dawna pocketed the cash and beamed up at him. "I know you will. Elyse is good people." Dawna offered her hand again and shook Ian's firmly. "It's been a treat meeting you. I like you a lot better than Elyse's last fellow."

"Ha!" Elyse pursed her lips. She definitely hadn't meant to laugh like that. After clearing her throat delicately, she admitted, "I like him more, too."

Ian ducked his head in a farewell to Dawna as he took the small bag of dogfood she offered, then he pulled open the feed store door for Elyse.

"Oooh," she said, emotional as hell because the cutest puppy was in her arms, and he was hers. Well, hers and Ian's, but secretly, she was going to baby it as her own.

Ian had frozen beside her and was watching her cuddle the little wiggling hellion. "What?" she asked, confused by the stunned look on his face.

"I just got this vision of you..." Ian shook his head and frowned. He let off a nervous-sounding laugh. "Nothing."

There was a bench just inside the doorway, and she sat on it so she could better stare at her new puppy.

"Are you happy?" he asked in a soft voice from above her.

"Yeah," she answered breathlessly. "Thank you. You've already done too much."

"Not too much."

"It feels like it. What can I possibly offer you? You've spent so much on me, and you've come out here at no benefit to yourself to help me out of the hole I dug myself into and—"

"Hey," he murmured, sitting beside her. "You're wrong. I have a stake in this, too."

"What stake? A dilapidated homestead out in the middle of nowhere?"

"No, woman. You."

Elyse sighed and rested the side of her face against his arm. Shaking her head with a soft scraping sound of her cheek against the sleeve of his jacket, she said, "I'll owe you for always."

Ian froze for a moment, hesitating, then lowered his cheek to the top of her hair. "That's not how this is supposed to work, and I think deep down, you know it. You're mine, Elyse, just like I'm yours. Sure, we didn't come about this the normal way—"

"You mean because I hired you?"

"Yeah, but so what? We aren't here to impress anyone but ourselves. I like you, you like me, I like to see you smile, so let me take care of you while I can."

"While you can?" Those words dumped dread into her stomach.

Ian frowned and stood. "You know what I mean. While we're together." He walked off and greeted Mr. Barns behind the counter as Elyse leaned back against the wall, troubled to her marrow by the thought of him leaving. She didn't know Ian's story yet. He'd shared so little with her that she was at a disadvantage. If he left now, it would hurt her. It would cut her worse than Cole had done because she'd let Ian in more than she would ever admit out loud. She'd grown hopeful and imagined their future stretching on and on. He made her feel good about herself. She felt whole around him, and braver, and more hopeful they would keep the homestead if they did this together. For the first time in years, she didn't feel any loneliness at all. The idea of losing him, of losing herself again, was too painful a pill to swallow.

She would have to become stronger so that Ian could lean on her as much as she was leaning on him.

ELEVEN

Ian stifled a chest-rattling growl just thinking about calling his asshole brother. He didn't get why things had to be so tense when he talked to Jenner and Tobias. Okay, their bears hated each other. Loathed each other and wanted nothing but to fight when they were close. That didn't mean their human sides couldn't get along, though.

He huffed three slow steadying breaths, then sat on the goat milking chair in the barn. He dialed Tobias's number and wasn't surprised one bit when he didn't pick up. A quick message about how he was throwing him some delivery business, and Ian hung up, leaned back on the stool, and waited.

Tobias might not like him any, but he was a bush pilot, too. If he wouldn't answer for a brotherly chat, he might answer for money.

Five minutes later, Ian's phone rang. Reception was spotty at best out here, so he stood and got two bars on his phone before he accepted the call.

"What business?" Tobias asked.

"Hey, brother."

A feral growl rumbled across the line. Okay then. "I have to take a break on deliveries for the rest of the season. I don't want to leave my customers high and dry, though, so I was wondering if you wanted to take them over for me."

Tobias huffed a humorless laugh. "Ian, if you give them to me for the season, they'll stick with me."

"Worth the risk. I'm settled now, and I can't get back to deliveries until after hibernation. If you took some of the load off my hands, I'd be grateful."

The silence from the other end was so heavy, it held weight. "What do you mean by settled?"

"I got a fiancé and a homestead."

"Fuck, Ian! Tell me you're joking. Tell me you're not shacking up with a human and threatening to expose us all."

"I know what I'm doing."

"Do you?"

Ian cast a look at the open barn door and lowered his voice. "Look, Tobias, I don't expect you to understand, but I love her. I'm ready to settle. I can't help it." He lowered his voice to a barely audible whisper. "This is my animal's choice. Instinct. I can't leave her."

"You can't leave? And what about in a couple months when you go into hibernation? What are you going to tell her?"

"I don't know."

"Ian—"

"Tobias! I don't ever ask anything from you, do I?"

Silence.

"Do I?"

"No."

"And I want to, man. All the time, I want to call just to fucking chat with you and Jenner, and I don't. I know you don't want the relationship, but I was so fucking lonely, and this makes sense to me. I have a purpose now. I get to take care of a woman. I didn't call for your blessing. I called to ask if you would take over my deliveries."

"Shit," Tobias muttered. He let off a loud sigh and said, "Well, tell me what she's like."

Ian straightened his spine and hooked his free hand on his hip. "She's a foot shorter than me and skinny as hell. She's had a rough go of it."

"She sounds weak—"

"I wasn't done. She's headstrong and running a homestead by herself, and she doesn't quit. She just doesn't. She works hard and long, and she woke up this morning before dawn just to get her day started and fuck it all, I respect her for what she's done with this place by herself. She doesn't need me emotionally, but I want her to."

"What's her name?"

"Elyse."

"You've got the McCalls hunting you, man. I saw your den on Afognak."

"What were you doing out there?"

"I like to go back home from time to time. I was checking that your shit is in order, and it definitely is not. You got Miller after you, and you're shacking up with someone he can and will use as leverage. You get that, right?"

"Yeah." Ian couldn't bring himself to admit Elyse was Cole McCall's claim. Tobias was actually holding a conversation with him—the first in years—and if he admitted how much risk he was really taking, Tobias would disappear and be a ghost in the wind once again.

"You gonna tell her what you are?"

"I haven't decided yet."

"It won't work if you don't," Tobias said in a defeated voice. "That's where Dad messed up with Mom. Secrets destroy pairings."

"I didn't know pairings were a thing for us."

"Yeah, well, your dumbass is mated, so it must be, right? Text me the deliveries and I'll get them taken care of. I've got to go."

"Okay, thanks."

"Ian?"

"Yeah?"

"She sounds real nice. Don't fuck it up."

The line went dead, and Ian stared at the screen as it went dark. Holy hell, Tobias had actively participated in a civilized conversation with him.

A sharp yip sounded from the doorway, and he turned, startled. The puppy came bouncing toward him, nothing but a ball of black and white fire and a curly tail.

"No!" Elyse whispered as she stumbled out from behind the open barn door.

"Elyse! What are you doing out there?"

She bit her lip and looked guilty as hell. "What happened was…I was coming out here to see if you could help me fix some broken fencing near the horses' gate, but then I heard you talking and I didn't want to interrupt, so I just stood there, waiting until you were done."

"So, eavesdropping."

Her cheeks were flushed like cherries now as she nodded once. "I didn't know you were talking about me at first, and then I couldn't pull myself away."

Panicked, Ian went over and over the conversation he'd had with Tobias, but he didn't think he'd given anything away about the bear that lived inside of him.

"You said I'm headstrong and you respect me." Her smile was faint as she looked up at him, then back down to his work boots.

Shoulders relaxing, he gestured her to him and hugged her close. "That was my brother."

"You have a brother?" Genuine shock painted her tone.

"I have two."

"Older or younger?"

"The same exact age."

"You're a triplet?" Her voice was so loud, it hurt his sensitive ears. When he hunched, she lowered her voice. "When will I meet them?"

"Probably never. We don't get along."

"Why not?"

"Well," he said, searching for a way to tell her without spilling their secret. "We can't. It's an instinct thing."

"You're competitive?"

"Massively competitive," he murmured, grateful she got it.

"Okay, so no holiday celebrations with them?"

Pain slashed through his chest as he thought about the holidays. He hibernated during the big ones, and he hadn't thought about her being all alone on Thanksgiving and Christmas before now. Even New Year's wasn't doable. Shit.

"No," he admitted low. "No holidays."

"Well, I want you to meet Josiah. He's good people. Maybe you won't be competitive with him," she said hopefully.

"Yeah, I want to meet your brother." He wasn't on a quest for friends, but Josiah was a big part of keeping Elyse's cattle safe, and her brother should know he had back-up from Ian during the warm months if he needed it.

The puppy was tugging at the hem of his work jeans and growling as he shook his little fluffy head ferociously.

"I've named him," Elyse said.

"Tell me."

"Miki. It's an Inuit name meaning—"

"Little," he finished, approving. The little furry terror had released his pant leg and was now barking and bouncing around him, trying to scare his denim apparently. "It's perfect. Do you want to bring him with us today?"

"Where are we going?"

"Far away."

"For our date?"

Ian dipped his chin once and eased out of her embrace so he could better see the green and gold in her eyes. Damn, she was beautiful.

"Maybe it should just be us today," she said, scrunching up her petite little nose. He wanted to kiss it, but big tough bear shifters didn't do cutesy shit like that.

"Good," he rumbled, picking up the pup.

The dog nipped him, and without thinking, Ian latched his teeth onto the scruff of his neck and let off a low snarl as a warning. Miki's growl died in his throat, and he hunched in submission. Good pup. Ian released his neck and nuzzled his little face as a reward, and got one timid lick on the nose in return. Then he set the puppy into the small enclosed stall he'd cleared out for him to sleep in until Miki was big enough to wander the yard when they weren't home.

"I can't believe biting him worked," Elyse muttered when he turned around. Her eyes were round, and she stood frozen in the same position she'd been in, her hands still out like she was surprised he wasn't hugging her anymore.

"Mmm," he said noncommittally, not about to explain dominance or how he knew so much about animal behavior. "Miki will be a good watchdog, but he has to learn who is boss. You ready?"

"After we fix the fence. I don't want the horses getting out while we're gone."

"Yep." Ian grabbed a box of nails and a hammer and followed Elyse out of the barn. They would need to hurry if he was going to take her to his favorite fishing spot. He was all about a date, but it would be the kind he understood. The multi-tasking sort where they brought meat home at the end of the day because winter was coming up, and fast. Hopefully she liked what he had planned.

One of the posts was rotted and leaning heavily to the side, so Ian clipped the wire and pulled it out while Elyse blocked the horses from escaping. He replaced it with a log he'd brought up this morning with the four-wheeler, all the while calculating how much lumber Elyse's wood burning stove would require for the winter. He didn't want her running out and having to go too far alone to haul and chop more. Not while he was sleeping and couldn't help her with the heavy work.

And when they were done, Ian packed the back of the truck with his nets and fishing poles, then opened the door for Elyse and laughed at her as she practically hummed with excitement.

"I know what we're doing! We're going fishing. Where? The Yukon? There's a stream off it near here that I've caught fish in before."

"This will be nowhere you've been and up in bear country."

"Bear country? Black bear or brown bear?"

"Both."

Her delicate eyebrows jacked up, creating little wrinkles of worry across her forehead. He wanted to kiss them smooth. "I'll keep you safe," he promised.

"Against a grizzly?"

Ian swallowed his smile down as he pulled out of the homestead. "Yes, Elyse. Against a grizzly. I brought the right weapons."

Sure, his high caliber rifle sat in the back of the truck, ready to be loaded and emptied into a bruin if they were charged, but that wasn't the weapon he was talking about. Ian had claws and teeth and had fought many a wild bear in his adventures in the Alaskan wilderness. Sometimes, his inner monster required a good fight.

He was much more afraid of what Elyse was doing to his insides than what a bear could do to his outside.

"Ian, I saw a bear once. A big one. It was the scariest moment of my life."

"Relax." He slid his hand over her thigh and squeezed it reassuringly. "Elyse, you're mine to take care of, and I wouldn't put you in a situation that was dangerous or that you couldn't handle. We probably won't see a bear, but if we do, you do exactly what I say, and I promise, I won't let anything happen to you."

"You are dangerous to date," she accused.

"It'll be fun. Plus we need to start filling that empty freezer of yours."

"Freezer of ours."

Ian pulled onto the main dirt road toward Galena. His plane was stored near the landing strip just outside of town. "Ours," he agreed, though he wouldn't be eating meat out of it this winter. He would be sleeping deep in a snowy den on Kodiak Island. The thought of being so far away from her suddenly socked him in the gut and stole his breath away. Kodiak Island was the natural choice that would make it hardest for Miller to track him, but the closer he got to Elyse, the more his instincts screamed to stay here, deep under one of those old cabins on the back of her homestead near his mate. His mate? Fuck. Tobias had been right about pairing up. Ian was deep, *deep* in this now. There would be no turning back or pulling away from her. Not after today.

Now the thought of her finding out about his bear was more unacceptable than ever.

TWELVE

Elyse pulled a hiking backpack from the floorboard and unzipped the biggest pocket. Ian seemed to need to eat constantly because he was built so muscular, so she'd packed him extra food for today. She pulled out an apple and handed it to him. "Here."

With a grin, he took it and bit a piece off, then handed her the apple, and she crunched off a bite. With a giggle, she gave it back and wiped the juice from her mouth with the sleeve of her thin sweater. Ian ghosted a hungry glance at her lips that turned her middle to churning hot metal.

"I didn't sleep that well last night," she said carefully.

"Why not?"

She gulped the sweet fruit down and stared out the window, too chicken to look at him when she said, "I was thinking about you."

Ian took another bite, and the crunching of the apple was the only sound in the truck for a while. "Thinking about me how?"

Elyse licked her lips. "Thinking about you, like I wished you would come into my room and sleep with me. Beside me. Sleep beside me."

"Did you...?" Ian canted his head and left the unfinished question hanging in the air between them.

"Did I what?"

"Never mind." He made his lips into a thin line and shook his head. "Nope. Not appropriate for a first date."

"I thought you didn't know anything about first dates, and besides, we're engaged, remember? Ask me."

"Did you touch yourself?"

Heat blazed up her neck and landed in her cheeks. "God, Silver." She definitely couldn't meet his gaze right now, so she kept her focus on the evergreens that blurred by.

"You don't have to answer."

"Yes," she answered on a rushed breath.

He inhaled sharply, and she huffed a laugh, shocked that she'd just admitted that out loud.

"Did you think about me?" he asked in a low gravelly voice that brushed chills over her skin.

Elyse covered her burning face when she whispered, "Yes."

"Shit, woman," Ian said, adjusting his dick and then gripping the steering wheel in a choking grasp. He was smiling so big right now. "Next time you feel like a slumber party, you let me know and I'll be in your room in a second flat. I was trying to give you space."

"In case I cried again?"

Ian nodded. "I listened for it last night. I had trouble sleeping, too."

Finding her bravery, she asked, "Did you touch yourself?"

"No, and now I'm going to fucking explode. I've thought about you a lot."

"A lot?"

"Yeah," he murmured, leveling her an honest glance before he pulled his attention back to the road. "An embarrassing amount a lot. It's hard to focus on the things I need to get done."

"I feel close to you," she whispered, terrified he would reject her sentiment.

Ian squeezed her leg again, this time higher up her thigh. "Me, too. I'm trying to take things slow with you, though."

"Why?"

"Because I want to do this right. Cole is still kind of fresh for you, and I don't want to be a rebound fuck."

Elyse laughed in shocked surprise. "Ian Silver, you are nobody's rebound. No one else compares to you."

"Not even Cole?"

"Especially not Cole. When I think about him now after spending time with you, I'm even more disappointed I stayed in that relationship as long as I did. I'm not crying over that man anymore." She took the apple from his hand on her thigh and chomped another bite.

Ian looked over at her several times, but whatever he was searching for on her face, she hadn't a clue. At last, he murmured, "Good," and took a sharp left onto an old dirt road right before they got to the Galena welcome sign.

"The river is that way," she said, jamming her thumb behind them.

"I told you, woman. We're going to bear country."

Elyse's mouth dropped open as she stared at the trio of small bush planes in front of them. "Did you hire a pilot? Ian, that's expensive."

Ian chuckled mysteriously and pulled the truck to a stop in a clearing near the landing strip. With a wicked grin, he opened his door and said, "Come on."

She helped him carry the nets and the basket of food he'd packed, as well as her hiking pack, but the closer they walked toward the planes, the more confused she became. If they were flying, there was no pilot here. Perhaps he was running late.

But Ian pulled a set of keys from his pocket and unlocked one of the planes—a red and white four-seater, and everything started to make sense. "You fly?"

"I do."

"And is this your plane?" Her voice jacked up another octave.

"It is."

"You're a bush pilot?" Any higher, and her voice was going to crack.

If his beaming grin was anything to go by, Ian was utterly amused. "I'm going to take you to my favorite fishing spot. The salmon have already run this year, but we can still get some fish in the freezer. And when hunting season starts in a few days, I'll go out and get you some red meat. Caribou and deer. Maybe even a moose. Along with the beef we butcher and the vegetables from the garden, you should be good all winter. And if things get tight at the end, you can take a few chickens. You won't go hungry if I get lucky on my hunts."

"And what about you?"

Ian's face went serious, and he busied himself with loading the back of the plane with their equipment. "I meant *we* will be good all winter."

Elyse narrowed her eyes at the back of his head. Mmm hmm. He'd been slipping up like that a lot. She opened her mouth to call him out on it, but he turned abruptly and kissed her into silence. As he eased away, he whispered, "I'm sorry. It told you I don't always say the right things."

Fidgeting with the gold ring on her finger, she nodded her forgiveness, but her hackles were still up. She hated the thought of spending the winter without him. Really, she hated the thought of spending any amount of time without him. Now that was an unsettling feeling, being so attached to someone this quickly.

"Have you ever ridden in one of these things?" he asked as he helped buckle her in.

"Yes." Most Alaskans had since bush planes were the main mode of transportation between towns and cities.

"Good, so no fear of heights?"

"I didn't say that." Her nerves had her heart pounding double-time.

"Don't worry. I haven't had a crash landing yet."

"How long have you been a pilot?"

"Nine years. I bought my first plane when I was twenty-one and took over the business my dad had left behind when he retired to Anchorage. Well, me and my brother, Tobias, took it over. He flies deliveries, too."

Ian closed her door and busied himself checking the plane. And when it seemed up to snuff, he got in and started flipping switches like his fingers knew exactly what to do. Seeing him so capable put her at ease a little.

The take-off was borderline terrifying, but smooth, and once they were up in the air, Ian seemed to lose whatever had kept him closed off about his life outside of Galena. "My other brother, Jenner, is a hunting guide. He's one of the best and gets clients from all over the world."

"What does he specialize in?" Elyse was trying her best to keep her eyes off the ground that was shrinking under them.

"Big game. Moose and caribou. Occasionally bears." The way he'd said *bears* sounded as though the word was bitter on his tongue, but when she glanced over at him, his face was wiped clean of any emotion.

"Does your mom live in Anchorage, too?"

"I don't know where she lives. My brothers and I were raised by my dad."

"Oh." Elyse reached over the space between their seats and rested her hand on his leg. "I'm sorry. That must've been hard."

"Nah, it was fine. She wasn't fit, and we were better off in Dad's care. Kind of."

"My dad wasn't in the picture when I was growing up, so I get it. My mom was kind of overwhelmed with raising me and Josiah on her own, so she sent us to the homestead whenever she could."

"In bush planes?"

She nodded and dared a glance at the green landscape below. "It's been a while since I've been up in one of these.

"Well, you're doing good, and we'll be there soon. You're a tough woman."

A smile commandeered her face at his unexpected compliment. "Really?"

"Really. Why did you kick Cole out of your cabin?"

"Lots of reasons."

"Tell me the last reason. The big one. The one that ended it."

Elyse winced. "He split my lip."

Ian's bright blue gaze drifted to the thin scar down her bottom lip, and he didn't look surprised at all. Perhaps he'd already guessed she was mishandled. "You kicked him out immediately?"

"Yes." Stupid shaking voice. She wanted to be strong when she admitted this. "I loaded a shotgun and pulled it on him when he wouldn't leave. Told him I'd blow a hole through him. He told me he didn't mean to, that it was an accident, but that's what they all say, you know? I don't want to be one of those women who sticks around for that shit."

"Like I said. You're a tough woman. A survivor."

"A tougher woman would've let him go a lot sooner. I knew he was using me, but I was scared of being alone."

"Why?"

"Because life out there isn't easy, Ian. Every day I run into something that could kill me, and being alone means I'd die alone. Josiah hardly ever comes my way unless we're driving the cattle either to the good pastures or back to my place for the winter. It could be weeks, maybe months, before anyone found me. Being with Cole was hard, but it took me a while to realize I'd rather die alone than be with someone who breaks me. Lesson learned the hard way."

"Is that why your advertisement said *Romantics need not apply*?"

"Yeah. I didn't expect this." She gave him a pointed look. "I thought it would be more like legally bound friends running the homestead. I was just so desperate for help that I did what my Uncle Jim did and put an ad out. He'd only wanted a helpmate, and Marta could've walked away any time, but I didn't want that. I wanted someone I could depend on. I got lucky and got you."

"Lucky," he repeated low, sounding unconvinced. She understood his reaction. She had trouble accepting compliments, too.

Ian spotted a place to land, and the panic set in, so Elyse did the only sensible thing and closed her eyes tightly until the bumping plane came to a complete stop. When she opened them again, they were surrounded on two sides by towering pine forest and wild grasses that swayed in the wind like ocean waves. Wild flowers dotted the landscape, and she was rendered breathless by the mountains that towered in the distance. This place was what calendars were made of. It was what mainlanders traveled hundreds of miles to see, and it was just a short bush plane ride away from her home.

"Do you like it?" Ian asked softly, as if her answer truly mattered.

"It's incredible."

Ian pulled off his headset, turned off the plane, and ran around the front to help her out. While she shouldered her backpack, he loaded himself down with most of their equipment like it weighed nothing, then he strode off toward the forest. She was stunned by how strong he was. Sure, she'd known by the way his muscles pushed against his clothes that he was powerful, but his easy gait and long strides up the side of a sloping hill were completely effortless.

Shaking her head, she hurried after him, resembling a tranquilized rhino next to his smooth strides. The hike through the woods lasted a good half hour at their fast clip, and Elyse gasped as they came out of the trees onto the bank of a stream. A small waterfall easy enough for salmon to jump in the right season flowed into the churning waters of the river. Ian kissed her forehead and then unloaded everything. He hopped over a set of rocks like a nimble mountain goat to the other side of the stream. If she tried that, she was going in the water, no doubt.

"We'll see if we can't get some lingering silvers with the net, and if not, we'll use the poles. Stand over there," he said, pointing right across from him.

"Oh!" she yelped as soon as the water splashed above her boots. "Good golly, that's cold!"

Ian frowned as he lowered himself easily into the water. "I didn't think about how the water would affect you. I should've brought waders."

Elyse stared in disbelief at him as he stood up to his waist on a rock below the churning water's surface. "You aren't cold?"

"I don't get cold easily." A troubled expression passed over his face as he dragged the net down through the deep water beside his standing rock. The giant net with the silver handle looked heavy to lift, but Ian did the practiced movement as though the weight didn't bother him at all.

It took half an hour to land their first fish, but he explained to her they were either here or they weren't. And he was right—once he caught the first one, the next ones followed quickly. They found a rhythm eventually. He caught the giant fish and pushed the net toward her where she pulled them out as best as she could manage and cut the gills with a knife he'd packed.

Usually, fishing was tedious and boring for her because she spent the entire time on the pole, thinking about all the things she still had to do back at the homestead. But today, she was having a blast. Ian knew the area and knew the exact fishing technique for this spot in the river, and they were on the fish. Each one they caught would feed them for several meals. Plus, she knew her workload at the homestead had been cut in half with Ian's presence, so she could let the never-ending to-do list go for a while and just have fun.

For hours, laughter mingled with the soft gurgling sound of the river as she and Ian teased each other. He was hard to look away from, smiling like this. He had dimples, which she would've never guessed under his beard. And time and time again, his eyes were drawn to her, as if he was having the same trouble keeping his attention away.

Finally, Ian said, "I think we have as much as we can carry." He hopped easily up the boulders, jumped the stream over to her, and pulled her against his chest, swaying as he dropped the net to the muddy bank. "You are my good luck charm. I don't think I've ever caught so many on one trip."

"We make a good team," she murmured happily. He was getting her all wet, but she couldn't even muster the energy to care. She was tired, hungry, and her arms shook with fatigue from hauling the heavy fish, but she hadn't ever been so happy. Maybe Ian was magic.

"You know what I keep thinking about?" he asked in a naughty, low voice as he scanned the woods behind her.

Oh, she could guess, but she would play along. "What?"

Ian dipped down and sucked on her bottom lip, grazing his teeth against her before he eased back with a wicked grin. "You touching yourself."

"I thought you said that wasn't appropriate talk for our first date," she joked.

"I changed my mind," he whispered, then kissed her again, deeper this time.

"Mmm," she moaned helplessly as he guided her backward. Her shoulder blades bumped against the rough bark of a tree, and she stretched up on her toes and whispered against his ear. "I'd like it better if you touched me."

Ian froze for just a moment before he leaned against her and asked, "Really?"

Elyse nodded and ran her hands up under his damp shirt to his warm skin underneath. His muscles were hard as bricks, and she flattened her palms against his abs just to feel them flex with every ragged breath he drew. Ian's lips were on hers again, kissing her slowly, thoroughly, as he popped the snap of her jeans open. He smiled against her lips and pulled her zipper down slow. Holy hell, she was desperate for his touch. Shifting his weight to the side, he slid his hand down the front of her pants under her panties.

"Cold!" she gasped out as his river wet hand cupped her sex.

"Sorry," he murmured, but he didn't sound sorry at all. He had that sexy, growly voice again.

Slowly, he slid his hand upward and back down, brushing her clit softly. "So wet already," he murmured, dragging a trail of fire down her neck with his lips.

"Please," she begged, needing more.

"Please what?" he asked innocently.

"Inside," she said on a breath.

His response was instantaneous, and so was the curious humming in his throat. He pushed his finger into her, and she cried out at how good it felt. She hadn't been touched like this in so long, and Ian had been building a slow burning fire inside of her since the day she'd met him.

"Noisy mate," he said.

Mate? Her thoughts were swirling. His words didn't make sense, but right now, with him moving his finger inside of her, it was hard to care. She moaned and closed her eyes, tilted her head back to give him access to her neck.

A low feral sound filled the air, and he whispered, "I like when you give me your neck, woman."

Desperate to feel more of his skin, she pushed the hem of his shirt upward, over his head, and threw it on the ground beside them with a wet sound. His arm and chest were flexed as he worked her closer to release, but the hard definition of his muscles weren't what had her drawn tight like a bow. He was marked up by dark red scars. Four long ones across his chest, and a mess of them across his ribcage. She wanted to know what happened—wanted to know everything, but not when she was so close to release. Right now, she wanted to appreciate his rugged sex-appeal. Burly, dominant, scarred-up man who had softened for her.

He pushed into her again, making sure to touch her clit every time until the pressure that built inside of her was blinding. So good. His touch was perfect. Just what she needed. He cupped her hard as she writhed against his hand, and then he pushed a second finger into her. She bowed against him and cried out his name as her body pulsed around him. So fast and so good, she was overwhelmed as he continued to stroke until every last aftershock was finished.

And when her legs locked under her, Ian was there, arm around her back, holding her against him and pressing his lips against her hair. Elyse hugged him as tightly as she was able. He couldn't understand how much that had meant to her. No one had ever cared about her pleasure before. They'd just taken from her, but not Ian. He was laying sweet kisses against her and holding her close, completely content not to take it a step further until she was ready. And something deep inside told her that Ian would only push for more if she was verbal about her needs.

"Ian?" she asked.

"Mmm?"

"I'm ready for more with you."

Ian eased back and smiled down at her, but when he opened his mouth to say something, he jolted to a stop and lifted a hard gaze to the woods instead. His nostrils flared as he inhaled deeply. Slowly, he maneuvered her behind his back and eased her toward the waterfall.

"What's happening?" she whispered, adrenaline dumping into her bloodstream, making it hard to move slowly as Ian was urging her.

"She has cubs," he murmured low.

Cubs? Elyse dared a peek around his wide shoulders and stifled the scream clawing its way up her throat. An enormous grizzly bear was walking slowly toward them, eyes intent on their pile of fish. And behind her followed two small cubs.

A whimper came from Elyse's throat as she tripped over the rocks that lined the bank. Ian didn't catch her or even turn around as she fell. He was unbuttoning his pants in what had to be the most inappropriate reaction to being stalked by a momma brown bear. Flashing his dick at the animal was not going to scare her away!

"Ian," she whispered, frozen to the rocks.

"Elyse, run."

"What?" You were definitely not supposed to run from a grizzly. Play dead. That was brown bear survival one-oh-one.

"I'm sorry," he whispered in a broken voice as the bear stood on her hind legs and roared. "Run!"

Elyse watched in horror as the bear charged, but Ian's neck snapped back and his shoulder joints hunched forward with the painful crack of breaking bones. He grunted an agonized sound as Elyse scrabbled for the rocks and up onto a higher bank. The bear skidded to a stop in front of Ian, but the second Elyse took off on level ground, she could hear paws pounding through the brush and the heavy breaths of the bear chasing her.

She let the scream out now because it didn't matter. Ian was broken on the bank and nothing would save her from this bear's wrath. Elyse pushed her legs harder than she ever had until she was almost flying through the forest, but still, it wasn't nearly fast enough. The bear was gaining and was so close, Elyse could almost feel her breathing down her neck, right behind her. Any step now, she was going to be on top of her. Terrified, she reached out, hooked her hand on a tree, and pulled herself sharply out of the animal's path. The bear skidded to a stop and gave chase. Elyse had only bought herself a few seconds at most. Damn it all, she'd been afraid of dying alone, and here it was—her death come early, and it was about to mean excruciating pain.

The bear clipped her leg with her long, curved claws, ripping her skin as she tripped her. Elyse hit the ground hard and shielded her face from the long canine teeth she knew was coming for her. But in the second she should've felt the puncture wounds, something huge barreled into the bear with enough force that their impact made a sickening thud and shook the air around her.

Elyse looked up in horror as another bear roared and slapped and sank its teeth into the first one. This one was much bigger than the other. A brawler if his torn ear and scarred body were anything to go by. She'd never seen such raw violence as the massive dark brown bruin pushed the smaller bear farther away from her.

She had to find Ian. She had to get them both out of here before the bears turned their murderous attention back on them. She tried to stand and cried out as her leg wouldn't bear any weight. The scent of iron was strong in the air, and her ankle was warm with the blood that was now soaking her tattered jeans. Sobbing, she crawled away as the roaring of the bears echoed through the forest. The best she could do was drag herself behind a tree and cover her face with her hands to quiet her panicked crying.

They would come back. Any minute now, those monsters would come back to finish her off. How could they not? Even she, with her dull human senses, could smell the thick scent of blood flowing from her leg.

Minutes stretched on and felt like an eternity as she sat there, afraid to move, afraid to breathe. The woods were quiet now. Not a bird chirped, and from here, she couldn't even hear the water from the river. With violently shaking hands, she reached over and grabbed a thick branch that had fallen from the tree. She stood on one wobbly leg and stripped the extra twigs until it was just one baseball bat-sized club. She'd played two years of softball in high school, and dammit, if she was going out like this, she was going out swinging for her life.

"Elyse," Ian said from behind her, scaring a scream and a swing from her.

With a loud crack, he caught the club before it hit him in the face. Then he yanked it out of her hand and hugged her so tightly to his chest, she couldn't breathe.

"It's okay. It's okay," he chanted. "She's gone, and she's not coming back. You're okay. I've got you."

Frightened sobs filled her throat, and tears blurred her vision. "What happened to you? I saw—" Elyse shook her head hard to try and sort out what she'd witnessed. "You were breaking, and I was alone!"

"You weren't alone. I had you. I just needed you to buy us some time."

"You had me?" Fury blasted through her veins. "You told me to run from a fucking furious grizzly bear and then you passed out on the river bank!" She shoved away from him. "And why the hell are you naked?"

"Shhh," he warned, eyebrows arched high as he scanned the woods.

"Don't you dare shhh me. Answer me, Ian. What happened back there?"

"I'm the bear." He straightened his spine and glared down at her, daring her to look away. "I'm the bear that protected you."

"Fuck off, Ian."

"Scars across the ribcage. Torn ear." He pulled his own ear in front of her and jammed his finger at a healed gash that had taken a small notch out of it. "Dark brown bear who pulled that grizzly off you. Why would a wild bear do that, Elyse? Why would he protect you if you weren't…"

Horrified, she asked, "If I weren't what?"

"Why would a male grizzly protect anything that wasn't his? You want to know why I haven't kept a woman? Why my eyes turned brown when I kissed you yesterday? You want to know why that growl rattles my chest when you affect me? Because I'm a fucking bear shifter, Elyse." He turned and gave her his back, which would've pissed her off right now if it weren't for the long, seeping claw mark down it. He gave her a sad stare over his shoulder. "I told you. Brown bear country doesn't scare me. I belong with the monsters. Always have."

Panic clogged her throat as everything clicked into place. Of course he was a monster. That's why a man who looked like him wasn't already married and running a home of his own. A tear trekked a warm stream down her cheek. "You're a bear?"

Ian looked sick and swallowed hard. "A bear and a man."

"I think I'm going to…" Elyse blinked hard as the forest began a slow spin around them. "Ian. I think…I'm going…to…"

Legs giving out from under her, the ground came at her face fast, but she didn't hit. Ian caught her, of course, but when she moved her lips to thank the bear-man, nothing came out.

And the spinning world went dark.

THIRTEEN

The sound of the steady beeping of a machine woke Elyse from a deep sleep. She cracked her eyes open, squinting against the light as her vision blurred and focused, blurred and focused on the man pacing outside the large window of her room. Ian.

She knew this place. She was in the medical center in Galena.

"She's my wife," Ian said. "Look at that ring on her finger. I gave it to her. I'm the one who brought her in here, and I don't want her waking up alone."

"Sir, calm down. No one here knows you, but we all know Elyse," Dr. Vega said, pointing into her room.

"Ian?" Elyse whispered, throat dry as a desert.

"See?" Ian said. "She just asked for me."

"I didn't hear anything."

"Ian," she said, louder.

Ian gave Dr. Vega a go-to-hell glare and threw open the door, then rushed to her bedside as the doctor and one of his nurses followed.

"Hey," Ian whispered. "I'm here."

"You were hurt, too," she said, worry unfurling in her chest. "He's hurt. Growly claws and babies, she was stealing our fish like a thrief. Thrief. Thief. Like a McCall." Why was she slurring? "She hurt my...Ian."

"No, baby, I'm okay," Ian said. Something sparked in his eyes. A warning?

She poked his cheek. "Your eyes are brown."

Ian leaned down and pressed his lips against her hand. "I'm okay, Elyse. Please." His voice was barely audible in his plea.

Elyse blinked hard to clear her thoughts and murmured, "Sorry, I think I'm confused."

"That's the pain meds talking," Dr. Vega said as he lifted the blanket from her leg. Her ankle was bandaged.

"Still clean," Dr. Vega murmured to his nurse. "I think she'll be okay to go home tonight if she can stay off it." That last part was directed at Ian.

"Of course," Ian said. "I'll make sure she takes it easy."

The fog was lifting from her mind by the second. "Is it bad?"

"No."

"Yes," Dr. Vega said at the same time. "You were attacked by a bear, Elyse. You're lucky to be alive."

Ian narrowed his eyes at the doctor, then dragged his dark brown gaze back to her. "Four cuts from the claw, only one was deep enough to require stitches."

"Six stitches." Dr. Vega grabbed her chart and gave her a significant look.

"I think I prefer my husband's bedside manner to yours tonight, Dr. Vega. Thanks for saving the leg," she said dryly.

Ian snorted, but covered it with a cough.

Dr. Vega narrowed his eyes at Ian and said, "She's free to go. Do see that you take better precautions from bear attacks next time you go gallivanting off into the wilderness."

Ian nodded once and gave him a little salute as the doctor ushered the nurse out and followed closely behind. After Elyse dressed in the cut-up jeans she'd been wearing earlier, the nurse came back with a wheelchair.

"Is that necessary?" She would limp, but the claw marks didn't feel wheelchair-bad.

"Afraid so. Vega is in a mood tonight. We don't get many bear attack survivors in here." At least the nurse didn't talk down to her, so Elyse smiled and acquiesced.

Ian wheeled her out front to where his truck was parked at an angle on the curb. The passenger side door was still hanging open, and their supplies had been thrown haphazardly in the back.

"The fish," she gasped.

"I got them."

"Of course you did."

Ian helped her into the seat and shut the door gently beside her.

Jamming the key in the ignition, he said, "Just so you know, it only took me about two seconds to get those fish on a line to carry."

"Wait, you carried all of our equipment, the fish, and me all the way to the plane?"

"At a dead sprint."

Elyse scrubbed her hands over her face. "Is that part of the bear-man stuff?"

"Strength?"

"Yeah."

He nodded.

"This is a lot to process, Ian."

"Elyse, you should know I've never told anyone about my bear. Never. You're the only one."

"Are you afraid I'll freak out and tell the world?"

"It's crossed my mind," he said carefully. "It's not just me who would be hurt by the backlash."

"Your brothers?"

He nodded again. "There are so few of us, there isn't safety in numbers. Do you understand?"

"Sooo, is this like a full-moon deal, or can you change into that thing whenever you want?"

"That thing," he repeated softly.

"Sorry," she said, eyes on his rigid profile.

"The moon has nothing to do with it, and neither does magic. It takes me a minute to Change, but I can do it when I want. Sometimes I do it when I don't want to. It depends on if my bear is being reasonable or not."

"Will you hurt me?"

"Never." His voice had gone hard as steel. "My animal loves..." A long tapering growl sounded and Ian shook his head hard.

"Say it."

He sighed a long exhalation. "My animal loves you as much as I do."

"Because I'm your mate? You said that in the woods. You called me your noisy mate."

Ian's Adams apple bobbed as he swallowed hard. "Yes. Because you're my mate."

"Okay," she whispered, dragging her gaze back to the dark woods that surrounded Ian's truck now.

"Okay?"

"Well, I need time to wrap my head around everything, but okay. I don't want you to leave because of this. I mean, I didn't know animal people existed before, and it's a lot, and I have horribly painful claw marks on my leg. And now I'm living with someone who can change into the biggest grizzly I've ever laid eyes on, or seen in text books or in a museum. I'm engaged to a bear. Man. A bear-man." She inhaled sharply and bit her lip to stop her rambling.

"There's more."

"Oh, for fuck's sake, Ian. What else could there possibly be?"

"You're right. We should talk about it later once you've had some time to deal with what I am."

"Well, spit it out now. Best to get it all out there at once."

"I hibernate."

Elyse cast him a prim look and said, "I'm sorry, what now?"

"Every October, I go to sleep, and I don't wake up again until April."

"Six months."

"Yep."

"You just sleep for half a year straight."

"Yep."

"That's fantastic. Fantastic news for me."

"You sound angry."

"I'm pissed, Ian!" she exploded. "You timed it just right, didn't you? You waited until I was head over heels in love with you before you told me this. I wanted a full-time husband! I wanted to have company in the winters so I wouldn't live another as lonely as the last one. You'll be asleep, and I'll be by myself, fighting cabin fever alone. How is that fair?"

"It's not," he said quietly.

"Then why did you answer that ad, Ian?"

"Because I wanted you." He let those words linger between them for a long time as they slowly bounced over the rough dirt road. "From the first time I saw you, I knew you were mine. And it didn't matter how much I fought it or how selfish I knew I was being, you were it for me. I want to protect you and provide for you." His voice cracked, and he slammed his head back against the rest. "Down to my bones, you feel like mine, and I hated what Cole did to you, and I wanted to do it better. I want to make you happy."

"But only half of the year."

"Do you think I want this? Do you? I've lived alone my whole life trying not to taint someone else's with my bear shit, and I was happy to do it until you came along. And then there you were, so perfect and brave and so goddamn beautiful, and you were asking me to stay, and I couldn't say no. There. There it is, Elyse. I'm weak, and I gave in to the idea that I could keep you. This right here is why I didn't want to marry you until you saw what life with me would be like. I wanted you to know the real me before you went all in. I know it's not fair what I'm asking. Six months of providing for you in the warm season, six months away. It's not what I want for us. It's not what I imagine a woman would be willing to put up with, but this is all I have to offer. Everything I have is yours. And I know it's not enough. I *know* it. But I guess I was hoping if you came to care for me enough, you'd at least consider me."

Tears were streaming her face now in uncontrolled rivers.

She'd almost had everything.

She'd been *this* close.

The silence was no longer easy, and neither one of them moved to turn on the radio. Instead, she allowed the weight between them fill the cab of his truck, and when Ian pulled to a stop in front of the cabin, Elyse couldn't escape fast enough. Her leg hurt, but that didn't stop her from hobbling into the house and into her room. She cried as she absorbed the thought of spending every winter alone. At the thought of losing him completely.

And tonight, just like the first night, Ian sat quietly in her bedroom doorway and waited for her tears to run out.

FOURTEEN

The new rooster was going at the morning sun with all he had, squawking and crowing the ugliest sound Elyse had ever heard. That wasn't what had woken her up, though. It was the smell of bacon and the soft sounds of Ian moving around the house that had dragged her from sleep. The rooster was too late. Elyse was already sitting up in bed glaring at the sunny sunshine that was filtering through the bedroom window. If the sun had a dick, she would kick it.

After hobbling into the bathroom, she washed the horrors of yesterday's misadventures from her skin, careful to avoid the bandage. She was still too chicken shit to look under it, but when Ian strode wordlessly into her bathroom as she was towel drying her damp hair, it was abundantly clear he didn't suffer from the same cowardice.

"Sit," he grunted, jerking his chin toward the edge of the bathtub.

He looked in as foul a mood as she was, and she wasn't up for a row this morning, so she waited an extra two seconds just to let him know he wasn't the boss of her, then sat daintily on the edge of the plastic ledge of the tub.

Ian knelt on the floor and lifted her foot onto his thigh, then removed the bandage from her leg as if he'd done so a million times. Gentle and efficient were his hands until, at last, the damage was exposed. Huh. She leaned forward and squinted. It wasn't that bad. Sure, it would probably leave four thin scars that would silver over time, but even the worst one was sewed tightly closed, and there wasn't even any redness or swelling around it.

"I thought it would be much worse," she admitted.

Ian didn't answer as he poured some kind of cleaning solution over her cuts and, mother fluffer, it felt like he'd poured boiling water onto her injuries. She gritted her teeth, refusing to make a noise. Quick as a whip, he had fresh bandages firmly in place and strode out of the room.

"Are you going to give me the silent treatment forever?" she called.

"Nope."

His boot prints echoed through the house as he made his way to and out the front door.

She narrowed her eyes at where he'd disappeared, then stood and dressed herself. The echo of the ax blasting into wood on the chopping block was loud. Much louder than the noise she made when she was chopping wood, but one look out the window explained why. It took her several strokes to get through a log. For Ian, it took one.

An overkill breakfast was on the counter in the kitchen, piled high on a plate and covered with a cloth napkin. It was cold, but good, and she ate every bite of it before washing her dish.

At the pump outside, she began to fill the bucket for the chickens' water dispensers, but Ian, with a saddle slung over his shoulder, jammed a finger at her and said, "I already did it. You're supposed to stay off your feet."

"What are you doing with my saddle?"

"Cleaning it. You have a fine saddle with horse shit splattered on it."

"Oh."

Grumpily, she sat on the rocking chair on the porch and watched him work with her arms crossed over her chest. She wasn't used to sitting around.

The man was a sight to behold, though. He'd chopped nearly a cord of wood while she'd readied for the day and ate breakfast, and the woodpile was looking much healthier, plus he had several logs lined up to chop later. He must've hauled them up with the four-wheeler this morning. He watered and fed the horses, milked the goat, and washed off a dark-stained table he'd apparently used to clean their fish sometime in the night if the dried scales were anything to go by. Out of curiosity, she hobbled around the house to the freezer and, sure enough, the bottom was covered in two layers of fish filets, neatly labeled and individually wrapped. Damn, it was good to see some meat in there.

When she came back, Ian was nowhere to be seen in the yard, but the telltale sound of tinkering echoed from the barn, so she hobbled closer and sat on an old rope swing tied to a tree in the yard. From here, she could see inside the double doors. Ian was working on the opened front of the broken-down snow machine. And from the pan of grease in the yard beside the generator, he'd been working on that this morning as well. Handy bear. She cracked an accidental smile at her little, silent joke.

Cocking her head, she tried to put the massive bear she'd seen yesterday to Ian's human form. Okay, so he was a bear-man. Or…a werebear? He changed into an animal when the feeling struck, and thankfully, he'd done it yesterday to save her. She'd be a lot worse off than a swatted leg if he hadn't been there. Undoubtedly, this place would be safer with him around. But spending winters without him would be brutal.

Perhaps she was thinking about this all wrong. She did love him. It seemed so strange to have that thought this soon, but there had been this instant connection between them. He cared about her enough to tell her what he was when he hadn't told anyone his secret before. Winters would be hellish, but at least she would get half the year. It came down to just warm-weather months with the man she was falling in love with, or cutting him loose and hoping to find a man who was less than Ian. And the more she thought about it, the more she considered that, for the rest of her life, this decision could cause her pain and regret. Who could compare to him? No one she'd ever met. If she cut her heart off from him and moved on, the most she could hope for was a relationship with a man half as good.

Elyse sighed. Half as good didn't sound good enough anymore. Not after he'd made her feel so deeply.

"Would you hibernate around here?" she called out, gripping the rough ropes of her swing.

Ian didn't answer, but Miki came bouncing out of the barn toward her. Ian muttered something below her hearing and yanked his hand back, shook it, and sucked on the side of his index finger. He wore a white T-shirt with grease smudges all over it, and old, worn-out, threadbare jeans that sat low on his waist. The brown had left his eyes. She could tell from here because, when he cast her a quick glance, it was all blue-flame sexy.

"Ian!"

"No, I wouldn't hibernate around here." He strode out of the barn, wiping his hands on a dirty rag as he sauntered toward her.

"Why not?"

"I have a proposal," he gritted out, pulling back the rope swing she sat on and pushing her forward.

"Oh, now you want to talk?"

"I didn't want to talk because I know what you'll say. And dammit, woman, I want to get shit done around here before you give me the boot."

"What are you talking about?"

"I saw the way you looked at me last night. Like I was a freak. That's part of the reason I didn't want to tell you what I am. And I get it. I do. I'm not normal, and this is a lot. But hearing you cry over what I am last night ripped me up. I know what's coming, but I still want to get you set up for winter before you kick me out."

"I wasn't crying for what you are, you ridiculous man. I was crying about missing you all winter."

He stopped pushing her and strode around front. "What?"

"You're a bear, okay. I can deal with that. It's a lot, yeah, but I thought about it, and the animal side of you isn't a deal breaker. Not after you used him to save me. It's hard to swallow being away from you for half the year, though. I already miss you." She shrugged helplessly and repeated softer, "I already miss you."

His chest rose with his deep inhalation. "Well, we have options on that."

"What options?"

"I can sleep six months as a bear, holed up in a den somewhere, or I can hibernate human. I'll wake up for about an hour a day to eat if I do that. The upside is that we'll be together an hour a day, the downside is I'll take up more of our food, and we'll have to work harder to feed us both through the winter." Ian squatted down between her legs and looked at her eye-level. "I don't want to leave you for winter either, Elyse. I wish I was human and normal for you, but I can't avoid this part of my life."

"So, if you hibernate human, you can stay here?"

"Yeah, but I'll be boring as fuck. My body slows down so much, I literally only revive for food so I don't starve. If I'm a bear, I don't need food. My body is more efficient at hibernating as a grizzly."

"So, technically speaking, if I had an hour, and you ate quickly, would you have enough energy for anything else?"

Ian gave her a baffled smile. "Like what? Card games?"

"Like sex?"

"Oooh," he said, lifting his chin as his eyes sparked with humor. "You're worried about your needs all winter."

"Whose selfish now, bear-man?"

"Still me...and that's bear shifter. I have no right to ask you to be okay with this."

"Will it hurt you to hibernate human."

He shook his head as the smile dipped from his face.

"Then will you do it for me? I don't want to dread the winter alone. I'll take care of your body when you're sleeping, and I'll have food ready when you wake up every day. I'll protect you."

His eyes went soft, and he leaned forward, pressing his forehead between her breasts. "Are you saying I can stay?"

"Well, if it's between having you half the year or not at all, I choose you, Ian. That's an easy decision for me."

Ian's striking blue eyes jerked up, and he searched her face like he couldn't believe what he'd just heard. "You choose me?"

"Mate," she whispered, running her fingers through his hair.

That sexy growl rattled his throat as his eyes rolled closed. "Say it again."

"My mate." The word felt strange, but exactly right on her tongue.

Ian let out a shaky breath and pressed his lips against hers. She still couldn't get over how easy it was to kiss him when he was clean-shaven for her, and with a happy giggle, she laid kisses over his cheeks.

Ian growled and bit her neck softly, and her instinct to freeze overpowered everything else. Ian wasn't being playful now. He was being sexy as hell. Feeling brave, Elyse slowly arched her head back, giving him more access to her throat, and as she did, his teeth disappeared and were replaced by his lips, gone all soft. A delicious shiver worked its way up her spine, and she let off a soft gasp as he lifted her off the swing.

"Careful," he rumbled deep in his throat as she brushed his hip with her bad ankle.

She was straddled on his waist but didn't have to do any of the work since her bear-man seemed to have infinite strength and carried her like she weighed less than a feather.

Her eyes rolled closed against the saturated morning sunlight as he sucked harder on her neck. The man knew how to use his lips.

Miki bounced along somewhere in the vicinity of Ian's feet, yipping in his little puppy bark as Ian toted her smoothly up the porch stairs and into the house. Anticipation zinged through her as he took a sharp turn directly into her bedroom. Oh, her mate was on a mission now, and she nuzzled his neck and smiled against his skin, then inhaled deeply. He smelled so good. Soap with a hint of oil from the machinery he'd been working on.

"Are you sniffing me, woman?"

"Maybe."

"Clever little human, using your nose like an animal. I like the way you smell, too."

"You do?"

Ian lowered her to the bed and spread her knees, then leaned down and clamped his teeth gently on the zipper of her jeans, then blew a puff of warm air through the denim. It tingled and, dear goodness, it felt better than almost anything she'd ever felt before. "I like the way you smell here best," he murmured.

She writhed and gripped his hair. This should be embarrassing, but Ian was kissing all of the discomfort out of her. And as he rucked her shirt up and laid those sexy lips to her stomach, fingers gripping her sides, she forgot exactly why she was supposed to be embarrassed. Ian was touching her as if he knew the exact map of her body, and his confidence eased any leftover nervous flutters.

Unrelenting, he pulled her shirt over her loose hair and unsnapped her bra, then slid it off her arms. His fingers were steady—slow and controlled. Heat pooled in her middle as he unsnapped the button of her jeans. The material tickled as he pulled it past her hips and knees, slower at her bandaged ankle, then off completely with a smile at the messy pile he was leaving on her floor.

The smile lingered as his gaze went first to her eyes, then lower and lower. His breath caught as he stared at her body. Running a soft touch over her knee, he shook his head as though he'd never seen anyone more beautiful. "I've imagined…" Ian swallowed hard. "It's not the same."

She wanted to cry at his admiration. Softly, she admitted, "I haven't ever let anyone see me like this. In the light."

A slight frown marred his face, making the color of his eyes intensify somehow. "Good. I want to be the only one who sees you like this." He ran his finger over the top of her thigh and whispered in a distracted voice, "Perfect. Your skin isn't even scarred."

Regret had tainted his tone, so she lifted her knee and rested her injured leg up on the mattress. "I have scars now, too, Ian. We match."

Pulling his oil-stained T-shirt over his head, Ian murmured, "I want to feel your skin against mine."

"Wait," she said as he settled a knee on the bed to lower himself. "I want to look at you, too."

Ian hesitated for a moment, then stood back up and rested his hands at his sides, clenching his fists, as if being scrutinized made him as uncomfortable as it used to make her. Strong, wide shoulders and a thick neck. A deep, shadowed indentation between his muscular pecs delved down to a defined eight-pack that flexed with every breath. There were scars, but now they'd been explained away. He was a bear, a big one, a dominant brawler who had been born to bear the long, red marks. She didn't mind them at all. In fact… "I think you're perfect, too."

His chin dropped, and his gaze lowered to the mass of red on his ribcage. For as strong and confident as Ian was, being marked by the struggles of his existence obviously bothered him. Elyse sat up and ran her hands lightly over his chest and the muscular curves of his arms, then down to his ribs to the scars. Pressing forward, she pursed her lips softly against the uneven skin there. "This," she whispered, "means you're still alive and here with me. Whatever happened and however you got it doesn't matter." She kissed it once more and looked up at him, then unbuttoned the top clasp of his jeans. "Have you shown them to anyone else?"

He huffed a small breath. "How could I explain them away to a bedmate?"

"So then they're only for me."

His face softened from a steely expression to one of thoughtfulness.

She kissed his ribs again and said, "This is mine, and you are mine, just like I'm yours, Ian. Don't regret them. I love them. I love everything about you."

"Even the animal?"

The rip of his zipper was loud in the silence that hung between them. "Especially the animal."

"Why?" he asked quietly as she carefully pushed his pants down his hips.

"Because without him, you would've been settled with someone else long before you found me."

Ian's oversize, calloused hand cupped her cheek gently, and his eyes filled with some emotion too big for her to understand. Elyse leaned forward and kissed just beside his belly button, then bit him gently on the strip of defined muscle that covered his hip bone. A shudder took his body as she pushed the elastic band of his briefs down, unsheathing his long, thick erection. It was every bit as intimidating as when it was shielded behind his jeans, and the nervous flutters were back in her belly with a vengeance.

She blew a soft breath over the swollen tip, and it throbbed once in a sexy reaction that drew a smile from her lips. Ian put his hands behind his head, gripping his hair as if he were trying to control his urge to hold her instead.

"You can touch me. Tell me what you like." Because sure as shit she wasn't going to be any good at this. Cole had been a man of many complaints.

Ian's chest heaved with his breath as he slid one of his hands around the back of her head and clenched her hair in a gentle grasp. His nostrils flared above her as he pulled her toward him. She slid her mouth over him, and his hips jerked. "Sorry," he murmured, loosening his grip.

She ran her fingertips up his powerful legs and took him deeper. Ian released a shuddering breath and pulled her to him faster. "Oh my God, Elyse." His voice was raspy and rushed.

Sensitive man, so easily pleased, and she should've known she would be enough for him. Gripping Ian at the base, she turned pliable in his grasp, heeding the pace he wanted and reveling in his reaction to the touch of her tongue against his shaft. His hips moved with her, pumping slowly into her mouth every stroke she allowed. And when his growl rattled him, she slid her hand up his stomach just to feel the vibration. She was so wet against the mattress under her, and for what? She hadn't been touched at all, but pleasing Ian was such a turn-on right now. She'd never found such pleasure in taking care of someone else, but now his abs were flexing every time she took him in her mouth, and he let off a low groan that said she was doing something right.

"Elyse, stop, stop, stop."

Or not. She pulled off him and glanced up, confused. "Did I do something wrong?"

"No." His eyes had gone a dark brown, and he was breathing heavy. "I don't want to come like that. I want to do it with you."

"Oh." She tried to hide the proud smile on her lips, she really did, but Ian had her feeling like a goddess right now. Her insides were practically glowing as he lowered her back against the bed and nudged her knees wider apart.

He lowered his hips against hers, and the head of his cock pressed right against her opening, teasing. This was it, and as she locked her eyes with his, gone dark and hungry, a moment of fear seized her. This was different from anything she'd ever felt with a man, and what they were about to do would change her. It would change them.

But when Ian lowered his lips to hers and kissed her so gently it stole her breath, the fear evaporated. She rocked her hips against him, enticing him. Ian pulled away with a smack of his lips and gritted his teeth, closed his eyes. "It's hard to stay gentle," he whispered.

She loved him for the admission. Admired him for his obvious effort not to hurt her. But she'd been worked up for days and was ready for him. Lifting her head off the bed to meet him, she kissed him and scratched her nails slowly up his back. His hips jerked, and his tongue slipped past her lips. He slid into her, stretching her. The burn was overshadowed by how good he felt inside her. Ian pulled her wrists above her head and bit her bottom lip harder than he had before. A needy moan left her lips as she spread her legs wider, allowing him better access. His powerful hips bucked forward again, harder, driving himself deeper into her. He was shaking now, trying to keep control, but he didn't need to anymore. She wanted all of him. Animal and man and teetering control, she wanted him to be himself with her.

"Harder," she pleaded.

A snarl ripped from his chest as he bucked into her so deep he bumped her clit. His eyes were midnight now, his face feral as he pumped into her again and again. His kisses were less controlled. Harder lips and grazing teeth as he trailed them from her lips to her neck, down her shoulder to the inside of her arm where he bit her hard enough to draw a gasp from her lips and make her writhe against him. He was losing it, and she reveled in the fierce abandon in his eyes. When he drew one of her nipples into his mouth and sucked hard, Elyse cried out as the pressure inside of her became too much. Pounding pleasure pulsed through her as Ian slammed into her again, harder and harder. He slid his body further up against hers, gripping the back of her neck as he buried his face against her collarbone and snarled out her name. Erratically, he slid into her, and she could feel it now as he let off a wild sound from his throat. Warmth shot into her with every thrust until he was emptied, and still, her aftershocks pounded on, long after he eased to a stop.

He lay there, connected deeply to her as she gripped him in slow, hard pulses. And when she was finished, he moved slowly within her, intertwining their fingers, and the next time she came, he watched her face. This one was softer. It was drawn slower. It was controlled and given because Ian adored her. She could see it in his eyes.

She'd been right when she'd had that moment of fear right before they'd slept together.

Elyse pulled one of his hands to her lips and kissed his knuckles. "Everything feels different now. Bigger. More important."

Ian rested his forehead against hers and closed his eyes as he let off a long, relieved sigh. "For me, too."

FIFTEEN

"Miki!" Elyse yelled. The pup bounded around the puddle of spilled goat's milk, curled tail wagging. "Little monster."

A loud whistle sounded from the yard and, immediately, the furry little cretin bunny bounced toward the door of the barn and out into the dim, early morning light.

"Yeah, you better run," Elyse huffed as she righted the pail Miki had knocked over. For whatever reason, Ian had complete control over Miki's behavior while the pup saved all of his naughtiness for her. At least he liked to snuggle her best, though, so she had that going for her. Ian was giving her lessons on being the boss of Miki but, so far, the little beasty pranced around here causing chaos wherever he pleased. He completely had her heart—when he wasn't spilling the goat juice.

Momma Goat stuck her tongue out and bleated a horrific scream, and Elyse hunched her shoulders against the grating noise. She was pretty sure Shayna Haskins had sold Momma Goat cheap because she was a screamer. Lucky Elyse. But, she kept them in the milk and cheese and wasn't a kicker, so Elyse had learned to take the good with the bad.

Next year though, she was going to keep one of the momma cows here to be a milker. And hopefully by then,

Miki will have gotten over his obnoxious fascination with the silver milk pail.

"Elyse, you ready?" Ian called.

Muttering a curse, she released the goat from the high pen and ushered her back into the big stall that housed the two nannies, the ram, and two half-grown kids. No milk today, but at least Momma Goat's teats wouldn't be swollen and sore. Elyse would be gone the rest of the day, cutting and storing hay with the help of Ian, Josiah, and the neighbors, Joanna and Ricky Fairway. Ian said it was just right to cut now for peek nutrition, and after the last two weeks of working the homestead with him, she trusted him completely. The man had a knack for guessing the weather, for animal husbandry, and a million other little talents that made her wonder just how she'd made it this far without his help.

Her heart sank as she sauntered out into the dawn and felt the chill creeping into her bones. It was mid-September now, only a month until Ian went down for the winter. And as much as she hated the cold and what it meant to her now, Ian seemed to feel the same urgency to get everything done around here. He'd even taken a couple days to help her store the vegetables in the root cellar, and he'd canned salmon one of the townies had traded him for some rabbits he'd snared. Next year, they couldn't miss the salmon run. Ian said his bear did best if he had a lot of fish in his diet.

Elyse snuggled deeper into her jacket and strode toward the hayfields behind the cabin. This was the second crop of the season, and a late one, but necessary since the first hadn't produced enough. They needed another fifty square bales for the cattle if they wanted to make it until the grass turned green again. For the millionth time since she'd taken over the care of this homestead, she was amazed at what Uncle Jim and Marta had been able to manage.

Ian would've scared her by jumping out from behind the cabin if Miki hadn't given him away. Elyse tried to run, but

Ian was too fast and had her thrown over his shoulder before she could even inhale once. She laughed and swatted his backside as he strode toward the hayfields.

"What took you so long, woman?"

"Ask that little hellion," she said affectionately as she wiggled her fingers down at Miki. He was much too little to reach her, but he tried anyway. If he wasn't so darned cute, he would be much easier to reprimand.

"The milk again?"

"Always."

Ian let off a little growl and set her down, facing him. "Good morning," he murmured, cupping her cheeks and kissing her lips. He'd been up before her, and this was the first she'd gotten to see him today. He was all mint toothpaste, three-day scruff, mussed hair, bright eyes and grins, and the stress of getting the animals taken care of before going out to the fields faded away.

Melting against him, she nipped his bottom lip and hugged his waist. "Morning."

"You ready?"

"Yes. No. There's something I should tell you before you meet my brother."

"Okay," he said, rubbing his hands up and down her arms to warm her. "Lay it on me."

"I didn't actually tell him about you yet."

"Ha!" Ian shook his head and jacked his eyebrows up. "Why not?"

"Well, because he knew about the advertisement, and he gave me so much shit over it, and I was afraid he wouldn't understand if he didn't meet you in person. I wanted to keep his pre-conceived judgments to a minimum."

"Trouble," Ian accused lightly as he draped his arm across her shoulders. He kissed the top of her head and led her down the dirt road that wound through dense, lush vegetation to the hayfields.

Unable to help herself, Elyse scooped Miki up and snuggled the wiggling puppy. "We like to keep daddy on his toes, don't we?" she crooned. But when she looked up, the smile dipped from her face at the expression on Ian's. "What?"

The corners of his eyes tightened as he walked beside her. "Nothing."

"Spill it, bear-man."

His jaw clenched in the early morning light as he gave her his profile. "I won't make a good daddy, Elyse. Best you don't get used to calling me that."

"Why not?"

"Why not?" He looked at her incredulously. "You want your sons to end up like me?"

"How do you know we won't have daughters?" she teased, but he didn't laugh.

"No daughters, Elyse. I can only give you sons, and when they turn sixteen, they Change for the first time and start hibernating. And trust me when I say, you don't want to deal with a pissed off teenager who can call a bear out of himself."

"Your dad did it?"

"Yeah, and me and my brothers nearly put him in the grave with stress."

"Maybe we won't have multiples, and one kid will be easier. And why can't bear shifters have daughters?"

"I don't know. Science. Maybe evolution decided females make bad bears or something. At least it's not like werewolves. They can have daughters, but they die at birth. Only the sons survive."

Elyse nearly dropped Miki in shock. "Werewolves? There are *werewolves*?"

The blood drained from Ian's flushed face, leaving him pale as a corpse. "Shit. Forget I said that."

"Not likely! Do they live in Alaska?"

"Elyse," Ian warned.

"Dammit Ian, this isn't an unreasonable question. I have wolf tags! Am I going to accidentally shoot some shifter?"

"Accidentally? No." Ian started walking again while she stood there with her head spinning, clutching Miki to her chest.

"What does that even mean?"

"It means if you get close enough to a werewolf, you'll know it. And that reminds me, after the hay is cut and stored, we're going to work on your marksmanship. You can't go into winter missing every damned target. I won't be awake to protect you."

"Protect me from what? Werewolves?"

A frustrated growl vibrated the air, but Ian didn't turn around, and he didn't slow down either.

"Ian!" He ignored her so she stomped her foot and let a pathetically human growl rip out of her. "I want kids."

"Cubs, Elyse," he gritted out, rounding on her. "They're called cubs. You know why? Because I'm a fucking animal, and your kids would be fucking animals, too."

"Don't you dare talk like that to me, Ian Silver. Don't you talk to me like I don't know the man I'm bedding. You aren't an animal."

"I *am*, Elyse." He stopped in front of her, eyes blazing and darkening by the second. "This is the gig. You can have me, but I'm not doing kids."

"Because you don't want them?" Damn her voice as it shook with anger.

Ian scrubbed his hands down his face and stared at her, shaking his head slightly in denial. "No, not because I don't want them. I wouldn't want to curse a kid. I don't talk to my dad for a reason, and neither do my brothers."

"You said it was because you were all dominant male grizzlies."

Ian ran his hands through his hair and linked them behind his head. "That's true of me and my brothers. But with my dad...shit." Ian spat. "He was always so proud of what he was and so disappointed when me and my brothers struggled. He's more bear, and we're more human, and we were always this huge mistake."

"Mistake?"

"That's what he called us. He said we didn't make sense, and that we were weak and not meant to be given bears. He raised us, but he didn't like it. We were on our own after our first hibernation. He'd moved to Anchorage by the time we came out of that first winter, skinny as shit and scared because he'd never thought to tell us what to expect. He'd thought we should just know. Instinct or something."

"Your first hibernation at sixteen?"

Ian nodded.

Utterly dumbfounded, Elyse murmured, "He just left you?"

"He came in and out for a while. I learned to fly and so did Tobias, so we picked up his deliveries in the summers while he lived in Anchorage. I get it. Me and my brothers weren't easy, but there is still a big part of me that hates him. Not just for pushing us out into the world early the way he did, but because he put the bear in me in the first place. I never want a kid hating me for cursing him."

"I didn't know," Elyse whispered, devastated for what he'd been through.

She imagined Ian as a child, scrawny after a hibernation, hungry as sin, and with no parental guidance—no mentor to tell him how to navigate a really difficult life. She respected him more for where he was now. He was not only alive still, but he'd bought a plane and found a job that made him a good living, and now he was here, a decent man who treated her sweetly. Who balanced a fine line between taking care of her and making her strong enough to stand on her own when he wasn't around. The way he was with her, Miki, and the other animals around the homestead, she would've never guessed he'd had a cold upbringing. He was so confident, and his anger was the quiet kind that he held in until he was ready to talk about things calmly.

Elyse set Miki down and wrapped her arms around Ian's neck.

"Woman, I'll get you an entire dog sled team of pups if you want, but I can't give you babies. It wouldn't even feel right leaving you to raise them while I sleep half the year away."

"Okay," she said, tears burning her eyes. She would keep taking her birth control and accept this for now. Perhaps in a few winters, he would feel differently, but this was something Ian was giving her a hard "no" on right now, and she had to respect it.

"I want to give you everything you want, Elyse—"

"It's okay."

"I hope I'm not interrupting anything," Josiah said quietly from ten yards away.

Ian started in her arms and turned, crouched slightly as he shoved her behind him. To stop the soft growl in his throat, Elyse rubbed his back and stepped around him. "Uh, Ian, this is my brother, Josiah. Josiah, this is my husband, Ian Silver. Er…not husband. Fiancé."

Josiah looked a lot like her. Sandy brown hair peeking out from under his winter hat, and the same odd-colored gold eyes they'd both inherited from their absent father. He was a lot taller though, much wider in the shoulder, and intimidating in his quietness to strangers. She knew her brother, though, and she adored him.

"Fiancé?" he asked, his face a frozen, emotionless mask.

Ian cleared his throat and straightened his spine, then strode over to her brother and offered his hand. "Nice to meet you. Elyse talks about you a lot."

Josiah's eyebrows quirked up. "Funny, she's said nothing about you. Fiancé," he repeated, ignoring Ian's outstretched hand. "Please tell me you didn't answer her advertisement."

"Josiah," Elyse warned. "It's not what you think."

"You didn't hire him to be your husband?"

Aw, shit-cicles. "Well, yes."

"Are you fucking kidding me, Elyse? I told you that ad was a terrible idea."

"Actually, it was an awesome idea because I met Ian."

"Well, forgive me if I don't throw my trust at you, Mr. Silver. My sister doesn't exactly have good taste in men. The last one she brought home was a worthless little shit." Josiah's lips lifted in a dead smile. "What do you want with my sister? Is it the land?"

Ian went rigid, hands hooked on his hips. He cast Elyse a ghost of a glance, then dragged his attention back to Josiah. "Look, I appreciate that you're protective of your sister, and I'm not asking for you to like me right now. I'm asking you keep your mind open to me, and I hope I earn your trust in time. Elyse and I met in unusual circumstances, yes, but I'm only interested in her land when I'm running it beside her, and I'm here because I care for her. We've got hay to cut and shit to do, so if you're up for it, we could use your help cutting and hauling it. I'll let you two have some time. 'Scuse me." Ian strode off in the direction of a pair of green tractors bouncing toward the fields.

"Why are you acting like this?" Elyse asked, mortified by her brother's behavior.

"Because look at him, Elyse? Does that man strike you as a mail-order husband? He can get any girl he wants. Think real long and hard about why he's here, Elyse. I can't fucking stand watching you go through another Cole McCall."

"I learned my lesson from Cole, you swamp turd."

Josiah's judgy little eyebrows jacked up even higher. "Did you?"

"Yeah, Jo, I did. You want proof? That man you just insulted has filled the hen house, fixed my snow machine and four-wheeler, and brought his own snow-machine, just in case you're comparing him to my moocher asshole late-boyfriend. Ian has been working himself to the bone chopping firewood, and he gets up earlier than me every morning and has my breakfast warming on the stove. He works until sundown getting our place ready for winter. He's gone on two hunts, has my once-empty freezer half-filled, and he protected me from a fucking *bear* attack without a thought for his own safety." She yanked up the hem of her pant leg and showed him the scabbed over claw marks. The stitches were still in the worst one. "And it's him who's been doctoring me without me ever asking, and no he doesn't need the money or the land, you snooty dick-weevil. He has a plane and runs a successful bush pilot career that he put on hold to come prepare me for winter. And," she growled, stomping past him, "I love the guy, so there's that."

"You were attacked by a bear?" her brother called after her.

"That was your only take-away from that entire tirade?" Elyse asked. "Seriously?"

The sound of Josiah's boots became louder and louder as he jogged to catch up. "When?"

"Two weeks ago. We were fishing, and a brown bear sow and her cubs went after our fish. And then after me." The memory still made the blood in her veins run cold.

"Why were you fishing in brown bear country in the first place?"

"Because my freezer was empty, Jo. I missed the big salmon run, and it wasn't hunting season yet, and we needed meat fast."

"Why was your freezer empty? Hey!" Josiah pulled her arm, yanking her to a stop. "Why were you that hard up for meat?"

"Because Cole drained me dry." Her voice shook with the admission of her weakness. She'd kept all this from Josiah. Sure, he knew that Cole had been bad news, but he hadn't known just how much Elyse had let him take advantage of her. "I know you thought that advertisement for a husband was stupid. I *know*. But I was desperate, and I got lucky as hell when that one showed up." She jammed her finger at Ian, who was talking to Mr. Fairway and his wife near the tractor with the baler on the back.

"Elyse, why didn't you tell me it was that bad? I knew you were losing weight, but I thought it was a vanity thing. You could've told me, and I would've hunted for you."

"Don't you ever get tired of taking care of me, Jo?" She let her shoulders hunch forward and sighed. "I do."

"As opposed to him taking care of you?"

"It's not like that. Ian doesn't coddle me. He's teaching me to snare rabbits, shoot worth a damn, and can food more efficiently. I even killed and plucked my first chicken last week because he thought I should know how to do that kind of stuff. He's not taking care of me. He's making me stronger."

Josiah took a step back and scratched at his beard as he watched Ian laugh and shake Mr. Fairway's hand. "I still don't like it," he muttered, but the vitriol had left his voice.

"You don't have to like it, big brother," she said, clapping him on the shoulder as she passed him by.

"And I'm not a swamp turd," Josiah called from behind her.

The stretch of her smile felt good. If her brother would give Ian half a chance, he would see the good man she'd fallen for. Ian and Cole were like night and day. Josiah was just being stubborn.

"Don't eat that," she said to Miki, who was chowing down on what looked like pebbled rabbit crap.

"He's a good lookin' dog," Josiah said, walking ten paces behind her.

"He's a hellion."

"They all are at that age. How's potty-training going?" There was a smile in his voice that said he already knew.

"Not awesome. How are my cows doing?"

143

"Fair enough. We lost one to wolves week before last. When do you want to come and get them? The temperature's dropping."

Like she couldn't feel the chill. Now she dreaded the winter for all sorts of reasons. With a sigh, she turned, waited for him, and didn't even kick his shin over the obnoxious grin on his face like she did when they were kids.

"My sister, the grizzly attack survivor. Shootin' and huntin' and plantin' and cannin'. Uncle Jim would be right proud of the Alaskan woman you turned out to be."

"Don't tease."

Josiah's voice went serious when he said, "I'm not."

When she dared a glance up at him, walking beside her, his eyes were sincere. Emotion swelled inside of her chest, and her throat went tight. "Thanks for saying that."

Josiah hopped on his four-wheeler he'd parked at the edge of the field and pulled it toward the first row of hay Mr. Fairway was already mowing down. Josiah turned on his seat and jerked his head in invitation. With a laugh, Elyse scrambled up onto the small trailer he was hauling and bumped and bounced along behind him as her brother managed to hit every danged pothole in the field to reach his destination.

She waved to Joanna Fairway as Josiah pulled to a stop and chatted with the neighbor until Joanna's husband was far enough ahead with the mower for her to start the baler on the line of cut hay. Elyse always paid them with a cow for their troubles, especially since Ricky had a gimp leg from getting kicked by a horse a few years back and had trouble hunting for them. Still, Elyse was extremely grateful they had been friends of her uncle's and offered to help bale the hay when she needed it.

The morning passed quickly as Josiah drove slowly beside the new, square bales Joana left behind her baler. She and Ian hauled them up into the back, stacking them high until her arms fatigued and she switched Josiah spots driving the four-wheeler. And when they had as much as the trailer could carry, she drove it slowly back toward the empty cattle pen. The storage building for the hay was dilapidated and half the wood rotten. She jogged inside the cabin and threw together a quick lunch for everyone while Ian and Josiah unloaded the bales from the trailer.

And when she came outside with a basket full of food, she smiled when she overheard Josiah and Ian's conversation. They were talking about fixing up the hay storage before Josiah headed back for his cabin.

They didn't know it yet, and she'd never admit it to them out loud, but they'd just given her a moment she never thought she would have. Cole and Josiah had fought like wolverines, and the tension had always added stress, but seeing her brother and her fiancé talking cordially about how to improve and expand the wooden hay shelter had her feeling incredibly relieved. She could imagine holidays together...

Wait. Elyse frowned and gripped on tighter to the handle of the food basket, causing the wicker to creak. Ian would be in hibernation and would only be awake an hour to celebrate the holidays. And how would she explain that to Josiah? Maybe one year she could convince her brother Ian was sick, but Josiah was sharp as a tack and wouldn't fall for that two years in a row.

A problem for another day because right now, she had a hungry bear-shifter to feed, hay to haul, and shit to do. And a puppy to wrangle because Miki was eating something unsavory again.

But when she pulled the puppy away from the horse-crap snack he was partaking in, she really looked at the homestead around her, and it became impossible to rush away from such a profound moment. Her brother and fiancé were talking low, the homestead was clean, the garden tidy and producing, and the hay was building up by the trailer-load. The woodpile was stacked high all along the side of the cabin and, in the distant barn, Momma Goat screamed her contentment. Sure, Miki's breath smelled like the south end of a northbound horse, but he wasn't nipping her anymore, and he stuck like glue to her and Ian wherever they went. And off in the field behind the cabin, she had kind neighbors who were helping out.

Elyse smiled at how far her life had come in such a short amount of time. It was because of Ian that she wasn't struggling and panicking right now, a mere month before the first snowfall would blanket this place in white.

Ian smiled at her as if he could tell she was thinking mushy thoughts about him, and she melted under his appreciative gaze.

Not even the chill or the threat of winter could dampen a moment like this.

For the first time in as long as she could remember, she was bone-deep, canyon-wide, ardently, and utterly happy.

SIXTEEN

Elyse gave Joanna a tight hug and waved to her husband as he drove the tractor back toward their own property.

"I'll bring the cow next week if that's all right."

Joanna smiled kindly and dipped her head. "That would be much appreciated. You have a good night now."

Elyse grinned up at Joanna as she climbed into the tractor with the baler on the back. "I think I'm going to sleep like a log tonight."

"It was a long day, but a good day. You keep those boys in line."

With a snort, she waved Joanna off. Elyse had as much a chance of keeping a grizzly-shifter and her half-wild brother in line as she did of controlling the Alaskan weather.

Her muscles had cooled as she'd said her farewells to the Fairways, so she zipped her jacket up to her chin and strode toward where Josiah and Ian were loading the last few bales into the trailer. "I will shamelessly bribe you to fix my hay storage," she said through a grin.

Ian gave her a grin and asked, "Bribe how?"

"Uncle Jim had this recipe for rabbit stew—"

"Sold," Josiah said, hoisting another bale. "I'm in. Dinner invitation accepted."

Ian let off a single booming laugh as he adjusted the stacked hay. "Well, get on then, woman. Josiah and I will be in later."

With a giggle, Elyse jumped into his arms and planted tiny pecking kisses on his cheeks until he chuckled warmly and hugged her waist.

"Bossy," she teased.

Ian's blue eyes sparked in the dim evening light as he leaned in and kissed her soundly. He set her on her feet and gave her backside a swat as she trotted away. And as she left the men in her life behind to bring in the rest of the hay, over Miki's puppy barks, she could've sworn she heard Josiah laugh low. And damn, it felt good to hear that. He'd always been a quiet man, more observer than participant in silly antics, but today, she'd seen him smile more than she could ever remember. Perhaps he'd been as lonely as her trying to make a life out here, or perhaps his worry over her had been heavier than she'd realized. And maybe, just maybe, Ian being here was good for Josiah, too.

Behind the cabin, the sunset painted the sky in vivid shades of pink and orange. Today had been one of those days that felt like summer. Not because it was warm. On the contrary, there was a nip in the air. But when she was a child, she'd looked forward to summers at the homestead all year long. The months in school would drag on and on, and the closer to summer it became, the more she was filled with the glowing feeling that soon she would be in the place she belonged. This place was magic. Here, mom's yelling and frustration with her and Josiah didn't exist. Uncle Jim was a patient sort of man, and Marta treated her and Jo like they were her own kids. It wasn't the impatient love that Mom forced herself to feel for them. Marta and Uncle Jim seemed to always have a smile when they watched them. The unforced kind that said they were really enjoying spending time with her and Josiah.

After Marta died, and then Uncle Jim, this place hadn't felt the same. It wasn't a retreat anymore, but instead a responsibility. But today had felt different. It felt like the old homestead again.

Miki bounced up the stairs behind her and into the cabin. She didn't run the generator unless she needed it, so she turned on the lanterns instead and built a fire in the stove with the pile of wood and tinder and newspapers Ian kept stocked by the door as a habit. She'd left the rabbit out to thaw when she'd made lunch, so she discarded the head and feet and chopped the rest up into twelve pieces. With a private smile for the sound of the four-wheeler and men's voices outside, she climbed down into the root cellar with one of the lanterns and filled a small basket with the things she needed. Thankfully, the garden had produced more once she'd gotten a hold on the weeds strangling her vegetable plants, and Ian had taken her around the property and showed her blueberry patches and a pair of apple trees that his oversensitive bear nose had picked up. The man had already eaten a tree's worth of the apples in his constant need to eat right now, but she'd preserved the rest along with a few buckets of ripe blueberries and would have jam and fruit for pies in the winter. She'd never had that before, nor had she known how to can and smoke salmon. Ian had proven himself invaluable.

She picked an onion, the smallest of the potatoes, and pulled a few cloves of garlic from the strands hanging from the rafters, then frowned at an unfamiliar coffee can that sat on the shelf with the jars of salmon. The can made a hollow clunk when she set it down on the small prep table. Inside was a wad of cash, mostly five and ten dollar bills, and a note.

If food gets low, don't go hungry.
I love you.
Ian

She read it several times to familiarize herself with his scrawled handwriting. She was both flattered and scared at the meaning of this coffee can. Ian was making sure she was taken care of. He was preparing for worst case scenarios, and for that, she adored him even more deeply.

But...

It was early to be making preparations like this, wasn't it? She still had a month with him, but he was already filling a coffee can with extra money. Maybe he was afraid his hibernation would come early this year. Last night's pillow talk had brought to light that he didn't control when he went to sleep, and that some years it snuck up on him.

She stuffed the money and the note back in the can and replaced it on the shelf. She would need that letter from him in dark winter when she was fighting off cabin fever and waiting for him to wake up for their mere hour of time together. Reading his note would be a good way to feel a connection to him when the loneliness became unbearable. That little scribbled paper was the closest she'd ever gotten to a love note. Sure, it was short and simple, but it was the meaning behind it that curled into her heart and warmed her blood. Ian was thinking of every way possible to help her through the cold months, even if he would be as good as a ghost.

Basket of vegetables in hand, she climbed up the steep stairs out of the root cellar and back into the kitchen. Thyme, parsley, bay leaves, butter, sugar, salt and pepper gathered, she seared the rabbit. Once the meat was ready, she got the stew simmering on the stove and finally removed her jacket.

Her muscles were so tired her limbs felt numb, but it was the good kind of exhaustion. It was a fatigue that said she'd had a productive day and would be stronger for it once the soreness left her in a couple of days. She hung her jacket on the coat rack, then strode into the bedroom and scrutinized herself in the mirror. She did this lately because for the first time in a long time, she enjoyed the way her body was changing. There was no wasting away or new bones protruding. She was on the mend and putting on weight that would cushion and insulate her in the cold months.

Ian liked the changes, too. She could tell because he couldn't seem to keep his hands off her curves now—her ass in particular. God, that man could make her feel beautiful with a touch.

Missing him, she meandered into the kitchen for a quick stir of the stew simmering in the cast iron pot before looking out the window. It was full dark now, and Ian and Josiah had lanterns lit on hooks around the hay storage. The sound of the chainsaw was loud in the stillness of the evening, and she could make out Ian making cuts into posts he must've dragged up from the old wood pile. Uncle Jim had always reused everything so he'd torn down the old horse shelter five years back and piled the wood behind the barn. His foresight meant Ian and Josiah weren't going off into the night searching for wood right now. Her brother was digging a posthole several yards outside of the shelter. Neither were talking, but they both seemed to know exactly what they were doing. Capable Alaskan men—there was nothing quite like them. She was proud of how self-sufficient her brother had become and proud that Ian had chosen her to share his life.

She refilled Miki's water and food bowls in the corner near an old blanket he usually slept on while she puttered around the cabin in the evenings. With cute little puppy snorts, he ate hungrily.

An hour and a half later of hammers on nails echoing through the homestead, she had fresh biscuits made, and the stew had thickened up nicely. Apparently Ian could tell the main course was almost done because he led Josiah inside at just the right time and wrapped his arms around her waist from behind. Resting his chin on her shoulder, he tasted a spoonful of the broth she offered him. The groan of ecstasy he elicited gave her a deep yearning in her stomach. Cheeks flushed, she nuzzled her cheek against the scruff of his jaw and murmured, "You go wash up. Dinner's on."

Ian leaned closer and clamped his teeth on her neck for just a moment before he eased away from her, leaving her back cold where he'd been so warm before. He did that a lot, and when she'd asked, he'd told her simply that his bear liked having his teeth on her neck. That it made her feel more like his. She didn't know what it said about her, but she thoroughly enjoyed him getting territorial and laying those sexy teeth on her skin. There was a sense of danger about it, having the mouth of a wild creature like Ian on her, but at the same time, she trusted him completely. With her life even.

Miki was passed out on his blanket by the time they filled their plates and sat down at the table. It was late, and the day had been long and hard, but that didn't seem to stop Josiah from stirring the shit. "If you saw Elyse when we were younger, you would run for the hills."

Elyse kicked her brother under the table and pulled more rabbit meat from the bone with her fork. "Piss of, Jo. I've been a looker all my life."

"What was she like?" Ian asked through a trouble-making grin as he slathered butter on his steaming biscuit.

"So one summer, Elyse decided she wanted to have a boy haircut like mine, so she begged Uncle Jim to cut it. Begged and begged."

"Josiah, stop it." Elyse was doing her best to hide her laughter. Her brother didn't need encouragement, and she had a sneaking suspicion where this was headed.

"So Marta told her she wouldn't look good with a boy cut and forbade Uncle Jim from going anywhere near her with the scissors. But Elyse here, being the head-strong person she is, decided she didn't need Uncle Jim, and she cut her own hair in the bathroom mirror before everyone woke up one morning."

Elyse's shoulders shook uncontrollably with her laughter now, and she set her spoon down with a clink on her metal bowl. "I was sixteen and had always wanted to try short hair. Marie Dryver had her hair cut in school, and she looked so cool I imagined I was going to look the same."

"Except Elyse shaved entire notches out of the back of her hair, and she was in braces for a pair of impressive buck-teeth at the time. She'd fallen off the porch a few days before, so she was sporting one helluva shiner to boot."

"And when Marta saw my hair, she burst out crying. I mean…body wracked with sobs kind of crying, and she said my mom was going to kill her. I'd done it at the end of summer and there was no saving the haircut without burring my head completely—"

"Which Uncle Jim did—"

"Okay, but in my mind, it was going to be short on the sides," she explained, gesturing to her hair, "and longer up top. I wanted to look like a badass."

"Yeah, but you used sheep sheers."

Ian was leaning back in his chair belly laughing now, and Elyse's cheeks were on fire.

"That was the year of no boyfriends at school."

"That was the one benefit to you looking like a deranged beaver," Josiah muttered.

"Oh God," Ian groaned, wiping moisture from the corners of his eyes. "I'm so attracted to you right now."

Elyse made a single clicking sound from behind her teeth and rolled her eyes. "Thanks a lot, Josiah."

Gold eyes dancing, her brother murmured around a bite of stew, "Anytime. I've got pictures at my cabin. I can show you them when you come pick up the cattle."

"I'd sure appreciate it," Ian said, dodging a swat from Elyse. "I want a picture of her to put in my plane anyway."

"Fantastic," she muttered.

"When are we driving the herd?" Josiah asked.

"Mmm," Ian murmured, looking thoughtful as he chewed. "I want to take Elyse up to Afognak in the next couple of days. Maybe get a deer or two. If we can get some venison, I'd feel a lot better about our freezer."

"Afognak?" Josiah asked, sandy brows rising high on his forehead.

"Have you been there?"

"Can't say I have, but I've heard things about that place. Haunted as shit if rumors are right."

"Nah," Ian said, ghosting Elyse a glance. "I've spent a lot of time there. No ghosts but there is wildlife as thick as the woods themselves."

"You have a boat to get there?"

"Yeah, I parked it on Kodiak Island in April. There are a few cabins on Afognak for hunters, and I figured Elyse and I would hole up there for a day or two and see if we can't fill a couple hunting tags."

"It's brown bear territory," Josiah warned. "Elyse got lucky the first time, but you can understand my concern, yeah? Besides Mom, she's all the family I have left."

"I get that. I respect that you are protective of her, and I promise to keep the risk as low as possible. I'm seeing zero sign of big game around here, though, and we need red meat."

Josiah leveled Elyse with a thoughtful look and nodded slowly. "When will you go?"

"Day after tomorrow. We'll do a two-day hunt, then come back here and ride up your way to collect the cattle if you have time."

"Yeah, that'll work for me. I can come out here on Wednesday and check your animals for you."

"We'd appreciate it," Ian said. "We'll take the pup with us, so it'll just be the chickens, goats, and horses. If we get anything, we'll bring you back a roast."

Josiah's face lit up, and he ripped open his biscuit. "I do love venison. You planning on getting a bear this season?"

As if she were lightning struck, Elyse jolted in her chair. "What?"

"Bear meat?" Josiah offered her a baffled look. "It's your favorite."

Elyse blinked slowly and gritted her teeth against the ill feeling unfurling in her stomach. She couldn't look at Ian even if she tried right now. "It used to be my favorite, but I don't have a taste for it anymore." Her voice cracked and dipped to a whisper. "Too gamey."

Ian's hand slid up her thigh under the table, and he squeezed her leg reassuringly. "No plans for bear this season."

Elyse intertwined her fingers with his against her leg. No plans for bear meat any season. Not when it reminded her so much of the massive animal that lived inside of the man she loved.

Except for the bones, Josiah scraped his bowl clean, then leaned back in his chair. "Elyse, this stew is as good as Uncle Jim's."

"You want to crash in the guest bedroom?" she asked hopefully, stalling for more time with him.

"Nah, I've got my own animals to feed. I'm gonna load the four-wheeler in the back of my truck and get going. Ian." Josiah shook his hand hard. "I will slit your throat if you hurt my sister. Formalities aside, I like you better than her last man. Cole never worked a day in his life, but I can see you're a real hard worker. I thank you for taking care of my sister."

Ian huffed a tired laugh. "Brother, you've got it wrong. Elyse takes care of me." He stood and followed Josiah with Elyse trailing behind him.

"Speaking of Cole," Josiah said, turning around at the door. "His brother was up at my place last week asking about Elyse."

"Miller?" Elyse asked, shocked to her bones.

Josiah nodded. All the humor had seeped out of his eyes now, and he looked more and more like the somber Josiah she was used to. "He was asking if you were done mourning and ready for a man and followed it directly with asking how your cattle are doing. Shit timing, too, because wolves had just taken one of the calves the night before, so I wasn't in a mood to answer him. He left pissed." Her brother dragged his gaze back to Ian. "Be wary of that one, okay?"

When Ian clenched his hands behind his back, Josiah couldn't see it, but she could. He was shaking, and a deep red flush of anger was creeping slowly up his neck. "Will do. Thanks for the head's up."

"Sure thing. Night," Josiah called over his shoulder as he strode toward his four-wheeler.

Troubled, Elyse watched Josiah straddle the seat of the ATV, rip the engine, and gun it toward the hayfields where he'd left his truck parked on the edge.

"Miller is Cole's brother," she explained softly.

"I know." Ian's voice was more growl than anything, and he strode out the front door and off the porch.

"How do you know who he is?"

"Small town," he answered mysteriously.

But that didn't make sense. Miller didn't live in Galena. He lived near Naluto, closer to where Josiah lived.

"Where are you going?" she called.

"To check on the animals."

Huh. Elyse leaned against the open doorframe, arms crossed over her chest as she frowned so deeply her face ached with it. It wasn't uncommon for Ian to check the animals right before they went to sleep, but they would likely be up for a couple more hours still. Josiah's admission that Miller had been asking about her had rattled Ian badly, but for the life of her, she couldn't understand why. Cole wasn't a threat to either of them, seeing as how he was cold and buried, and Miller could ask about her all he wanted. That butt-faced moocher wasn't laying a hand on anything she owned ever again. She was Ian's now, and he was the biggest, baddest man there was. With everything going on around here, a drunken McCall brother should be the least of her mate's worries.

Gooseflesh rose in waves across her skin, and she grabbed her coat off the rack before she shut the door behind her. Shrugging into it, she made her way carefully over the dark yard, but when she got as far as the tree with the rope swing, Ian suddenly appeared out of the dimly lit barn. His nostrils flared slightly in the warm glow of the lantern light, and his eyes were dark as pitch, as though his bear was right there, just below the surface.

"What is it?" she asked, drawing to a halt. Chills rippled up her spine.

Slowly, Ian lifted his face to the sky, and in that moment, she felt it. Something cold, as if the finger of a corpse brushed her cheek. No. Elyse gasped when a snowflake floated down in front of her face. Before Ian, snow hadn't meant anything. It was a way of life and expected, but now? Suddenly the small, cold flake melting on her cheek stung like acid. Dread seeped into her as she wiped it off and shook her head in despair. "It's too soon."

Ian's chest was heaving as he watched her. She could see it in his eyes—he was rocked to the core by the early snow, too.

"It's too soon!" she repeated louder, walking toward him. She picked up her speed, then bolted into his open arms.

"Shhh," he said against her hair, hugging her so tight she couldn't breathe.

Or perhaps it was the crushing realization that her time with him was growing so short.

"I'm not tired yet. I'm not. Elyse, it's okay. Shhh. Don't cry."

She was gasping, holding in her sobs and trying, but failing, to be strong for him as more snowflakes floated down to the ground around them.

"I'm not going to sleep on you yet, woman. I'm not. Listen." He eased back and cupped her cheeks. "We've still got things to do together. It's just the first snow, and it's not even warm enough to stick yet."

"I'm not ready, Ian. I just got you."

"I know." He leaned forward and kissed her, then rested his forehead against hers. "I know, and I'm not ready for it either. We've still got time."

"How much?"

Ian shook his head helplessly. "I don't know."

Warm tears streamed down her cheeks. "Will it always be like this? Dreading the winter, dreading the snow?"

Heartache slashed through his dark, inhuman eyes, and then he pulled her in close again. His lack of an answer was answer enough. Clutching onto his jacket with trembling hands, she watched the soft snowfall over his shoulder. She had to do this better—appreciate more the time they had together. She could see exactly how their years would progress, six achingly short months together, and then six that dragged on for eternity as she waited over his body for him to wake up for an hour every day. She had to figure out a way to savor every second he was awake.

"Ian," she said on a frozen breath, clinging to him tighter. "I love you."

A wrecked sound wrenched from his throat, and his mouth crashed onto hers. He pushed his tongue past her lips and gripped the back of her hair. With a growl deep in his throat, he yanked his jacket off and tossed it to the ground, and then his hands were on her again, reaching into the open zipper of her coat, lifting the hem of her shirt. Fingertips brushed up her ribcage, over her bra, then slipped in to cup her breast. How was he so warm when the rest of the world was so cold? Nipping his lip, she pulled his shirt over his head and reveled in how touching his chest thawed her frozen fingertips.

His voice was tinged with desperation as he gritted out, "Touch me." Then he pulled her hand down the mounds of his abs and into the front of his jeans. He shuddered when she gripped his thick, hard shaft and pulled a slow stroke.

She understood this—the desperation to be close. To connect. Soon, this wouldn't be an option for them. He massaged her breast harder, dumping warmth into her middle and pooling wetness against her panties. He could always do this. Ian had the uncanny ability to rev her up in seconds. She pulled his erection again and again, until his hips rocked with the pace she set, all the while kissing him as if she would never get the chance to be in a moment like this again.

She was on fire. Writhing, gasping, panting his name as he slid his hand down the front of her pants and drew his fingers through the wetness he'd conjured there. The soft growl in his throat turned feral. He leaned forward enough to pick her up by the backs of her knees, and then carried her toward the barn. His shoulders were hard as steel under her hands as she gripped the muscular curves of his body. Tears still warm on her cheeks, she slipped her tongue past his lips. Ian opened for her, daring her. Tempting her, and she lost herself as she tasted him. The snowfall outside was just like the rest of the world right now. It didn't matter. All that mattered was that she was here, safe with the man she loved. Treasured and adored by the man she respected most.

The barn was warmer without the wind brushing a chill against her cheeks, and he strode directly for a work bench and raked his arm across it, scattering all of the tools onto the splintered wood floors. Ian was breathing ragged now, and he sucked hard in a line down her neck as he set her on the table and pushed her jacket off her shoulders. Eagerly and with trembling fingers, she unsnapped the button of his jeans and pushed them down just enough to unsheathe him.

Ian's hands and lips were everywhere, setting her on fire with every touch, every kiss. He pulled her sweater smoothly over her head as she kicked out of her boots and shimmied out of her pants. She needed him. Needed him inside of her, filling her, giving her silent promises that no matter what kind of separation they would face with his hibernation, he still adored her.

As he unsnapped her bra and exposed her breasts to the cold night air, she tilted her head back and closed her eyes just to focus on how good his hands felt against her skin. A moan pushed past her lips as he pulled her taut nipple into his mouth and brushed his tongue against her. His kisses trailed lower as he pulled her pants from her ankles and tossed them onto the ground.

"Ian," she pleaded as he lifted her up and shoved her jacket between her bare backside and the rough table. She didn't even know what she was begging for. He wasn't denying her anything.

Ian's eyes were as dark as the night sky, and the sound in his chest said he was half-wild and rutting right now. His teeth were rough on her skin as he sucked and bit his way down the center of her stomach. He lifted his gaze to hers, a dark challenge in his eyes as he went to his knees and lifted one of her legs over his shoulder. They hadn't done this before, not that he hadn't let her know he was willing. She hadn't been ready to give herself so completely to a man before, but as he grazed his teeth against her inner thigh, her back arched instinctively in a silent plea to keep going. His focus drifted from her eyes down, down to between her legs. When he leaned in and kissed her, brushing his tongue against her slit in a sexy tease, she came undone. She moaned loudly and ran her fingernails against his scalp while he took his time slowly laving his tongue against her. God, he was beautiful, bobbing between her legs. The pressure in her middle was already blinding by the time he sucked gently on her clit, and when he directly followed it by thrusting his tongue deep inside of her, she cried out helplessly.

"Fuck, I'm coming already," she gasped. "Ian, I'm coming."

He thrust into her harder, and she exploded from her middle out. She came so hard and so fast, she gripped his hair and yelled his name.

"Want to feel," Ian growled out, pulling her from the table until her feet were planted on the floor. He spun her until she faced the table, but the dizziness didn't last long as he jammed his knee between hers and spread her legs wider.

Lost in the aftershocks of her release, Elyse gripped onto the table and arched her back for him. Ian had always been controlled and gentle in their bed, but this wasn't like before. Now, everything was different. Now, they were on borrowed time, and he was letting her see the real him. The feral animal side she'd only seen glimpses of before now. With a snarl, he slammed into her from behind. One arm around her stomach, holding her to him, and one hand on top of hers on the table, gripping her, intertwining their fingers as he slid into her harder. His body was strung tight, iron against her back as he pumped into her faster and faster. God, he felt good inside of her, slick as he eased back by inches, then back in. The snarl in his throat was constant now, and the second she cried out with her second orgasm, he rammed into her so hard the table creaked under her. His teeth brushed her skin again, but this time he didn't hold himself in check. This time, as he swelled inside of her and bucked into her again, he bit her hard.

Bowing back, she squeezed her eyes tightly closed as pain warred with pleasure. Warmth shot into her over and over until it became too much for her to hold and trickled down her inner thighs. With a snarl of her own, she pulled away from him and spun, then gripped the back of his hair. His eyes went from dazed to shocked the instant before she clamped her teeth against his chest as revenge for him marking her.

Except when she bit him, Ian didn't seem angry as she'd been. Instead, he tossed his head back and gritted out her name, then slid into her from the front. Hand cupped against the back of her head, he pulled her closer and in a low, gravelly voice demanded, "Harder."

And she did. So hard, she could taste blood. Something instinctual bloomed within her. Some impulse to claim her man that had long been buried. His shaft throbbed inside of her, but he was moving more slowly now, heaving breath as she pulled her teeth from him.

With a slow, savage smile, he pulled the back of her hair and angled her face up to his. There was red on his lips when he murmured, "Good mate, letting the world know who I belong to. I've wanted to put my mark over Cole's since the first night I saw it."

Elyse clenched her teeth at the memory of the awful night Cole had given it to her. He was drunk and had hurt her. "You can see it?"

Ian's eyes narrowed to dangerous slits. "Not anymore. You were never meant to be McCall's claim, Elyse. You were meant to be mine."

SEVENTEEN

Ian poured the last pot of hot water into the tub near Elyse's feet. The heat must have been too much because his mate scrunched up her knees and clasped them to her chest, avoiding the steaming front of the tub.

She hadn't said much since their coupling in the barn. Instead, she'd drawn into herself and allowed him to pamper her in silence. He'd cleaned her gently with a cloth, then had given into his need to care for her by drawing her a bath.

Josiah's admission about Miller earlier had Ian's bear roaring for blood, but he couldn't explain that to Elyse. Not now. He would tell her everything on Afognak when he showed her his burned den and explained all the secrets he'd been keeping from her, including the note he kept hidden in his things—the one Cole had asked him to deliver.

Ian needed to tread softly so he didn't lose her.

"Did you not like it?" he asked low, kneeling down near the edge of the tub. "I won't be that rough again. I'm sorry."

Elyse rested her cheek against her knees and gave him a shy smile that buckled his insides. "Don't make that promise, bear-man. I liked seeing the real you."

"If I'm ever too rough—"

"You weren't." Her gold-green eyes were sincere in the flickering light of the candle he'd lit and placed on the sink.

With a relieved sigh, he ran a washcloth gently around the torn skin on her shoulder. She winced when he got too close, and he hated himself. Hated that he wasn't human and better for her. She shouldn't have to deal with an animal's whims.

"Why didn't you tell me you could see Cole's bite mark?"

"I thought you hadn't mentioned it because it hurt to think about. I hated it, though." Ian shook his head to ward off the new wave of rage that threatened to take him. "Elyse, I'm sorry. I didn't intend to hurt you. Not ever."

As soft as a breath, she asked, "What does it mean?"

"My mark?"

She dipped her chin once.

"It's a claiming mark. I never thought I would give a woman one, but then…"

"Then you met me?"

"Yeah. You're important."

She reached across the porcelain ledge and drew a wet finger gently over the half-healed bite mark she'd made on his chest.

Ian swallowed hard and closed his eyes against how good her touch felt on his skin. "Can I tell you something?"

"Tell me everything."

"I was so fucking proud when you bit me back."

"You're proud of me?" Why the hell did she sound so baffled by that? Could she not see she owned him, heart and soul?

"Elyse, whatever Cole made you feel about yourself, he was wrong. You are the strongest woman I've ever met. You've been dealt blow after blow, and still you are here, fighting and clawing to keep the life you love. You're a badass."

"A badass," she repeated dreamily. "You know, I think I like that compliment even more than if you told me I'm beautiful."

He smiled and ran his fingertip across her soft cheek. "You're both."

"I think I'll grow to hate the snow," she whispered.

The moisture that rimmed her eyes split him open and laid him bare. For the first time in his life, he hated the snow too. Snow meant change. It meant winter was on its way. The cold, white powder was Mother Nature's reminder that they would be separated by sleep soon. "I wish I was different for you."

A single tear slid from the corner of her eye and dropped into the bath water that rippled around her. Elyse slid her hand up the back of his and pressed his palm against her cheek. "I don't. You're perfect the way you are."

Ian let off a shaky breath and leaned his chin on the tub just to be closer to her.

"Ian?"

"Hmm?"

"When you wake up next spring, I'll still be in this. I'll still want you to be my husband."

This woman... Ian swallowed hard and brushed a strand of damp hair from her forehead. She was everything good about his life now. How anyone so brave, determined, loyal, and beautiful had picked a man like him, he wouldn't ever understand. All he could do was try his best to make her happy when he could because that right there, her slow smile, was the thing he coveted most in this world.

He pulled her left hand to his lips and kissed the gold band on her finger. "Big wedding or small?"

"Small. And I want it to be here."

"Done," he promised.

Elyse leaned her cheek onto the bathtub ledge, right near his, so he let his lips linger on her wet hair and ran a light finger up and down her spine.

She bore his mark now, and he bore hers, and he would do anything to keep her.

And now, while he was awake enough to be of use to her, he would give her the tools she would need to protect herself from what was coming.

Elyse didn't understand yet, but she would. Miller asking Josiah about her meant she hadn't ever really escaped the McCalls. That crazy werewolf had killed one of her cows. It wasn't vengeance that made him hunt her herd.

Miller was marking his territory.

And Ian would be damned if he went to sleep without teaching Elyse how to defend herself from the wolves.

Starting tomorrow, his beautiful badass would become a weapon.

EIGHTEEN

"Again," Ian murmured.

Elyse lifted the rifle to her shoulder and put the scope on the target of the wolf Ian had sketched out on brown butcher paper and nailed to a tree a hundred yards off.

"Tighter to your shoulder. Even tighter. Spare your body the kick so you won't be sore."

"Ha," she muttered. Tomorrow was going to suck. No doubt she would be black and blue since she hadn't listened to Ian's advice the first hour, and now her shoulder ached like she'd taken a solid kick from Demon's hoof.

"Remember what I said. Repeat it in your mind, and with enough practice, it'll become second nature."

Keep your finger off the trigger until you're ready to shoot. Sight on the target. Focus on your muscles. Don't shake. Hold the gun tight and steady. Three slow breaths, and on the third, hold it, and brush your finger on the trigger. Don't jerk it. Brush it like paint on a canvas.

Boom!

Reload in case the animal needs a second shot.

Ian had been working with her for six straight hours on every gun she owned. She now knew the name of each and its ammunition, and what gun was best for each situation.

"Good," he said low. "You want to see the damage?"

"Yeah." Not because she needed to see if she'd hit the mark. Bark had flown with each shot so she knew she'd been on target, but her shoulder needed a rest. Ian didn't have to know that little tidbit, though.

Elyse turned the gun back over and shoved the bullet back down out of the chamber and safely into the magazine, then slid the bolt in place with a satisfying click of metal to keep the bullet out of the chamber. This was the first layer of protection, and the second was when she physically clicked the safety into place. Chambering the bullet was as easy as pulling her bolt handle back, slamming the bullet forward, and releasing that safety button right before she pulled the trigger. She and Ian had worked on that over and over until it was as natural as breathing. He seemed just as determined to have her constantly aware of gun safety as he was of working on her marksmanship.

Anticipation surged through her as they hiked closer to the target, and she saw where she'd really been hitting. This was her closest grouping all day, and the grin on Ian's face said he was proud of her improvement, too. He hugged her against his side and said, "Woman, I think you've got this."

Damn, that man knew how to lift her up. He was a good teacher who didn't ever put her down. If she messed up, he would simply go over and over the correct way until she understood the how and why. His comments weren't ever biting either. Ian was patient, calm, and generous with letting her know when she did something right. And the beaming smile on his face now made her heart swell. She was glad she hadn't given up earlier when her arm had first begun to get sore. From the start, she should've trusted him. The tighter against her shoulder she held the weapons, the less recoil she endured when she pulled that trigger.

"I need to eat," he said.

"Again?" He'd been eating constantly all day.

His smile turned sad. "That's how it gets…"

"At the end? Like real bears do…you have to eat a lot right before you go to sleep, right?"

Ian led her back toward the table he'd dragged out for the rifles. "Right, but I still don't feel tired, Elyse. We still have time."

He kept saying that, but he could never tell her how much time. Shouldering a couple of her rifles while he shoved ammo into his pockets, she said, "I've got work to do in the house today."

"Yeah?"

"Laundry. Contain your jealousy."

"I can help if you want."

Imagining him washing her delicates with his big, rough hands, she snickered and shook her head. "Polite decline."

Back in the cabin, Ian rummaged around the kitchen while she gathered dirty clothes. Hers were spread out here and there as was her habit—some in the corner, some over the chair in their bedroom, some on the end of the bed, and a small pile in the bathroom. Ian was cleaner by nature than her. How much of that was animal instinct, she couldn't tell.

The soap was bubbling up nicely in the tub, but the water was slow as molasses today, so she dumped the clothes in and left the spout running as she strode across the living room into the guest bedroom, humming to herself. At the kitchen table, Ian was tucking into leftover hamburger pie smothered in cheese. The aroma was a delicious temptation, and while the laundry soaked in the tub, she was going to eat a piece with him.

Ian hadn't slept in the guest room in weeks, but this was where he kept his belongings, piled neatly on and around the rocking chair in the corner. And beside an empty trash bag he'd used as luggage was a small mountain of wadded up clothes. She dug through the pockets of his pants, grinning at the empty bullet casings and small tools she found, and when she came to a back pocket with a folded piece of white paper, she rushed and put it with the small pile of treasures she was building on the dresser. It was the writing on the other side that caught her attention, though. It read *Elyse*.

She froze, and the pair of jeans she was rifling through fell from her hands onto the floor near her boots. That wasn't Ian's handwriting.

Dread filled her as she frowned at the familiar scrawl. Small letters and all capitalized, and she'd only seen one man write like this. Cole.

Slowly, she pulled the folded paper from the dresser and stared at her printed name. The paper crinkled as she opened it, fold by fold, then held it up in the window light so she could better see the small lettering.

Elyse,

If you are reading this, well, then I'm already gone. This is my seventh attempt at writing this damned note. It's hard to explain myself or to tell you how sorry I am without giving too much of my life away. My secrets are better off buried with me. I disappointed you, and me. I should've never raised a hand to you, but my mistakes started long before that, and you and I both know you held onto me longer than you should have. You're good, Elyse. The best woman I've ever met, and I strapped you with my shit. It wasn't fair. There was never a chance for me to be okay or to be a good match for you. It has become really fucking obvious as I sit here in this cabin thinking on all the bad I've done to you that I never had a chance of making you happy. I can't even remember you smiling when we were together. Only crying.

It's the end of my life, and that's okay with me. Don't mistake this for a plea for understanding. I've done horrible things. More than you even know, and I deserve the end that's coming.

I just wanted to say I'm sorry. For all of it.
Cole

Elyse gasped quietly against her tightening throat and put her hand over her mouth as twin tears streamed down her face. Why the fuck did Ian have this note?

Miller's voice whispered through her mind. *He died of a bear attack.*

Blinking hard to clear her vision, she looked out the bedroom door. From here, she could see Ian's legs under the kitchen table as he ate, but nothing more. In a daze, she shuffled from the room and held up the note.

Ian glanced up, and the greeting smile fell from his face as he stared at the piece of paper she clutched in her hand. "I can explain."

"Did you kill him?"

Ian stood slowly and held out his hands. "It wasn't like how you're thinking, Elyse."

"Did you kill him?" she screamed. "I don't give a fuck about anything else except 'yes' or 'no' right now Ian." She swallowed a sob and whispered, "He died of a bear attack. That's what his brother told me. Was it your bear that did it?"

Ian angled his face away, but his bright blue eyes never left her. He swallowed hard and nodded once.

"Say it out loud."

"Yes," he admitted.

The word rocked her back on her heels. Yes? Ian had killed her ex-boyfriend, and now he was here, eating at her table. She felt sick as she stepped backward. Her shoulders hit the wall as she shook with sobbing.

"Elyse, I was going to tell you everything—"

"When, Ian? When were you going to tell me you murdered him?"

"It wasn't murder." Ian paced behind the table and gave her a warning look. "He knew I was coming for him."

"You killed him, Ian!"

"Because I had to!"

She let off a furious shriek and bolted for the key hook. She yanked the jangling keychain from it and startled when Ian gripped her upper arm. He was too fast. Faster than he'd ever let her see. "Get your fucking hands off me!"

"Elyse, don't go like this. Just let me tell you what happened."

"I need space. If you care for me at all, you'll give it to me."

Ian was shaking his head, eyes wide and churning, chest heaving.

"Please, let me go." She shrugged out of his loosening grasp and bolted out the front door.

Ian watched her drive away from the front porch. His hands were linked behind his head, and his face…she'd never seen such despair in a man's eyes.

She ripped her gaze away from him to spare herself more pain. He'd brought this on himself.

And as she blasted down the dirt road away from the homestead, she forced herself not to look back.

Sobbing, she threw Cole's note into the seat beside her and hit the gas on a straightaway. She'd made mistakes with Cole. Held onto him as he stole her happiness. Stealing, cheating, hurting her. She'd turned into a zombie for a man, and it had changed her from the bones out.

She wouldn't do that again. Overlooking a man's deep-rooted faults for love wasn't something she was willing to do anymore. Not after Ian had showed her she deserved better. Goddammit, he'd *been* better. He'd pushed her to become stronger than she'd ever been, and for what? The entire time he had been hiding this from her. The sting of betrayal was like a slap against cold skin. She screamed at the pain in her chest and slammed her open palm against Ian's steering wheel over and over.

How stupid she must seem to him. How naïve. He'd killed Cole, then made a move on her. The first moments she'd met Ian came back into blindingly bright focus. He'd been holding Cole's letter then and seemed confused by the advertisement. He hadn't been there to apply to be her husband at all. He was there to deliver a dead man's message. A message from a man *he killed*.

She'd lost sight of what she wanted. The advertisement was meant for an older Alaskan man made of gristle and bone, who was willing to be a friend, legally bound to her and her land. The entire point of mail-ordering a husband had been to leave love, romance, and feelings out of it completely. This was supposed to be an emotionless transaction. One that her closed-down heart could handle.

Instead, she'd fallen for a pretty face, a pretty body, and pretty lies.

And now she was breaking apart. Shattering into a million pieces. She was a mirror, and Cole had carelessly slammed his fist into her. Her heart had barely survived that man. All of the good parts of herself had been sacrificed in the last couple of years, and she'd been so determined to discover something strong about herself again. She needed a man to help her with her homestead, but she didn't need him wrecking her heart.

Her mistakes stretched on and on across her mind, vast and endless like a desert, and everything Ian had ever said to her was a mirage.

The landscape of her homestead passed in a blur outside the windows as she cried her anguish. She'd lost so much, and dammit, she'd never complained. She'd accepted her father's absence and had worked through her childhood insecurities that he'd somehow left because of her. Lash. She'd stayed quiet under Mom's constant criticism. Lash. Marta's funeral. Lash. Uncle Jim's funeral. Lash. Cole had laid her heart wide open because she'd been ready. She'd wanted someone to stick around so badly, she'd clung to a horrible man. Lash, lash, lash.

But the biggest pain of all was this. She'd told Ian everything. Shared all of herself, her fears, her hopes, because she'd been so sure he was doing the same for her. She'd been convinced he'd laid himself bare in those quiet moments between working their fingers to the bone, and in bed after intimacy, and in the early mornings when the snuggled closer to avoid the coming day, and when he tracked her down and interrupted her chores just to hold her and tell her everything was going to be okay.

She'd believed him. She'd believed in him.

Elyse had fallen completely while Ian Silver had only cared for the wounded bird left reeling by the man he'd murdered.

She hunched into herself as the ache in her middle doubled.

This wasn't love—not for Ian.

This was guilt and pity.

****

Elyse nodded when the bartender, Eric, asked if she wanted another. She fingered the edge of the folded note and wiped her damp lashes on the sleeve of her jacket. Whiskey was the only thing that made her feel better. It numbed her. The scorching amber liquid made the smallness she felt less important.

Even the darkest end of the bar top wasn't near black enough for her right now. The light above her had gone out, and though it flickered to life every once in a while, it was the only corner in this whole place that felt comfortable.

"Just the woman we're in town to see," Miller slurred from behind her, raising the hairs on her neck.

She slid the note smoothly into her pocket and gave him a sideways glance as he sat on the stool next to her. His youngest brother, Lincoln, sat on his other side, all mussed dark hair and irritated grey eyes scanning the bar as though he wished he was anywhere but here. Miller, however, was staring with an empty smile, like there was nowhere else he'd rather be than pissing her off.

"What do you want, Miller?"

"You."

With a frown of disgust, she pulled the shot the bartender gave her closer. "You're not my type."

"I'll have what she's having. Make it a double," he said to Eric, though from the slur in his voice and the reek of alcohol that wafted from him, Miller was already two sheets to the wind.

"You still owe me from a couple months ago," Eric said low, his bushy gray eyebrows lifting high.

Miller slammed his fist on the counter. "Give me my fucking drink."

Eric tossed her a quick glance, then began pouring another shot.

"Now," Miller said in a calmer, saner voice as he arched his attention back to her. "You and I both know I'm exactly your type. You like trouble, Elyse. You like being roughed up. You like taking care of a man, just like you did for Cole. I look just like him, don't I?"

Frozen, Elyse swallowed the bile that clawed its way up the back of her throat.

"Look at me, Elyse."

Breath shaking, she clutched the shot glass and refused.

"Look at me!" Miller grabbed her chin and yanked her face toward him. "I've come to tell you I'll be courting you."

"I don't want you."

"Miller, let's go," Lincoln murmured, hand on his brother's shoulder.

Miller lurched out from under his little brother's hand and said, "Shut the fuck up, Link. This is why we're here. To get our girl."

"She ain't our girl, and this is on you. I'm not after her. She's Cole's claim. Not mine and certainly not yours."

Cole's claim. The way he said that dumped ice into her veins. The fine hairs on her arms electrified with chills, and she inched away from Miller.

His rough hand jerked her to a halt, and before she could stop him, he tore the neck of her sweater downward with a *riiip*. With a curse, she pulled away from him, shielding Ian's new bite mark, which was still red and painful and hadn't scabbed over yet.

"Did you see that, boy?" Miller growled in a voice she'd never heard before. It was low and snarly, and a long growl rattled his chest. What the hell? "Cole's dead, but she's still marked. She's a McCall claim."

Elyse stumbled off the stool and flung her shot of whiskey into Miller's face. "Get the fuck away from me."

Too fast to be human, Miller grabbed her by the throat and pushed her backward until her shoulder blades hit the wall behind her. His eyes were blazing such a light color they looked like snow against his flushed, whiskey-soaked cheeks. "Careful, girl." He pressed his hard erection against her. "I like my women feisty, and you're gettin' me all excited in this public place, you kinky bitch."

"Miller," Lincoln growled out.

Elyse was struggling to draw air into her lungs as Miller's grip tightened around her throat. Soft choking sounds slipped past her lips, but she couldn't scream.

Scrambling, she reached into her pocket for the knife Ian had told her to always carry. She flicked it open with a jerk of her wrist and pressed it against Miller's neck. She was going to pass out soon, but she could take this sadistic asshole with her. Desperate for air, she shoved it harder against his skin and a stream of crimson trickled out of him. "Get off me or I'll slit your fuckin' throat," she gasped out.

Miller smiled and cupped her sex hard, then leaned into her blade, the psychotic sonofabitch. Spots dotted the edges of her vision now, and his smile shook and blurred. He opened his mouth to say something, but the crack of a gun being cocked drowned out everything. Miller's eyes narrowed.

"Get your hands off her," Eric gritted out, jamming a sawed-off shotgun hard against the side of Miller's head. "Are you deaf? I said get your hands off her!"

Miller let off a single, humorless laugh, then released her. Stepping back, he raised his hands in surrender. "Don't get your panties in a bunch, bartender. We're just having a lover's spat."

"Get on out of here, Elyse," Eric said in a steely voice.

Clutching her aching throat and struggling to draw air into her body, she rushed past Miller.

"I'll see you soon, baby," Miller called after her.

In the front seat of the truck, she looked at the red blade of her open knife and dropped it to the passenger's seat in horror. She'd cut a man. The blade had sliced into his skin so easily. Nausea made her swallow hard, over and over— she couldn't puke here. She needed to escape to somewhere safe.

Safe. This morning *safe* had been Ian and the homestead, but now everything had changed.

Miller and Lincoln exited the bar with Eric right behind them, so she threw the truck into reverse and blasted out of town toward home.

She was caught in the middle of something big. Much bigger than she'd thought when she'd kicked Cole out of her life. Miller wasn't human. He wasn't. His eyes had changed colors, and he'd growled a feral sound like Ian sometimes did.

And he'd known about Cole biting her. He'd even called it a claiming mark. She knew what that was because Ian had given her one. But when Cole had bitten her before, she had assumed he was just being cruel.

Werewolf.

The word breezed through her mind.

Ian said bear shifters were rare, but there were also werewolves, and from the way he talked about them, they were bad news. As much as she wanted to reject anything Ian said as truth right now, Miller had always been a half-deranged pill. His mishandling of her in the bar said he was losing his fucking mind. He'd asked if he looked like Cole. Well, he definitely reminded her of Cole at the end. Something was wrong with that man, and her instincts said Ian knew more about the McCalls than he'd let on. And now the realization that Cole had been a werewolf and so easily hidden such a huge part of himself slammed into her middle.

She tightened her strangle hold on the steering wheel and hit the gas.

Ian had mountains of explaining to do.

NINETEEN

When Elyse blasted through the final grove of trees and into the clearing in front of the homestead, Ian was sitting on the porch. His eyes reflected strangely in the headlights as she pulled around and parked the truck.

Her anger had grown into an inferno on the forty-five minute drive back. No longer was she in oh-woe-is-me mode. She was in punch-everything mode. Ian had lied about so much, then she'd been choked, threatened, and felt up by a fucking werewolf, and now her rage was infinite.

Pursing her lips over the urge to curse him out immediately, she grabbed the knife and the note and stomped toward him. Miki bounced around her legs and yipped a puppy greeting.

Ian had a lantern hung from a peg over the porch stairs, so she could see just fine when his eyes narrowed on her knife. Then he lowered his gaze back to the half-plucked duck in his hands and went back to ripping feathers from the breast. He had a small pile of the water fowl beside him and a bucket for the feathers a couple stairs below, between his knees. Their first major fight and what did she do? Weep and chug whiskey. Of course Ian had gone and done something productive, such as hunt down a couple week's worth of meals. Pissed at the world, she kicked a cloud of dirt into the air and started jacking up the water pump handle.

"Who did you stab?" he asked conversationally.

"A werewolf."

The sound of plucking stopped, but she didn't look at him. Instead, she washed the blade off and contemplated which question, out of the billion rattling around in her brain, she would ask him first.

"No, you know what. I'm not going to ask questions right now. Why don't you just tell me everything so I don't have to decipher your infinite mysteries, Ian?"

"Okay. Why don't you come sit beside me?"

"I feel like standing." *So I don't punch you in the face.*

Nodding, Ian reached behind him and handed her a large, brown envelope. "This was waiting for me at my den on Afognak when I woke up from hibernation this past spring."

"What is it?" she asked, moving closer to take it from his hand. When she did, there was a bloody thumbprint from where he'd held it.

Ian went back to plucking. "It's a kill order for Cole McCall. I'm not just a bear shifter, Elyse. I'm what shifters call an enforcer. All bears take that title because we're the biggest of the predator shifters. My brothers have taken jobs like this, too."

"Are you paid to assassinate people?"

Ian huffed and lifted his narrow gaze to her. "Do you really think so low of me?"

"I don't know what to think, Ian."

"No, I don't get paid, and it's not called assassinating. It's called 'putting them down.'"

"Like animals."

"Yes."

"Why?"

"Because they *are* animals."

"Cole was a little crazy, but he wasn't—"

"He was. You don't need me shit-talking your ex though, Elyse. I can see how little you trust me. That folder contains most of your answers."

Elyse stomped up the stairs, then dragged a rocking chair loudly across the porch to the ring of soft, glowing light. Then she pulled out the stack of paperwork from the envelope and read silently, her heart breaking with every word. It was a history on Cole—a list of all the things he'd done to call attention to himself. Some of them she'd known, but the last several pages made her sick to her stomach. There were photos of two trappers who had been attacked by a wolf. One had survived and one had not, and whoever had put together the file for Cole had included the after pictures. It was the next two pictures that drew a horrified gasp from her lips. One was a posed school picture of a little girl. Dark hair and dark eyes. Alaska Native perhaps. She had a snaggle-toothed smile. The photograph that followed was of the little girl in a hospital bed.

Elyse had read about this wolf attack in the newspaper. Her doctors thought the girl would make it for a while, but she hadn't.

"Cole did this?" Her voice was no better than a wisp of air.

Ian nodded his head and set the naked bird down beside him, then picked up the next to pluck. "The McCalls all go crazy. It's in their blood. Most of them are smart enough to recognize their expiration date and not involve a mate, but Cole, for whatever reason, felt like taking you down with him at the end."

"Was this all that was in the file?"

Ian shook his head, his back to her as his body jerked with every rip of the feathers. "There was one last thing." Leaning to the side, he reached in his back pocket and pulled out a folded photograph.

When she opened it, she found herself staring at the camera with a hollow look. Someone had photographed her from the woods near the garden. She almost didn't recognize herself, as skinny as she was. Dark circles hung from under her eyes, and her lips were chapped. This picture had been taken right after she'd kicked Cole out of the house. Her lip was still split.

"Why was this in your pocket?"

"Because I fell in love with you from that picture. I carry it everywhere." When he cast her a glance over his shoulder, his eyes pooled with such deep vulnerability. "It can't touch the real thing, seeing you in person, but I like the feeling that you're always close. My bear chose you before I even met you."

"So you being here isn't some way to get rid of your guilt over killing Cole?"

"Fuck, woman, is that what you think? I called you, do you remember?"

"When?"

"At the beginning of the warm season I called you asking where Cole was."

Elyse's mouth fell open, and she rocked back against the chair. "I remember. I felt better, more hopeful after I talked to you. You said I could call you if I needed anything."

"And I meant it. I would've dropped everything and helped if you ever called. I waited, hoping you would. Not hoping that you needed me, but to hear your voice again. Cole knew I was coming. He didn't even try to hide from me. He told me he was hoping I got to him in time because his wolf wanted you."

"Wanted me how?"

"He said he'd given the wolf that little girl to buy him time so he wouldn't come back here."

"He wanted to kill me?"

"His wolf did, Elyse. You have to understand. Cole wasn't right. The McCalls have bad bloodlines. They have for centuries. Most werewolves are okay, but the McCalls always end up losing control of their animals."

"And you put them down."

Ian went back to plucking as he darkly said, "Sometimes me. Sometimes my brothers. Cole didn't deserve it, but I gave him an honorable death. He asked me to give you the note, and I told him I would."

"An honorable death. Tell me."

"Elyse," Ian warned.

"Tell me, Ian."

He sighed and dropped the duck into the pile, then lifted his jacket and sweater out of the way, exposing the worst of his scars across his ribcage.

"That was Cole's doing?"

"Nah, that was his wolf's doing. It was a fight to the death, animal versus animal. His wolf knew he was beat, so he attacked while I was Changing. I couldn't do anything as he ripped into me, but I can't really blame him. He didn't deserve to live, but he still wanted to. Survival is a powerful instinct, even for the broken. This is the gig, Elyse. If a shifter goes wild and wages war on humans, or if they take innocent lives and threaten to expose us, I get the order to put them down."

Elyse swallowed hard at the thought of a wolf tearing into Ian while he was mid-Change. Of the damage his body had sustained to keep the awful scars that he did. "Why did you wait so long to come find me to give me the note?"

"Because I knew I wouldn't want to leave if I saw you. If I talked to you in person, I knew I'd want you. I just meant to give you the letter and say sorry and leave, but you were determined to hire a husband, and dammit, Elyse, you were standing there, so fucking beautiful, offering me everything I hadn't known I wanted, and I was weak. I couldn't say no. Every instinct in my body screamed that I could take care of you where Cole had failed. I could provide for you and make you stronger. I could make it so you never came out of another winter so skinny. And as time went on and I got to know you better, I got terrified of losing you. I've wanted to tell you about Cole a million times. I've laid awake after you've gone to sleep just thinking about it. The thought of losing you was so painful. No, I'm not here out of guilt. I'm here because I fucking need you more than the air I breathe. I love you more than I've loved anything. Any life without you would be empty. I told you before, and I meant it. You weren't ever supposed to be Cole's mate. You've always felt like mine."

Elyse clutched the picture of herself. This wasn't the black and white *he-killed-my-ex* scenario she'd assumed. This was about a different set of rules for shifters to follow, about Ian putting down someone who was dangerous and who'd taken innocent lives. She thought about the trapper and the little girl. About their families, who would forever be changed for the worse because of Cole's actions.

Life out here required sacrifice. No one made it without getting blood on their hands. Taking life, like those of the ducks on the porch stair, was a part of living. It was a cycle. Cole had become a kink in the chain and disrupted the balance, and Ian drawing out his bear and fighting Cole to the death wasn't the betrayal she'd thought. He'd avenged the people Cole had killed. He'd given justice to their families. Ian Silver had placed himself between Cole's dark intentions and the rest of the world and taken scars upon his body to keep her and everyone else safe from that werewolf's descent into madness.

And he'd saved her in the process.

She didn't even want to imagine what Cole would've done to her if left to his own devices. If she read his letter again now, every sentence he'd written would have a different meaning.

Ian had gone back to plucking, but Elyse slid off the chair and squatted down behind him. Slowly, she rested her cheek against his back and wrapped her arms around his middle.

With a long sigh of relief, the tension left Ian's body, and he relaxed under her. He angled his head back toward her as if he wanted to be even closer. "I'm sorry."

"Were you really going to tell me everything when we went to Afognak tomorrow?"

"Yeah. I had it all planned out. Afognak has always been home to me. Miller found the cave I hibernate in. I'd built a cabin inside, but he burned it to ashes."

"Oh, Ian."

"It's fine. I was going to show you and bring the folder and tell you everything—let you see all of me. I couldn't have gone to sleep for the winter without coming clean. It's part of why I wanted you to wait to marry me until you'd been with me through the cold season. I want your eyes wide open when you take my last name."

Her eyes felt puffy, and she had a headache from crying so much today, but some of the tension had left her shoulders as well. She hugged him tighter, then released him and sat down on the stair. Pulling a duck into her lap, she began to work in silence beside him.

And for a while, they just were. It wasn't until she was working on the last duck that he turned to her and asked, "Are you going to tell me who bruised your neck?"

She swallowed against the lingering ache there. "Miller. He came in the bar drunk. I know how Cole was at the end, and his brother is headed down the same path, Ian. Maybe he'll be worse. I don't know. He seems to think that mark Cole gave me makes me a McCall claim."

A snarl ripped from Ian. "You're not. You're mine."

"I know I am." No longer able to shoulder what had happened in the bar, she murmured, "Miller choked me, and I put the blade against his throat. Then the bartender, Eric…well, he put a gun to Miller's head and got me breathing proper again." She dragged her gaze to Ian and rested her elbows on her knees with the limp, half-plucked bird hanging from her hands. "Ian, he's going to bring us trouble."

"That's what they do, Elyse." Ian's eyes turned fierce, darkening like storm clouds. "The McCalls always bring trouble."

TWENTY

Ian opened his eyes to the pitch blackness. He blinked rapidly a couple of times, trying to remember where he was. The bed was as unfamiliar as the room, and as his eyes adjusted to the darkness, everything that had happened yesterday crashed over him like stormy ocean waves.

Elyse had forgiven him for hiding the truth, but he would have to work to earn her trust back. Tonight, he was sleeping in the guest room in an effort to give her space to process all he'd kept from her. It had taken him forever to fall asleep, and apparently he was still restless without his mate in his arms because he was awake again, only—he looked at his watch—two hours after he'd gone to sleep.

The soft clink of metal sounded from the other side of the house near Elyse's bedroom. Miki let off a low growl. Ian slipped out of bed and padded out of the guest room and through the den, careful to miss the creaky boards.

He hadn't just woken up restless. Something had his hairs raised on end, and by the time he reached Elyse's room, he could smell it—the stink of a werewolf. Elyse was lying in bed on her side, facing him, fast asleep and unbothered, but Miki was looking out her bedroom window, his dark lips curled up, exposing a row of needle-sharp puppy teeth. Little brawler.

Ian heard it again. Metal on metal. Mother-fuckin' Miller was trying to steal from Elyse.

Ian's rage started in his middle, unfurling like a poison as it filled him. Gritting his teeth, he swallowed down a growl and padded out the front door because it was a silent opener. The air nipped at his bare chest as he slunk silently around the cabin. A figure stood beside the freezer, shoving a small key into the padlock with a muttered curse.

If he hadn't recognized Miller's voice, he sure as shit would've recognized the pungent aroma of unwashed body and wet dog.

Ian leaned against the log wall. "Your little thief key don't work anymore, McCall."

Miller started and spun, his eyes blazing white. "S-Silver." He cocked his head and straightened his spine from the defensive crouch he'd sunk into. A deep frown making him even uglier, he asked, "What the fuck are you doing here?"

Inside, Miki went mad, barking in a much deeper voice than the pup had ever used before.

Ian offered him a dead smile. "My territory now. I'd suggest you get the fuck off it before I rip your throat through that hideous mouth-hole of yours."

"Your territory." Miller took a step back and leaned on the padlocked deep freeze he'd been trying to rob. He slid a slit-eyed gaze to Elyse's bedroom window, then back to Ian. "Your territory? I think you're lost. See, this is wolf territory, along with that pretty little bitch inside."

Ian didn't hide the snarl in his throat now. Miller should see his death coming. "She chose me."

"Bull—"

Ian lunged, grabbed the back of his head, and slammed it against the edge of the freezer so fast Miller couldn't even finish the curse. He shoved his bowed body onto the dirt and gritted out, "You laid a hand on her today. Choked her, so I heard."

Miller was crawling away, one hand gripping his forehead as dark streams dripped through his fingers. "She's marked."

"By me now. Your shit brother's mark is covered up, and even if it wasn't, even if she bore his scar, that wouldn't make her yours or any other McCall's, and it wouldn't justify you stealing her meat."

"Ian?" Elyse's voice was high-pitched and scared as she flew around the corner, flashlight beam bouncing across the ground in front of her. When it illuminated Miller, she skidded to a stop, her white nightgown billowing around her knees. "What are you doing here?"

Miller scrambled upward and jammed a finger at Ian. "What's *he* doing here? Do you know who he is? Do you know what kind of monster you're fucking, Elyse?"

The flashlight beam shook in Elyse's hand, but her voice didn't sound scared at all. It sounded like steel. "The only monster I see here is you. Get off our land."

"Our land."

"Yes, our land! You are trespassing on our property, and for what, Miller? To steal from me again? To clean me out because you aren't man enough to fend for yourself? You're too lazy to provide for yourself so you have to prey on other people? Well, fuck you. You're not welcome here, and let's face it. You never really were."

"He killed my brother!" Miller screamed. Half of his face was covered in red now, but he was a fast healer. He probably wouldn't bleed out from the head wound. Pity. "Did you hear me? You're sleeping with your mate's murderer, you stupid bitch!"

Elyse's eyebrows arched primly like she gave exactly zero fucks. "Cole who killed that trapper? Cole who killed that little girl? Cole who cheated on me, stole from me, hurt me, and nearly fucking starved me because he didn't want to work when he could drain someone who loved him instead?

Ian did the world a favor. Your brother was shit. Just. Like. You. Get out of here before my mate kills you."

Miller rocked back on his heels and looked back and forth between the two of them.

Ian clenched his hands. They tingled to strangle the life out of him, but Clayton hadn't given the order for Miller, and killing a shifter un-sanctioned was against their laws and would bring punishment on him and Elyse both.

Miller huffed a laugh that echoed through the clearing, followed by an insane giggle that toppled from his lips as he hunched forward. Hands on his knees, he laughed from his belly, louder and louder until the air shook. "You stupid fucks." Miller spat red, but the crazy smile still lingered on his lips. White eyes, red blood, yellow teeth. "Do you feel that?" Miller inhaled loudly and lowered his voice. "Can you smell it? Winter is almost here, and you," he murmured, locking his inhuman eyes on Ian, "you're gonna go to sleep for a long time. I told you I was gonna hunt you slow. I told you I was gonna hurt the people you loved." He backed toward the woods, step by careful step. "Sleep tight, Silver, 'cause when winter comes, I'll be hunting your girl."

"Clayton will put a kill order on you," Ian warned. All he wanted to do was kill Miller now. Rip him limb from limb. Maul him because Miller didn't deserve the honorable death he'd given Cole. He didn't want to wait, but he had to. Clayton gave the orders. Clayton was judge and jury.

"Nah, he won't get to me in time, and some things are just worth it, you know? Like with you. I told you I'd hunt you and anyone you loved if you killed my brother and what did you fucking do? You tracked him down. Did you think I was joking, Silver? Did you think I was talking to hear myself speak? You aren't untouchable!" Miller's voice pitched high and shaky, and he shook his head hard and gripped his hair. "Not untouchable," he muttered to himself through gritted teeth, slapping the side of his bloody face. Crazy wolf. Miller dragged his narrowed, blazing eyes to

Elyse and jammed a finger at her. "I'll see you soon, pretty bitch." With one last empty smile, Miller disappeared into the thick grove of trees.

"Ian," Elyse said in a frightened voice.

"I know," he said, pacing the tree line.

"Ian!"

"Get inside," he gritted out, right before he sprinted for the trees.

Waiting on an order from Clayton wasn't going to work. Ian's bear was already ripping out of him and seething for Miller's blood. He'd threatened his mate, and the price for that was death.

Gritting his teeth against the pain, Ian's bones snapped and his body reshaped and grew. Dark fur shot out of his skin, prickling like millions of needles, and long, curved, black claws replaced his fingernails. Shaking off the last tingles of the Change, he inhaled deeply and bolted through the woods. A long, lone wolf howl lifted and echoed through the night woods, a taunt that urged an answering snarl from himself. He was going to kill Miller. Hang shifter laws, he was a fucking McCall, and he was sinking deep into insanity just like all his ancestors. And now, that crazy sonofabitch's attention was on Elyse in some twisted game of vengeance. Miller couldn't live another day to plot and plan against everything that meant anything to Ian. He couldn't be allowed to hurt his Elyse.

Rage pounded through his blood, urging his heart beat faster, like a pounding war drum. Perfect—because this was war.

Ian pushed himself faster through the woods, around pines and western hemlock, yellow cedar and spruce, across the prickling pine needles that blanketed the floor. The moon was half full above him, peeking through the trees and casting the wilderness in blue rays of light that trickled through the canopy.

Miller's scent was stronger now, and he dug his claws into the earth, pushing his muscles faster. Ian was at his prime at this time of year. Strapped with muscle and power, not yet affected by the fatigue that would come for him soon.

The sound of a car engine revved. No. Ian pushed himself harder, faster, panting as he charged through the woods behind that crazy wolf.

He could see taillights now, and from the open window of an old beat-up, mud-brown Bronco, Miller's insane laugh cackled. Miller hit the gas just as Ian swiped the back end, sending the SUV spinning. Ian skidded sideways through the loose dirt and scrabbled for traction behind the Bronco.

Miller was accelerating, getting away as Ian dug his claws in and gave chase. He was fast, but Miller had worn a path through the woods where he'd probably parked to steal from Elyse many times, and he was hitting forty miles per hour, then fifty. Fuck!

The back-end of Millers ride faded in the distance, and then his red taillights disappeared altogether.

Ian skidded to a stop and arched his head back in rage.

And then the woods were filled with the roaring of his bear.

****

Elyse clutched the gun tighter as an enraged roar rattled the woods, raising all the fine hairs on her body along with it. Birds lifted from the trees, the cicadas went quiet, and inside her veins, blood pounded with adrenaline and fear.

She trusted Ian—trusted him with her life. Yes, even after he'd lied about how he'd known Cole, she could still feel his love. He would protect her from Miller's dark promises.

Her hands trembled badly as she waited by the open front window. Wolf or bear—which one would come back for her?

Please let it be my bear.

But if it was the wolf, she was going to fucking annihilate him.

Movement captured her attention in the dark woods, and she lifted her rifle through the window and put the crosshairs on the form meandering through the trees. Deep breath. *Click*—the safety was off.

A soft grunt sounded from the animal, and a long, frozen puff of breath steamed in front of him. Much too tall to be a wolf, Ian's bruin bear ambled from the woods.

Click—the safety was back on, and Elyse lowered her weapon.

Her mate didn't look injured, but he swung his weight from side to side in agitation. If he hadn't Changed back, it was because he couldn't. Perhaps he'd gone too long between shifts, or perhaps he was too close to hibernation to Change back. No, no, no.

Elyse threw the door open and ran to the edge of the stairs. *He won't hurt me.*

"Ian," she said on a scared breath. He just couldn't be Changed for the winter season already.

At the muscular hump between his shoulders, the bear was taller than her by a few feet, and even though she knew it was Ian, it was hard to advance on the massive grizzly. He wouldn't hurt her. He wouldn't. She was his mate.

Gasping, she stepped down the stairs slowly, hand out, shaking fingers outstretched.

"I love you, I love…you," she murmured, her voice as meek as a mouse's.

Ian grunted again and stopped swaying. He averted his dark gaze and angled his head, giving her his neck. She blew out a long, trembling breath as she slowly approached.

If she'd had any lingering doubt he was her bear before now, his ripped ear put her at ease. Still, five feet away, she couldn't make her legs move forward. She stood there frozen, fingers out, helpless to move toward him any farther.

Ian ghosted her a glance, then lowered his head and took two powerful steps forward, forehead against her middle. She stumbled backward and held onto his big, block head just to stay upright. There was a humming in his throat that filled the air as she slowly rested her cheek on top of his head, near the ripped ear. The nerves left her slowly as they stood there, touching. Animal and human, bonded so deeply that neither one of them could be whole without the other.

Slowly, Ian lifted an intimidating claw and wrapped it gently around her back, then settled back on his haunches and pulled her toward him. She didn't fight him. Couldn't. He was hers, and if he wanted to be closer, she understood the instinct. She couldn't stop stroking his coarse fur. Her thin nightgown wasn't meant to meet air this cold, but Ian sat up and pulled her against his massive chest as the gown billowed around her legs and her hair lifted in the chilly breeze. Here, in his powerful arms against his heavily furred torso, the chill was banished and her fear along with it. Ian was so big, so powerful and protective, she couldn't help but feel safe from the rest of the world—Miller included.

Elyse tucked her arms between them and rested her cheek against his chest. His breath was deep and steady, and the drum of his heart beat had slowed to match hers. Neither one of them were scared here in the dark yard of their home.

Ian rubbed his giant muzzle over her face, and his lips lifted against her skin. His gleaming teeth grazed her, and as he eased back, he snuffled loudly against her hair. He scented her gown and between her breasts as if he was allowing his animal to put everything about her to memory.

"My mate," she whispered.

Ian responded with another soft noise in his throat.

"Tell me you can Change back, Ian." Tears burned her eyes and blurred her vision. "Tell me you aren't Changed for the winter."

Ian released her and backed away, shaking his head sharply. With a soft roar, he strode for the woods.

Baffled, she waited for her beloved to return. Without his warmth, the autumn air lifted her dress and chilled her blood, raising gooseflesh over every inch of her body, but still, she waited. And when Ian, human and naked, strode from the tree line, blue moonlight illuminating his bare torso and powerful legs, her face crumpled with relief. Her Ian was still here.

"I didn't catch him," he said in a gravelly voice. He looked sick about it.

Elyse held her arms open and sighed as he lifted her off her feet and spun her slowly. "I can't protect you when I'm sleeping, Elyse." The gravel in his voice turned to glass, and a slow, angry rumble vibrated against her belly.

"Oh, Ian. You don't have to." She eased back and cupped his cheeks, so certain of her destiny now. "You protect me during the warm season, but now it's my turn to protect you. We're a team."

Miller's threats had opened up something dark within her. Something fearsome that had only existed in the shadows of her soul before. He'd made threats on her mate and on her, but her fear had changed in those minutes she'd been waiting for Ian to return from hunting that damned wolf. If she wanted to keep Ian, she had to be his protector when he hibernated, just as he'd done for her this past month.

She'd always thought herself too weak for this life. It had been her greatest fear, but she'd been wrong. Ian had shown her how strong she could be.

As it turned out, she wasn't the damsel in distress.

She was the knight.

And she'd be damned if anyone hurt what she and Ian had built here.

TWENTY-ONE

Elyse's boots splashed onto the beach as she jumped out of Ian's boat and helped him drag it up the bank, out of the way of the changing tide. She'd never been to Afognak before, but even from here, she could see where the rumors of its haunting came from.

The morning fog rolled in waves across the pine forest, and the forest floor was like none she'd ever seen. Covered in moss and intertwined tree roots, it was a lush kind of green that only existed in dreams.

Ian didn't speak, but then, she wasn't surprised. He'd explained to her that the island required silence if they wanted to take red meat from it. Sitka black-tailed deer were abundant here, but so were brown bears. This island could give and take away so much.

Even Miki trotted silently beside her, brushing her leg every other step like the Velcro dog he was becoming.

It didn't surprise her at all that Ian had called this place home. He was tough as leather and his inner animal was as wild as these woods.

The second she stepped onto the squishy moss forest floor, chills blasted up the back of her neck. It was so quiet here. Ian was always silent when he moved through the woods, but here, with the lichens under her rubber-soled hiking boots, even she, in her natural human clumsiness, was silent when she moved.

Ian handed her a backpack, then pulled on his own. In silence, they chambered a round of ammunition in their rifles and checked the safety on each, then shouldered the weapons and made their way up a small trail that led upward between two moss-covered boulders.

Ian pointed out a set of enormous grizzly tracks on the beach sand headed up the same trail, then cupped the back of her head and whispered, "How old?"

She squinted at the prints, bigger than her head, and remembered everything Ian had taught her about tracking animals over the last month. These were half dry on damp sand. "A few hours at least," she whispered against his ear.

As a reward, he leaned down and sipped at her lips, massaging the back of her hair gently. "Good. Keep alert, but he should be out of the area. They're on the hunt right now, not sleeping much, trying to build up last minute fat reserves for winter."

Ian had been doing the same thing. Even nervous about following a grizzly trail, she smiled. While her backpack was full of ammunition, deer tags, hunting knives, and a bedroll tied on the outside, his was full of food.

The deeper they hiked into the Afognak woods, the eerier they became and the thicker the fog rolled in. Sometimes they walked blind in the thick cloud cover and other times hiked through a clearing, surrounded by the thick fog. She relied on Ian's instinct to guide them because she couldn't see any great distance in front of her. They could be hunted right now by a brown bear, and she wouldn't know, but Ian constantly turned his head at every sound. This way and that, he angled his ears, and she could almost see him identifying each one and tossing them away as non-threatening.

The claw mark on her leg was almost healed, but it tingled here in the quiet wilderness of the haunted woods.

The remembered pain from that bear raking its six-inch claws through her flesh made it hard not to panic and give in to the claustrophobia that the island pressed against her.

Deeper and deeper Ian led her into the heart of the island, each step silent against the spongy moss. The vibrant green lichens grew so thick on everything, she could be walking over boulders, tree roots, or bones of the dead, and she would never be able to tell the difference.

Ian's need to bring her to Afognak wasn't just about hunting or showing her his charred den. He hadn't been able to get a hold of Clayton to tell him about Miller's threats, and Elyse knew a piece of her mate was hoping there would be an order for the crazy wolf waiting at the entrance of his winter den where they'd always been delivered before.

They weren't hunting now, though Ian's eyes were always scanning their surroundings, as were hers. It was natural to search for opportunities now that she'd been on hunts with Ian. He was slowly adjusting her instincts, honing them to look for wildlife that could serve as food during their long winters. She was more aware of her surroundings than she ever had been.

Over a rocky ridge, a Sitka doe bounded away. Ian's gaze followed her until she disappeared, but he didn't seem inclined to track her. Not now. Instead, he turned and offered his hand up the side of a slick, exposed rock surface, helping Elyse up. And after what seemed like hours of hiking, half-afraid of what would charge out of the fog, Ian led her into the small mouth of a cave. She had to crouch down to get through the opening. Once inside, she could stand.

Ian squeezed her hand, pulling her to a stop, then kissed her forehead. "Welcome to the Monster House. Stay here," he said on a breath as he clicked his flashlight on. "Let me make sure it's clear." *Of grizzlies claiming my den.* He didn't have to say the last part, though. She was understanding more and more about Ian's life and of the wild animals he had to live alongside.

Two minutes later, and he was back. He jerked his head in invitation, and she pulled a headlight from her backpack, slid it onto her forehead, and clicked it on.

The cave smelled like smoke and charred wood, and when she laid eyes on the rubble, she hated Miller even more.

He'd taken Ian's home from him.

There were burnt remains of what looked like a cabin built into a corner. She moved through a scorched doorway and bit her lip as she arched the beam of her headlamp over the rubble. Everything was ash and blackened wood remnants, and she couldn't even tell what the furniture had looked like before.

"I slept there," Ian whispered, pointing to a corner. Only a few spruce limbs remained. Pine and smoke clogged her throat, and she pulled the front of her jacket over her nose so she could breathe easier. "Over there was a dresser. Nothing fancy. I made it one year when I miscalculated my hibernation and had a week to kill up here." He faced her and dragged her waist closer, then dipped his lips so close to her ear she could feel the vibration of his murmured words. "Over there was a stool I stacked my clothes and pack on, ready for when I woke up. I always kept money from my deliveries in a safe so I could go find food immediately when I woke up."

"Tell me about your first hibernation."

He let off a soft breath and hugged her closer. "It was the only one my brothers and I did together. Our bears were juveniles then, and we could stand to be around each other. And we were so scared about what was happening, it was a comfort not to be alone. We were sixteen, and Dad hadn't told us what to expect. Whenever we asked him, he would say, "It's instinct, boys. You'll know what to do.""

"And did you?"

Ian shook his head slowly, the scruff on his cheek rasping against hers. "No. We were all scared shitless, and when Tobias went down while we were out in the woods, Jenner and I dragged him under a rock ledge. Only, he hadn't Changed into his bear before he fell asleep, so he woke up a few days later, starving, and we had barely any food between us. He woke up the next day, too, and Jenner and I didn't know what to do. We were getting tired and didn't know how to feed Tobias if we were asleep. The fifth day, Tobias Changed into his bear when he woke up, but he wasn't right. He was what they call a winter bear, ravenous. He almost killed Jenner."

"Oh my gosh, Ian. What did you do?"

"Sewed him back up as best I could. His healing had already slowed down like the rest of his body, and Tobias was in the wind, hunting for anything that would sustain him. Jenner and I figured out we needed to sleep as bears or starve, so we Changed and waited, scared, clinging to that shallow rock face, scared that Tobias would come back. Scared that he wouldn't. Tobias showed up on the sixth day. He was still a bear, but the crazy was gone from his eyes. He was dragging his body, exhausted, and we all tucked ourselves in that tiny den and went to sleep. It's a wonder a hunter didn't find us. We were so close to the hunting cabins here, and we nearly froze because the den we'd chosen was too shallow. And when we woke up after hibernation, it was war. We were starving to death, emaciated, and none of us had the sense to Change back. We just went to battle, bleeding each other until we were all nearly dead. That was the first and last time we hibernated together."

"I can't believe your dad let you go into it blind like that. It makes me sick to think of you that young, trying to figure all of this out. It's too much on a kid. Too much." She squeezed her eyes tightly close and thanked God Ian had survived at all.

"Shhh," he crooned, brushing her hair off her shoulder. "It's done now."

With a sigh, she looked out the burned door to the dirty cave floor. "There's no envelope."

"I know."

"It's okay, Ian. Miller won't get to us. I won't let him. Not ever."

"Strong mate," he murmured. "Do you know how sexy it is watching you come into your own? Soft to steel." He kissed her gently, then walked her backward until her shoulders rested on the cave wall. "Watching that determination flash across your eyes. I thought I couldn't love you any more than I already did, but then I watched you learn so much." He brushed his fingertips up her neck and cupped her cheek. "You work harder and longer than anyone I've ever met, and you never get frustrated when I'm teaching you something new. You just try harder until you get it. My wood-chopping, rifle-slinging, fierce-as-hell Alaskan mate." He sipped her lips again. "I've never met a woman stronger than you."

And that right there was the difference between Cole and Ian. A weak man was intimidated by a strong woman. Cole had lashed out as she'd discovered herself little by little. He'd stunted her to make himself feel more in control. But Ian, *her Ian*, had worked to push her from the ashes like a damned phoenix and fell more in love with her as she'd transformed into a better version of herself. That's what love was supposed to be—not some power struggle. It was both people pushing the other to be better. To be stronger.

Breath shallow, she shoved the straps of the backpack from his shoulders and set his gun gently against the wall. She took her time unzipping his jacket. And after she shoved it off his shoulders, exposing his sweater with the top button undone, she traced the strong lines of his muscular neck down the deeply shadowed indentation between his pecs.

He'd never shared this place with anyone else. He'd never shared this part of himself, but for her, he'd opened up and let her in. And she knew how scary that was because she'd been learning to trust him, too, and damn it all, it was terrifying to let another man really see her after Cole had stripped her bare and exposed the ugliest parts of her.

But Ian wasn't running. He wasn't throwing his hands up and telling her she was "too much work." He wasn't leaving for town just to escape her. Instead, he was showing her the bottomless adoration a good man was capable of. He was telling her without words that she deserved everything he could give her.

That she was worthy of unconditional love.

That she was *enough*.

Ian slipped her headlamp off and let it fall from his fingers to the floor, then he cupped both of her cheeks and kissed her. This wasn't the desperate passion-saturated love-making they'd done in the barn. This was an apology for hiding from her before. It was a promise that he would always be with her, trying. It was a declaration he would work as long as necessary to gain her trust back after his secrets had been exposed.

"I hated sleeping away from you last night," she whispered against his lips.

"Then I won't do it again." He undressed her slowly as his lips moved gently against hers. He shifted his weight from side to side as he removed her clothes. Angling his face, he slipped his tongue past her lips.

She melted against him as he slid his hands up her bare ribs. How were his hands so warm? Somehow, he seemed to run hotter the closer to winter it became.

Writhing against him, she gripped the back of his hair and brushed her lips against his throat. Tugging at the neck of his sweater, she exposed the mostly healed bite she'd given him. She kissed it gently, and a shudder took his shoulders. A soft growl filled the small space, and she smiled. It was easy to tell when she had him.

He dragged her waist closer and rocked his hips against hers in just the right spot to draw a gasp from her lips.

"Ian," she sighed, and the name echoed off the cave walls.

The jangle of his belt and the slow rip of the zipper dumped warmth into her middle, and now his teeth were on her, grazing, nipping down her neck, and working back up until his lips crashed onto hers. God, she loved him. Loved him claiming her body in his den, making her a part of this place.

His eyes were dark in the muted light that her discarded headlamp provided. Here, in the place he'd spent so much time, vulnerable and asleep, she felt more connected to him than ever. She felt safe here and could understand why he'd chosen it as a den. Outside, the world spun on. It was harsh, cold, and the constant struggle for survival was unending, but in here, with the man she loved more than her own life, she was safe. For the first time ever, she felt whole.

Ian lifted the back of her knee and deepened his kiss, stroking his tongue against hers as he brushed her wet entrance with the tip of his swollen cock. A needy sound wrenched from her throat as he pushed in an inch and slid back out, teasing. She clawed down his back to punish him, but he smiled against her lips as though he enjoyed it.

"Please," she whispered.

Holding her close, Ian pushed into her, stretching her slowly as she arched her head back and gasped at the intense pleasure building in her center. He eased out slow, then slammed into her. Closing her eyes against the cold cave walls and shutting her senses off to the lingering smoke, she pushed her nose against his throat and inhaled his scent instead. She plucked at his skin there with her lips, then sucked hard as he bucked into her again.

She rocked with him, meeting him with each blow until his body shook and his control slipped. His next thrust was faster and harder, and he pulled her off the ground completely, wrapping her legs around his waist as he slammed her backward against the cold, smooth cave wall. It should've hurt, but she didn't feel anything past the way he was filling her. Her mate wasn't gentle by nature, not when they were together like this. He tried for her, but it always ended up satisfyingly rough. The room filled with the slick sound of their love-making as he rammed into her faster, pressing her against the wall as the snarl in his throat turned feral. One arm around her waist, he pulled her hand above her head with the other into a submissive position that begged her to trust him.

Pressure built, bigger and wider, until she was lost on a wave of pleasure. The cave didn't exist anymore, and neither did any of their problems outside of here. The constant threat of his hibernation disappeared because, in this moment, it was just her and Ian—alive and healthy and together. The only thing that mattered was her mate and this overwhelming bond that was building between them. His powerful hips thrust against her over and over, harder until she moaned, hanging right on the edge of release.

Ian held her tighter, his arms flexed hard as he bucked into her, and with his name on her lips, she detonated around him, pulsing, gripping him as pleasure flooded through her in tidal waves. He gritted out her name and buried his face against her shoulder as he slammed into her again and froze. His pulsing release matched hers, filling her with warmth.

"I love you, Elyse. I love you," he panted.

The raw, thick desperation in his voice shocked her to her core, so she hugged him tighter. "Shhh. I'm not going anywhere. I promise."

She'd never seen Ian scared, but here, in the dark of his old, charred den, he'd just given her a glimpse of something she'd never realized.

He was just as terrified of losing her as she was of losing him.

TWENTY-TWO

Miki was fast asleep in Elyse's lap when Ian pulled the truck to a stop in front of the cabin.

She was shocked to find Josiah chopping wood near the porch.

"Jo?" she asked, getting out with Miki cradled in her arms.

The pup woke up and wiggled to be set free, so she let him down, and the little hellion went bouncing toward her brother, letting off his big pup bark.

Josiah left the ax in the chopping block and knelt down, offering Miki his hand. Ian pulled the tailgate of his truck down and started unloading while Elyse followed the dog's path to her brother.

"Is everything okay?"

Her brother looked up at her with those somber gold-green eyes that were so much like hers. "We lost two more cattle last night to wolves."

"Oh my gosh. Which ones?"

"The bull and one of the mommas." Josiah sat down in the dirt and pulled Miki into his lap. "They have to be rabid or something. They left the half-grown calf and went after two big ones. And that ain't all. The wolves didn't even eat them. They just killed them for sport. Makes no damned sense this close to winter."

Elyse swallowed hard and looked up at the churning storm clouds above them. The McCalls had done this, led by that asshole, Miller.

"I brought the calf with me, but we need to get back and bring the rest of them in. They're exposed out there, and every day they spend out in the open now, they're at risk."

"Did you see the wolves?"

"Nah, they're being crafty, only taking the cattle in pitch dark. I can hear them, though. Howling and calling like a fucking celebration every time they take an animal."

Ian nodded to her once. Even from the truck, he'd heard the devastating news. Cattle were expensive and hard to come by, and that bull would cost them a lot to replace. Fucking Miller. He was hunting them from all sides now, taunting them with how much he could destroy their lives. He might not have the right key for the new padlock on the freezer, but he was still stealing from her.

Ian strode forward and reached down, gave Josiah a mannish handshake, then helped him up. "Thanks for letting us know. I'll need a couple of hours to cut up the venison we got, and then we can head out."

"Good hunt?"

"We filled two tags."

Josiah laughed. "You mean *you* filled two. I know my sister. She won't shoot anything bigger than a ptarmigan."

"You're wrong," Elyse said. "We both had a good hunt."

Josiah's dark eyebrows arched high. "No shit?"

"No shit, man. She even dressed hers out."

"Damn," Josiah murmured, shocked. "I wish Uncle Jim was here to see this."

The flattery heated her cheeks as Elyse dropped her gaze. That was as close to a compliment as her brother ever got. "Me, too."

"Okay, well let's get the table out. I can help and cut the work in half while Elyse saddles up the horses."

As much as Elyse wanted to take a shower after their two-day hunting trip, it was already mid-morning, and they were burning daylight. She took her and Ian's rifles and checked that they were unloaded, then put the safety back on both before she climbed the porch stairs and settled them against the railing where they wouldn't fall over. And when she turned to head for the horses' shelter, Josiah was watching her with a slight frown.

"You're different."

"Thank you," she clipped out as she strode for the gate where the horses waited.

Ian chuckled from behind her, and she grinned to herself.

A bucket of grain was the only thing that was going to keep Demon from pinning her against the fence. Bribery worked best with this black-coated beast. As she brushed his thickening coat out, she lifted her gaze time and time again to where Ian and Josiah were preparing the venison and wrapping it in brown paper. They talked low and easy, but she couldn't hear anything from here.

Demon tried to bite her when she put the saddle blanket on him, but he always did that, so she was ready and dodged his teeth. Irritated, he kicked, as if his near miss put him in a worse mood, and she rolled her eyes at what a little monster he could be. He was the taller of her two horses, so she had to give the saddle a strong swing upward to get it on. Demon pawed the dirt near the fence where she'd tied him, but at least the bucket of grain distracted him enough that he didn't try to bite her again.

Milo was much better behaved and always had been. He was a chestnut horse with a big white blaze down his nose. He didn't need the bribery, but she gave him a bucket of food to munch on to be fair. She could've sworn Demon was glaring at her the entire time she sang to Milo and saddled him, but she didn't care. Ian was going to handle that horse's foul mood, and she was going to have a nice, peaceful trail drive with her dependable horse.

She was finished before the men, so she left the horses tied to the fence and ready while she went inside and packed another backpack of food for Ian's ravenous appetite. They would only be roughing it one night, but it still required preparation, so she busied herself with packing them so Ian wouldn't have to worry about it.

Supplies sitting next to the guns outside, she rushed in and changed her clothes. Thermal pants under her jeans, two pairs of wool socks in her hiking boots, and a double layer of sweaters under her winter jacket. She glanced at herself in the mirror, and it shocked her to a stop. Her cheeks were filling out and tinged the rosy color that had left her during the hard years. She stood taller and didn't have her chin to her chest, staring down at the ground like she used to do. The dark circles under her eyes had disappeared, and deep within her strange-colored eyes, she saw something she'd never seen before and almost didn't recognize. Pride.

She'd taken a deer, and respectfully. It had been a good, clean, painless shot, and her effort would help to keep her and Ian fed this winter. And as she stared at the stranger reflected in the mirror, something within her clicked into place. She could do this. No longer was she living each day thinking this winter would be her last. Her confidence in her own abilities were growing.

Ripping her gaze away from the mirror glass, she pulled a dark green winter hat over her ears, then tugged her warmest work gloves on and left the house to pack the horses' saddlebags.

Ian's lessons repeated in her mind as she checked the weapons one last time for safety before she slid them into the leather sheaths on the saddles and strapped them into place. And when Milo and Demon were ready, she allowed them a good drink, then pulled them behind her out of the gate. Josiah waved as he trotted toward his truck, a black trash bag of meat dangling from his other hand. "I'll meet you there. I've got them penned up on the south side of my property."

"Okay, we'll see you tonight."

"Yep!" Josiah nodded his farewell to Ian, who was locking up the freezer.

Ian gave a soft whistle, and Miki left the bowl of food he'd just devoured on the porch and trotted toward them.

Demon lurched to the side as Ian put his foot in the stirrup, but that moody gelding was no match for him. Ian swung over the saddle smoothly and jerked his reins as the beast reached back to nip his leg. Of course he knew how to handle himself on a horse. There was likely nothing Ian Silver couldn't do.

Ian gave a troubled look up at the storm clouds, then back at her. "You ready?" But his eyes looked different. Hazy. Tired.

Dread snaked through her, but she nodded. "Ready."

A stark sense of urgency was a constant companion as she led Ian toward Josiah's homestead. She pointed out the landmarks along the way. Even though it was only a twenty mile journey, it was easy to get lost in Alaskan wilderness like this. And out here, getting lost meant death. Everything out here was designed to kill the weak. Weather and predators were king, and mistakes meant dying alone in the unforgiving wilderness.

Miki made it a mile before he tired out and Elyse zipped him up in her jacket. He fought it at first, but he settled against her chest soon enough. The smooth gait of her horse lulled her into a quiet comfort as she and Ian rode along in silence. His lack of speaking was more troubling when highlighted by the way he slumped in the saddle, then straightened his spine, then slumped again.

He wasn't saying it out loud, but she could see it clear as day. His body was preparing for the long sleep. He'd told her he would get tired at the end. No, not tired, *exhausted*, as if he'd taken tens of sleeping pills all at once. It would get worse and worse until he couldn't stay awake anymore.

Sometimes it happened slowly, but more often, it happened fast.

And they had to be back at the homestead before he fell asleep for the winter.

As if Mother Nature had heard Elyse's silent challenge, the clouds finally opened up. Snowflakes floated all around them, and there was a moment when Ian turned in his saddle and locked eyes with her. They were a somber blue that said so much with just a glance.

Winter's here.

I can't stay much longer.

We'll be all right.

You're ready for this.

Remember everything I taught you, always.

And last but most importantly, *I love you.*

He turned and kicked his horse, and Demon responded under him, trotting immediately. And by the time he got him into a run, she could feel it, too. Time was closing in on them.

Ian wasn't turning back and letting her drive the cattle by herself. He wasn't playing it safe—not while she was exposed to the werewolves out here.

Their horses ran on and on beside each other. And as the snow steadily blanketed the landscape around them, it was hard not to look at her mate. Time and time again, her gaze was drawn to him.

Beside her, Ian's jaw clenched in determination to finish this last chore before the cold season swallowed him up completely.

Winter's here.

I can't stay much longer.

TWENTY-THREE

"Is Ian okay?" Josiah asked low, his horse swerving so close, he bumped Milo's side.

"He's just tired. He didn't sleep much on the hunt or last night, and he's been going for a while," Elyse lied.

In fact, when they'd slept in the tent last night near the cattle, she'd had trouble waking him to head home this morning. He'd been so limp when she'd shaken him that, for a few minutes, she'd been terrified she wouldn't be able to wake him at all.

Josiah didn't need to be saddled with her burdens, though.

At the other side of the herd, Ian was listlessly riding after a stray heifer. He wasn't even yelling and cussing as she and Josiah did when they wanted to get the cattle moving.

Really, three riders was overkill, since the herd was now only ten strong with the ones she'd lost to wolves, the calf already in the corral, and the one Josiah kept back as payment for watching them through the warm months. It made for an easy drive, though. Two more miles, and they would be home. Two more miles, and she wouldn't have to live in fear that Ian would fall from his horse and not wake up. Two more miles, and he would be safe to fall asleep without her having to explain any of this to Josiah.

"Hup!" she called, holding the extra length of her reins and waving them side to side over Milo's neck to get the cattle moving over a slick straightaway. The temperature was dropping so fast it was freezing the bottom layer of snow that had melted. Dangerous conditions for clumsy cattle.

Behind them, a howl lifted into the air. Pissed, Elyse swatted at the raised hair that tingled on the back of her neck. The snow was falling harder now, making it difficult to see any distance, and those damned McCalls sounded close.

Josiah narrowed his eyes behind them. "What the fuck do they want? It's like they've stayed the same distance behind the whole day. There's still two dead cattle out on the marsh for them to eat."

"Jo, I think you should take Ian's truck back."

"What? No. You need that, and besides, what would I do with Renegade?" He patted his buckskin's neck.

"I'll keep him for now, but I don't want you range riding when those wolves are out like this."

He frowned behind him again. "They are acting strange."

"Please, Jo."

"Bossy. You remember I'm the big brother, right?"

"And I'm the worried little sister. I don't ask you for much. Just this once, take the truck. I'll be on a snow machine from here on, anyway."

"Yeah, all right." Josiah cast her the tenth worried look he'd given her today and trotted off toward a trio of cattle that were breaking off.

Usually, the herd stuck together like glue, but they'd watched some of their own attacked by wolves this season, and the howling had them spooked. Elyse couldn't blame them one bit for scattering.

Ian slumped forward again and almost went over. Shit. Elyse kicked her horse and bolted for where Ian was struggling to stay awake on a side-stepping Demon.

She pulled up beside the black gelding and steadied Ian in the saddle. "Baby, you have to make it just a little while longer. We're almost there. Look." She pointed to the jutting rock formation that was snow-capped like a miniature mountain. "We're almost on our property. Almost home."

When Ian slid her a glance, she swallowed down a gasp. He looked like a shell of himself—like walking death. Eyes dull and bleary, he was as pale as a ghost.

"Ian, can you ride ahead? Can you make it? Josiah and I will bring the cattle in. Just let Demon into the coral, and I'll take care of him."

"Elyse," he slurred, heartbreak in his eyes.

"I know, baby," she whispered, blinking rapidly. He couldn't see her weak. Not right now. "I'll see you when you wake up."

"It'll be a few days before the first hour we get."

"Okay." She hid the devastation from her face. "Can you make it to the cabin?"

Ian nodded once. "I love you, Elyse. Remember." One eyebrow arched before he leaned over and kissed her.

He kicked his horse into a trot, and then into a gallop as he clung to the saddle horn.

She knew what he meant.

Remember all her lessons.

Remember how to defend herself.

Remember to be strong.

She doubled over Milo's neck at the pain in her middle. She felt it down to her marrow—that had been goodbye. From here until April, she would only get a borrowed hour here and there.

As Ian disappeared into the falling snow, the weak tears she hadn't allowed before slipped to her cheeks. He'd thought he would hibernate in mid-October, but the weather had turned bitterly cold early, and now two weeks had been stolen from them.

Wiping her damp lashes with the back of her work glove, she turned Milo and made her way toward the bawling cattle.

Across the herd, Josiah's faint silhouette sat atop his mount, arm slung over the saddle horn as he hunched forward, face turned toward her. She couldn't see his expression under the low rim of his hat, but she imagined it was marred with confusion and worry.

Elyse swallowed a sob and laid into the back of the herd with a new sense of urgency. Even if it was only for a little while, she didn't like being separated from her mate.

Not when he was this vulnerable, and not when those damned McCalls were this close.

The last two miles took an eternity, and when she and Josiah had driven the cattle into their fenced pasture, she put out a couple bales of hay, broke the ice in their water trough, then pointed her attention to Demon, who was screaming like a banshee and running around the coral with his saddle still strapped to him.

He probably hadn't enjoyed carrying Ian that last bit of the way, smelling like fur and predator. His nostrils were flared, and he huffed breath after steaming breath as he ran, ears back.

"You want me to unsaddle him?" Josiah asked, frowning at Demon.

"No, I'm going to let him tire himself out first. Don't worry about it. You go on." She handed him the keys to Ian's truck. "Get home before this weather really opens up. I'll keep Milo and Renegade in the barn until Demon settles."

She took both sets of reins from where Renegade and Milo were tied at the fence. She made to head for the barn, but Josiah said, "Elyse?"

She froze and turned. "Yes?"

His eyes held a deep understanding that said he wasn't as in the dark as she'd intended to keep him. "I know you're stronger now. I can see it, but life out here still gets hard. It gets dangerous. If you need help this winter, you call me. No matter what it is, you call. You hear me?"

She swallowed hard and nodded. "I will."

Josiah gave her a lingering, hard look, then strode for Ian's truck without another word.

And as the engine roared to life and he drove away, she stood there watching until the glowing taillights disappeared altogether.

Then she turned her gaze on the dark house and let off a long, shuddering sigh.

Stalling, she put up the horses, unsaddled them, fed and watered them, and checked the goats. She wanted to cling to precious moments before she accepted what she already knew to be true—winter had defeated them. It didn't matter how fiercely she loved Ian, she couldn't keep him. Inside, her mate would be limp on the bed, and her heart would ache until he woke again.

The walk from the barn to the house was surreal, as if she was floating like the flakes of white snow that kicked up in the breeze all around her.

Inside, she turned on a lantern. He'd struggled to get through the house, and the entryway table had been knocked over. All of the ammunition that had been stacked there was scattered across the floor. The rug was flipped on the corner, and she stepped carefully over the mess to right the fallen vase on the kitchen table. Ian had filled them with late season flowers for her a few days ago, and now they were dry and dying. She felt like those withering flowers as she lifted the lantern into the bedroom and saw Ian lying at an angle across the mattress. From here, it was obvious how much his body had already slowed down. He was barely breathing.

She set the lantern on the dresser and curled up beside him, burying her face against his shoulder and inhaling his scent.

Ache bloomed wide and deep as a canyon inside of her.

Now, she was really alone.

And in the distance, the wolves howled on.

TWENTY-FOUR

Ian had lied. Unintentionally, sure, but it had been five days, and still he hadn't woken up.

Other than the slow breaths he took, there were no signs of life from her mate. And now she was watching the man she loved waste away, and she couldn't do anything for him. It had been a mistake to ask him to hibernate human just so she could selfishly keep him for an hour a day. It wasn't natural for him, and he was suffering because of her.

She felt like grit.

The days had melted together, one after the other as she'd watched over him, day and night, waiting, always waiting, for him to come back to her.

She was only able to sleep for a couple hours at a time, curled up beside him and wishing she was a bear just like him so they could hide all winter in a den somewhere on Afognak and lose this time together. Her restlessness wasn't all because of Ian, though. Most of it stemmed from the howling wolves outside.

Each night they got closer, louder, more excited. This was their taunt. They could've come for her at any time. Perhaps they were waiting to make sure Ian was really down for the winter, but more likely they were waiting because the hunt was the fun of it, right? Once the kill was over, the McCalls would have to go back to their mundane lives of stealing and drinking themselves into oblivion as they waited for their inner monsters to drive them mad.

What an empty life. She pitied them. Elyse loaded another shell into her shotgun. Well, she almost pitied them.

They were close tonight, yipping between the haunting notes of their death song, as if they couldn't contain their excitement, their bloodlust. She hated them.

Elyse stood and set her shotgun in line with the others, strap toward her so she could grab it quick.

She should be scared, but other than an occasional nervous flutter, she didn't feel anything. Only resolve to protect Ian at all costs. At all costs.

A six-inch blade hung in a sheath from her hip, and on her other side, she'd fashioned a loop for her hatchet. These were her last-resort weapons. If she got down to her blades, she was probably already dead and just stalling on her fate. She'd used Ian's phone to call a contact named Clayton again and again. She'd left him voicemails, but the head of Alaska Shifter Enforcement apparently didn't get involved unless human life was already taken.

Too bad her life was the one that would be sacrificed to gain that kill order.

Miki growled at her feet, his black lips curled back, his teeth gleaming, his bi-colored eyes narrowed on the door. It didn't matter that he was a puppy. He could look terrifying when he wanted to.

She'd locked the horses and goats in the barn but even from inside the cabin, she could hear them screaming and kicking the stall doors.

Owooooooo. Ooooo. Ooooowooooooo.

The song of the wolves lifted and fell, and for the hundredth time, she tried to decipher between the voices. Tried to guess how many were coming for her. Cole had told her he had relatives all over Alaska, and apparently Miller had enough sway to call them all to go on a man hunt. Or as it happened, a woman hunt.

Miki's growl grew louder and ended in a bark. The hairs rose all along his back and, in a rush, she scooped him up and shoved him in the guest room. God, she hoped she would be okay enough to let him out after this, but he would be killed for sure if he went after the wolves with her.

"I'm sorry, Miki," she blurted out as she closed the door. Inside, the quarter grown pup went mad, barking constantly.

She bolted for the rifles on the wall, but the door exploded inward, spewing splinters over the living room.

Miller stood in the open doorframe naked and scarred with an empty sneer on his lips. His eyes were white and horrifying, and the first wave of fear washed over her.

"Where is he?"

Elyse gripped the handle of the knife at her hip. "Go to hell."

"Been there for a long time, pretty bitch." He lifted his chin, and his nostrils flared as he drew in a noisy breath. Then he strode past her toward the bedroom where Ian was hibernating. With a screech, she pulled her knife out and brought it down into his back.

Miller roared in pain and swung around. The back of his hand blasted across her face, and Elyse flew against the wall as the world spun on its axis. On hands and knees, she blinked rapidly, trying to see straight again as her ears rang with pain. Her face had a pounding pulse, and beneath her, red dripped onto the floorboards. Rage, dark and consuming, tinted her vision, and she spat crimson, then stood in time to see Miller dragging Ian's limp body past her.

The guns were stacked on the opposite side of the door—too far. Rushing Miller, she tackled him and beat on him with her closed fists, so hard, her hands felt like they were breaking. With a scream, she clawed his face so hard her nails ached and loosened. Miller's face was terrifying as he rounded on her, but she was ready. Ducking out of his way, she pulled on Ian's leg, dragging him back into the heart of the house as best she could.

Miller shoved her off Ian and pulled him toward the door.

"Ian, wake up!" Elyse screamed, pulling on his leg.

"Let go!" Miller yelled.

"Ian!" She pulled the hatchet and swung forward, catching Miller across the cheek before he could pull away.

"Fuck," he raged, holding his face. He jumped over Ian's body and caught her by the throat and the wrist. "You stupid cunt. Can't you see I'm trying to save you for last? I want you to savor this with us. Why are you so determined to mark me?" The rage slipped from his face as his lips twisted up in a cruel smile. "You would've made a beautiful breeder. You could've given us McCall pups for the next generation, but you chose him instead."

She fought like a wild, injured animal, snapping, kicking, and writhing against his grip. She reared back and spat on his face. "I'd never breed with anyone so broken."

"Broken?" Miller let of a low, empty chuckle. "Am I broken, Elyse? Was my brother broken?"

"Yes!"

"Wrong!" He slammed her back against the wall. "Cole was coming into his own. A true man-eater, just like the old days. Back in the times where shifters didn't cower in the shadows. We took what we fucking wanted and we bathed in the blood of humans because they were prey. They were lesser." He lowered his lips to hers and kissed her with the violence of a tornado, then pulled back before she recovered enough to bite him. "You're lesser, Elyse." He pulled the hatchet from her hand and leaned in close, pinning her with his weight. "A mark for a mark."

"Ian!" she screamed, struggling against Miller. "Wake up!"

Miller gripped her neck and slammed her head backward, and before her vision cleared, it was done. Just one swipe of the sharpened blade down her cheekbone, so deep it didn't even hurt yet.

With a smile, he whispered, "Beautiful." Then released her neck and let her fall to the floor, gasping.

Warmth trickled down her face as she watched Miller drag Ian's body out the front door by the leg. She blinked hard as time slowed. She'd thought it would be hard to kill a man. Had thought about it countless times over the last week, but this, right here, changed everything.

A strange calmness washed through her as she stood and strode for the row of rifles. She shouldered the straps of five and grabbed the satchel of ammunition. The last gun she aimed as she walked out of the house and into the cold evening. "Let him go." She didn't recognize her voice. It was low and steady.

When she chambered a bullet and clicked the safety off, Miller froze. In the tree line, animal eyes glowed, and in the background, Miki's desperate barking sounded over and over.

"This is my house, my property, and you're filthy fucking hand is on my mate. Let him go, or I'll put a hole in you."

"You shoot me, and all those wolves in your woods will attack."

She shrugged one shoulder and moved closer to Ian, her gait smooth as she held the barrel of her rifle in the general vicinity of Miller's chest.

Miller gave a disbelieving laugh and dropped Ian's leg in the snow with a thud. "Cole told me all about you, Elyse. He said you were weak. Easily manipulated and soft-hearted. All the things that get you killed out here."

His eyes narrowed to white slits, and a snarl ripped from his chest as his head snapped back and fur sprouted from his body.

Elyse planted her feet and held a quick breath as Miller stood crouched before her, an oversize black wolf with murder in his eyes. Teeth bared, he lunged for her, and she pulled the trigger.

The sound of the shot was deafening.

As the wolves in the tree line charged the clearing, she lifted the rifle from Miller's limp body at her feet and took aim at the next.

Determined to protect the man she loved, she murmured, "Cole was wrong."

****

Ian, wake up. You have to wake up.

Ian shook his head and tried to open his eyes. That voice. He knew it. Needed it. That voice was everything that anchored him to this world.

"Ian!"

With a massive effort, he opened his eyes, but he didn't understand the scene before him.

Shot after echoing shot filled the air. Snow falling down, and *her*, standing above him like an avenging angel. Her eyes were blazing gold next to all that dripping red on her face. Warrior. *Elyse.* The name brushed his mind. His Elyse. She was hurt.

She aimed the shotgun. *Boom.* Her rifle swung over his body to something else.

Growling, snarling, snow crunching, the stink of wolf so close he could almost feel their teeth on his back. The fine hairs on his body rose.

"Hold your breath," Elyse murmured, then pulled the trigger again. "Reload." Her fingers were steady as she cracked the shotgun open and shoved two more shells into it. "Remember, remember." Her voice dipped to a whisper as she yanked the barrel back into place. "Ian, please wake up." Her voice sounded so soft, defeated, as if she'd given up on him.

Ian clenched his hands, willing himself up. The wolves were threatening his mate. She was hurt. Bleeding. He would kill whoever had done this. Kill them. Kill.

He mustered every ounce of his energy, conjured his monster, called on the snarling bruin inside of him. This was

222

it. His animal had always wanted to rampage, and here was his chance. Bones cracking, he gave himself to the bear.

Changed, Ian stood to his full height and roared his fury. So many wolves. How were there this many? Ian charged, drawing their attention away from Elyse. He stumbled, so exhausted, but he had to protect her. Had to draw them back into the woods so she could get away. Get inside and lock the door.

Run, Elyse!

Teeth sank into his back, and he spun, caught a gray wolf with his claws as three more attacked. He was surrounded, but this was the way it was supposed to be. Elyse was supposed to live.

The sounds of high caliber rifle shots echoed now, one after the other, and the wolf at his throat dropped like a stone under him.

In desperation to buy her time, he clawed and fought. Pain slashed at him, but he had no thought save mauling the next wolf, and the next.

"Lincoln, help us!" Elyse yelled.

Lincoln? He was one of them. The enemy. A McCall.

"Please!" Elyse begged.

Another shot rang out.

Two wolves were fighting now. Dissention in the ranks, but it wouldn't be enough. Ian had four on him, and his fur was matted with red. Pain, pain, pain.

Another shot and another, and Ian couldn't stand on his own anymore. Too little energy left. Too much ache. Too much red snow.

He hit the ground hard, but the teeth left him. Inhaling deeply, he pried his eyes open. Elyse was sprinting for him, boots crunching against the deep snow, rifle up as her blazing gold eyes followed something he couldn't see. Warrior. Badass. Fearless. *My mate. Mine.* It was okay to go like this, looking at *her*.

Elyse stood over his body, weapon trained on something in the woods, but she didn't move to pull the trigger anymore.

Her hand brushed his fur. So comforting. "Ian, it's okay to sleep. I've got you." She looked at him with such fierce determination and repeated, "I've *got* you."

And then the winter woods faded, leaving only Elyse's fearless gold eyes for a moment before the world went dark.

TWENTY-FIVE

November
December
January
February
March
April

TWENTY-SIX

Ian grunted and pushed upward, paws against something cold and unfamiliar. Wooden floors? He forced his eyes open and looked around the den. Not his den on Afognak, but he knew this smell. *Home.*

He was starving, but he didn't need to go far. There were wooden crates of food, filled with sawdust and shelves of canned meat. Strips of smoked venison hung from the rafters above. He needed to Change back but couldn't fight the gnawing hunger long enough. Ravenously, he yanked down the long strips of venison and tore into them until every bit of the meat was devoured. Only when that was gone did he brave the pain of the Change after the long winter.

His human body was smudged and emaciated, but that part was expected. What he couldn't comprehend was why there was a web of new scars across his legs and torso. What the hell? His stomach still felt so hollow he was nauseous, so he pulled the canned meat from the shelves and ate that, too, then moved onto the remaining carrots in the wooden crate. Only when he'd eaten everything in the root cellar besides the strands of garlic did he crawl up the ladder and out of the den.

Even muted, the light in the living room was blinding, and he had to blink several times to bear it. Elyse wasn't here. He couldn't hear her or Miki, and a sliver of worry took him as the memories of Changing mid-hibernation crashed down on him. He stumbled toward the bathroom. It smelled like her. Even the shampoo she used lingered, so she must be okay. Still here, protecting him. He ran the water in the shower, but it was just a trickle and cold as balls. Still, he scrubbed his skin clean. He ghosted a glance at his reflection in the mirror as he brushed his teeth, but his face looked just as wretched as it always did. Hollow face, long beard, dull, sunken eyes. A vain part of him didn't want Elyse to see him like this.

Outside, an unfamiliar dog barked out a deep timbre. Ian ran his hand over his damp hair and then noticed the pile of neatly folded clothes in the corner of the bedroom. The stretch of his smile felt good after so long, and when he lifted the garments to his nose, they smelled like the soap Elyse made. No dusty, musty clothes like he usually changed into when he first woke up from hibernation.

He dressed as quickly as his aching muscles allowed, then stumbled to the living room. He pushed the thin curtain back from the window and froze. The dog wasn't unfamiliar. Miki was just grown. He stood in the middle of the yard, looking up at something with a dog grin, his tongue lolled out to the side. He was big, much bigger than Ian had ever thought a runt would grow. Strong legs, a straight back, and a thick black and white coat that had a healthy sheen. White eyebrows over his mismatched eyes gave him a humanlike expression as he barked again.

"Beggar," a soft voice said.

The smile fell from Ian's lips as he pulled the curtain back farther. Elyse chucked a big stick into the woods and laughed a tinkling, happy sound as Miki bounded off toward it.

Ian's breath froze in his throat. A long red scar ran down the length of her cheekbone now, though she didn't favor it. Her smile was still just as big. She looked different in other ways, though. Her hair was longer and hung around her shoulders in soft, pretty waves. She wasn't rail-thin anymore. She was stronger, and her posture was straighter. Her laugh echoed through the homestead and warmed him as Miki danced proudly back to her with the stick.

Unable to keep from touching her another second, Ian pulled open the door.

Elyse's eyes jerked immediately to his, and she let off a tiny shocked sound. "Ian."

Unsteady, he strode down the porch stairs as she sprinted toward him. He wasn't strong enough yet to catch all of her weight as she launched at him like a torpedo, so he fell backward with her, cradling her from the fall as he laughed. Back in the mud, he clutched her to him. She felt so damned good against him, all warm and clutching his shirt. She was crying, so he held her even tighter and kissed the top of her hair.

Miki was bounding around him, whacking him with the stick in his mouth, so Ian let go of Elyse just long enough to rough up the dog's fur on his head.

Elyse eased back, her eyes rimmed with moisture and her cheeks damp. "Ian, say something to me. I've waited so long to hear your voice."

He cleared his raspy throat and whispered, "I love you." That should be the first thing she heard from him. And from this spring onward, he swore to himself he would always start their warm-weather life with those words.

"I love you, too." She nuzzled against his neck and curled her body over him. "I love you, I love you, I love you. And also, you should know I had to tell Josiah what you are."

"You did?"

"Yeah, how else do you think I dragged your big furry ass into the root cellar? We had to borrow a damned tractor from the Fairways just to get you to the porch. Oh my gosh, I have so much to tell you. So many stories. Books I read and all the trouble Miki got into and one of the cows had a late season calf and I snared a rabbit all by myself and Ian, I missed you so much!"

He chuckled under the tiny kisses she laid all over his face, but that wasn't what he wanted. Holding the back of her head, he pulled her close and leaned up. Her lips met his, and he closed his eyes against how damned good she felt. It could've been minutes or hours before he eased back.

Above him, the sun was shining behind her head like a halo as Elyse smiled down at him. His mate was so stunning she stole his breath away. Gently, he ran his finger against the long, red scar on her face.

The smile slipped from her mouth, and she shrugged. Dropping her gaze, she whispered, "I've been nervous about you seeing me like this."

"No," he whispered, his throat tightening. He knew that feeling. He'd had the same insecurity about her seeing him right after hibernation. "Elyse, look at me."

She couldn't seem to, so he rocked upward and pulled her into a straddle across his lap, then hooked his finger under her chin and lifted her striking green-gold gaze to his. "You're the most beautiful thing I've ever seen. And that scar? Sexy as hell. You got that protecting me, didn't you?"

Her face crumpled, and her chin trembled with emotion, but she was holding his gaze now, his brave mate. She nodded once as a tear slipped to her cheek. "Yes."

Ian closed his eyes against the heartache. She was marked forever because of him. But another emotion overwhelmed any sadness that would take away from her moment of triumph. She'd waged war on an entire pack of werewolves and won. And then she'd gone through something unspeakably hard in the aftermath—healing and dealing with the trauma all alone. And here she was, healthy and strong, filling their yard with laughter and gifting him easy smiles. "I'm so proud of you."

Elyse laughed thickly and buried her face against his neck, hugging him up tight. She was crying again, but that was okay. It didn't make her soft. He'd seen her go to battle for him and knew what she was capable of.

"I saw you standing over me, firing at any wolf trying to get to me. Bleeding and fearless. You stunned me, Elyse. My beautiful badass."

She sighed a happy sound and snuggled into his embrace, as if she could never be close enough to him.

He smiled over her shoulder as Miki lay down and began gnawing on his stick. Ian inhaled deeply and looked around the homestead to the barn, then to the pasture where the small herd of cattle bawled occasionally, chewing on their hay. He looked to the horses' corral where Demon was acting ornery as ever, bucking and nipping at Milo.

Everything and nothing had changed.

"Ian?" Elyse whispered against his throat.

"Yes?"

"You said to give you a winter season."

His smile deepened. Oh, he knew what she was asking. He eased her back and kissed the long scar on her cheek, then let his lips linger on hers before he drew back and asked, "Knowing everything, are you still in this?"

Her lips trembled into a smile, and she nodded. "I am."

Ian swallowed hard and brushed her wavy hair behind her ear so he could better see her. Lifting his gaze to hers, he asked, "Elyse, will you marry me?"

She laughed and gripped his wrists, held his palms to her cheeks as they flushed pink and warm under his touch. "I thought you'd never ask."

"Is that a yes?"

"I already bought a dress."

Ian chuckled and searched her dancing eyes. "Is *that* a yes?"

And then Elyse, his Elyse, pursed her lips and nodded an answer that changed his entire life for the better in the span of an instant. With a shuddering sigh, she rested her forehead against his and smiled. "The answer was always yes."

EPILOGUE

Elyse bounced nervously as she waited for the truck she could hear coming. Ian had been on a delivery, earning them money that would help them carry through the year, and damn, she missed him fiercely when he did trips like that. Even if they were sparse and short, any time spent away from him was hard after the long, lonely winter.

"There he is," Josiah said from beside her. There was a smile in his voice, and she understood it. She couldn't wait to see the surprise on Ian's face either.

The old brown and white Ford crested the hill and bumped and bounced down the muddy road toward them.

She grinned big at Tobias and Jenner, and the latter, Ian's dark-headed brother, looked down at her with an exasperated expression in his vivid blue eyes, as if her mood was catching and he couldn't cling onto his grumpiness hard enough. "I already told you. He's not going to like us in his territory."

"We'll see," she sang, completely unconvinced.

Tobias, who looked eerily like Ian but with emerald green eyes, stood stoically on the other side of Jenner with a slight frown marring his thin features. Hibernation hadn't been easy on any of the Silver brothers.

Ian slid out of the truck and walked around the front, eyes on his brothers, as if he was seeing ghosts. "Tobias?

Jenner?" He jogged toward his brothers, but then stopped right in front of them, expression unsure. "What are you doing here?"

Jenner nodded toward the preacher that stood on Elyse's other side. "We're standing for you on your big day."

"The woman who hired you to be her husband begged us," Tobias clarified, his blue eyes tightening.

"Elyse," she said happily, undaunted by Tobias's grousing. "My name's Elyse. You should probably learn it since you will be my new brother."

"In-law," Tobias muttered. He cleared his throat and stuck out his hand to Ian with a low growl. "It's good to see you."

"D'aaw, love!" Elyse said, scrunching up her face and hugging her wildflower bouquet tighter.

Ian blinked hard and glanced at her white dress, then the preacher, then back to Tobias's extended hand. Instead of shaking, Ian leaned in and hugged him roughly, clapping him hard on the back, and then moved on to Jenner and greeted him the same way. "It's damn good to see both of you, too."

All three of them were growly, snarly, beastly men until Ian moved farther away, but that was okay. Nothing could dampen today.

Glancing down at his jeans and thin, black sweater, Ian asked, "Do you want me to clean up?"

"I think you look perfect," Elyse said, jumping into his arms and hugging his neck.

His chuckle was so deep, genuine, and warm, it vibrated against her chest. Walking her backward until they stood in front of the others, he smiled politely at the preacher.

With a slight frown, Ian leaned back on his heels and glared at Lincoln McCall, who was standing quietly on Josiah's other side. "What's he doing here?"

"Well, I'm a big fan of Link's since he helped me out of that little wolf situation this past winter," Elyse explained with a significant look at Ian. "And besides, you have two groomsmen, and I need two bridesmaids to make it even."

Lincoln and Josiah both groaned.

"Seriously, Elyse," her brother gritted out, "stop calling us that."

"Men of honor?" she said.

"Whatever," Josiah said, clasping his hands in front of the suit he'd dug up from somewhere. "Let's start this already. I'm hungry."

"That's the spirit, bridesman."

A muscle twitched under Josiah's eye, but he smiled instead of arguing.

"I'm hungry, too," Ian's brothers said in unison.

"Ha!" Elyse rocked forward on the toes of her hiking boots she wore under her dress and murmured to the preacher, "We'll take the condensed version, if you don't mind."

With a nod, the preacher began the ceremony. "We are gathered here today to witness the union of Ian Silver and Elyse Abram…"

His words faded to a murmur as she looked up into Ian's eyes. She was stunned with how happy he looked. He glanced back at the wedding party, who stood behind them, then back at her.

Thank you, he mouthed.

And she understood the deep gratitude that swam in his bright blue eyes. He'd missed his brothers. Even if their bears didn't get along, this was a big day, and they were family. They should be here, standing beside him, just as her brother was here, showing his support.

She hadn't planned on Ian when she put that advertisement in the newspaper, but standing here with him, holding his hands in hers, staring up into his adoring eyes, she knew their struggle had been worth it. They had fought for each other. They bore scars for each other, and loved each other beyond all faults.

She had given herself completely to a worthy man and been rewarded with a bond so deep it left her breathlessly happy.

And as she said "I do," she was giving so much more than the simple vows the preacher had asked them to repeat.

She was promising to walk this difficult life hand in hand with her mate, no matter what danger came.

She was giving her solemn oath to spend every winter protecting him and every summer loving him unconditionally.

Her eyes were wide open going into this. Winters would always be long and hard, but summers...oh, those warm months held the potential for indescribable happiness.

"You may now kiss your bride," the preacher said.

Up on her tiptoes, Elyse met Ian's lips. This was the moment she would remember for always—holding Ian in the front yard of their homestead, newly married, vows still warm on their lips as the people who meant the most clapped softly behind them.

Ian rocked back and looked down at her. With the pad of his thumb, he wiped away a tear before it touched the scar on her cheek. "Elyse," he whispered. "I've *got* you."

She smiled slow and squeezed his hand, then said the words that were just as important as their other vows. "I've got you, too."

Want More of These Characters?

Up Next in This Series

Bear Fur Hire
(Bears Fur Hire, Book 2)

About the Author

T.S. Joyce is devoted to bringing hot shifter romances to readers. Hungry alpha males are her calling card, and the wilder the men, the more she'll make them pour their hearts out. She werebear swears there'll be no swooning heroines in her books. It takes tough-as-nails women to handle her shifters.

Experienced at handling an alpha male of her own, she lives in a tiny town, outside of a tiny city, and devotes her life to writing big stories. Foodie, wolf whisperer, ninja, thief of tiny bottles of awesome smelling hotel shampoo, nap connoisseur, movie fanatic, and zombie slayer, and most of this bio is true.

Bear Shifters? Check
Smoldering Alpha Hotness? Double Check
Sexy Scenes? Fasten up your girdles, ladies and gents, it's gonna to be a wild ride.

For more information on T. S. Joyce's work,
visit her website at
www.tsjoycewrites.wordpress.com